BROKEN NIGHT

A NEW YORK KNIGHTS NOVEL

BOOK FIVE

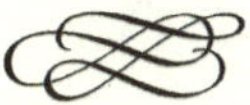

S.M. WEST

Broken Night

ISBN 978-1-989881-05-7

Cover Design: Najla Qamber Designs
Editors: Evident Ink & Leanne Rabesa
Photographer: Lindee Robinson
Models: Francina Juncaj & Chad

Even the darkest night will end and the sun will rise. ~ Les Misérables, Victor Hugo

PROLOGUE

MIA

Twelve Years Ago

"Mia, he's heeere." Kylie's sing-song voice hits me as I exit the break room.

"Hmmm." I tighten the elastic band of my ponytail, still preoccupied with thoughts of my upcoming exam. "Who are you talking about?"

I'm not ready. It's hard to believe I spent the entire night studying and I still don't feel ready. Why did I agree to this shift on the same day as one of my toughest exams?

"Mister Yum-o-licious came in the second you went on break." My co-worker babbles and bounces, causing those waiting in line for their coffee to stare.

It's on the tip of my tongue to tell her to help me with the line, or just go on break, when the next thing out of her mouth sends my insides into a pretzel.

"He's waiting for you." She's oddly robotic as she tries to speak without moving her lips. Hilarious.

While I'd normally laugh, I'm stuck on the news that my crush, the object of my nighttime fantasies, is here. A wild fluttering ripples through my body and I force myself to get a grip.

Mister Yum-o-licious comes back to me. The name is new, but she isn't wrong. Patrick Townsend is dreamy. Definitely delicious.

"Never try that again. Just don't," I say in hushed tones, stiffening my lips. *Great, now I'm doing it.*

"He's watching, and I didn't want him to know we're talking about him."

Despite her words, she points in his direction. For the love of… grabbing her arm, I slap it to her side and step closer so we're barely a foot apart.

"Kylie, just stop. Everyone, and I mean everyone, is staring."

"Don't you mean Patrick is staring?" Her teasing tone and megawatt smile do nothing to calm me.

"He's watching?" My brain turns to mush and my insides become one big out-of-control mess.

Reality sinks in and she smiles smugly, turning to take a freshly brewed cup of coffee from Alice, the other barista and the only one who appears to be working at the moment.

Kylie hands a college jock his order and I stand frozen, facing the storefront. My gaze drifts from the line of people to those at tables scattered around the coffee shop. Sure enough, he sits in the far corner at a table for two.

Our eyes collide and a mischievous grin steals over his gorgeous face. Straightening his spine, he crooks a finger at me.

With a shaky smile and equally unstable insides, I nod and hold up a finger, needing a moment. Or maybe five thousand. I'm not so sure my legs and feet will carry me across the store.

"Um, Kylie, Alice, are you guys okay if I go talk to a friend for a sec?" I'm horrible at hiding my nerves.

Alice arches a black brow, staring at me unamused—her normal state of being. "Didn't you *just* take a break?"

I resist the urge to roll my eyes. I want to ask what's it to her, seeing as she already took her break and it was twice as long as allowed. But I don't say shit. She can be vicious.

"Yeah, yeah, go ahead." Kylie sticks her tongue out at Alice and hops to the cash register, finally calling the next customer.

I feel less guilty for taking an extra few minutes knowing customers are being served. "Thank you."

"It isn't like I'm dying to talk to my boyfriend or anything." She's joking, as we both know she spends every free minute with her boyfriend.

"He's not my boyfriend."

As much as I wish he were, it's too late for that. He just completed his undergraduate study and oddly enough, instead of doing his law degree here, he's going to Columbia University in the fall.

I think it has something to do with expenses based on his comments. He lives in New York City so it would be easier. Even so, he isn't coming back here. And let's not forget, there's the minor fact that we're just friends.

"Not yet anyway." She pours the milk into a carafe. "You two have been sniffing around each other for the better part of a year like dogs in heat."

Alice releases a pig-like snort and I wrinkle my nose. "Yuck, must you?" Stepping from behind the counter, I take one last look at her over my shoulder. "I'll make it quick."

"Take your time. Young love is oh so grand."

I laugh. Outside of work, Kylie and I don't hang out, but I like her. She's a freshman living with her high school sweetheart and has no declared major, whereas I'm a twenty-two-year-old virgin with one more year to my undergraduate degree before starting law school.

On wobbly knees, I make my way to Patrick, the guy I've been crushing on for two years. He hasn't made a move and neither have I. We have this thing going on where he flirts, I stammer and blush, and then we retreat to our respective lives. It's awesome and frustrating.

"Hey, Patrick." I fiddle with my apron strings for something to do with my clammy hands. "What's up?"

His blond hair flops over his forehead and his smile widens. "Mia, Mia, Mia."

My cheeks warm. "Is that the best you've got?"

"Hey, I was warming up but would you rather I just say *I can't stop thinking about you*?" His voice is low and gravelly.

My heart beats faster, almost a gallop, and I want to slap my hands over my cheeks to hide the rising burn. Did he just say what I think he did? He's good. *Get it together, Mia.*

"Okay, whatever." I try to play it cool, something I'm not and have a hard time pulling off.

He could mean anything by it. He's flirting. Or maybe he really can't stop thinking about me? But why would he say that now? We're at the end of the school year and this is goodbye. I'll never see him again.

"I'm serious. You have your last exam today, right?" He pauses and I nod, trying to ignore the growing lump in my throat.

"My house is having an end-of-school party tonight and I wanted to invite you." His lazy smile causes my stomach to flip.

"I've got an exam to take." Why did I just say that? My exam is this afternoon and will be long over by the party.

He cocks his head to one side, gifting me with a lopsided grin, and his dimples pop. "Even more reason to let loose tonight."

Let loose? What does that even mean? To me, it's spending the day in my pajamas watching movies, eating ice cream out of the carton, or splurging on takeout for dinner. I'm so out of my depth.

"What about you? Don't you have any more exams?"

"Nah, I'm done." He casually shrugs, beaming. "Come tonight."

"Um, but I'm leaving in the morning. I've got to…"

A lame excuse. Parties aren't my thing, but how can I say no? How can I say yes? I'm socially awkward, painfully shy at those kinds of things.

"That's tomorrow. Come for a bit. It'd be fun to hang out. Please." His eyes are as big and as blue as the ocean and I just want to dive in.

He's never asked me out before. Is that what this is? A date?

"If you're done with exams, then this is it? Goodbye, Cornell and hello Columbia." I inwardly cringe at how corny I sound.

It's another lame attempt, this time to switch topics, unable to wrap my head around his invitation.

He waits a beat or two before gifting me with another one of his sexy grins. "So, what do you say?"

I want to go. This could be my only chance. He's leaving and I'll never see him again. What if something amazing happens between us? Could I live with that? But what if I walk away from my chance? I couldn't live with that.

"Um, sure." What on earth did I just agree to?

I can't go to this party and do what I'd normally do, which is sit in the corner tongue-tied. He'll regret inviting me and I can't watch him with other girls, been there done that and have the scars. Ugh. No, thanks.

He stares up at me, a playful glint in his gaze. A bundle of nerves, I hook my thumb over my shoulder and shuffle from foot to foot.

"I should get back to work."

"Cool, and I should get going." He stands and I have to tip my head back to maintain eye contact—he's several inches taller. "Here's the address."

He hands me a postcard with all the details for his frat's big school blow-out party. My heart drops, realizing he's most probably asked many girls to this thing.

It looks like it'll be huge. I might not even find him with all the people there.

"Thanks. See you later." I turn on my heel, shoving the card in my apron pocket and trying not to think about the fact that this might be the last time I ever see him again.

Well, I'm going to have to find him tonight. This is my chance. *Mia, you better make the most of it.*

"Hey, Mia." His deep voice sends shivers down my spine and stops me in my tracks.

"Yes." I swivel around and his fingers glide down my arm, stopping at my wrist, where he gently grips the simple leather bracelet.

"Where's mine?"

It's burning a hole in my apron.

I blush, feeling guilty for not giving him the bracelet any of the many times I've seen him over the past two weeks. I make them with my younger sister, Emily, and we sell them online.

Our small business has been a windfall, since I don't make nearly enough at the café to cover living expenses and food. We'd had a conversation about my bracelet weeks ago and he asked me to make him one.

"Sorry, I've had it for a while." I pull the small black pouch from my front pocket and a rush of heat prickles along my neck.

I'm not ashamed of my work, actually the opposite, but I never gave him the bracelet because I wasn't sure if he wanted it. I thought he was being polite.

"How much do I owe you?" He takes the pouch and our fingers graze. Tingles explode throughout my body like fireworks.

"You don't owe me anything."

His eyes widen, expression thoughtful. "No, this is your business. Let me pay." He puts his hand to his chest. "I'm a customer."

"And I want to give this to you." My tongue suddenly feels heavy and useless. I want to add "in friendship," but would that ruin my chances tonight? Would I be putting myself in the friend zone?

"Mia, thank you." His gaze flickers with something unknown, making my heart do a somersault.

He pulls the drawstring wide, sliding his fingers into the pouch. I nibble at my bottom lip, now second-guessing my choices—every element was chosen with him in mind—and also hoping he likes it.

I hold my breath as he removes the bracelet. His gaze is fixed on the simple yet masculine brown leather band, braided like rope.

Knees weakening, I'm bowled over when he lifts his head and hits me with a blinding smile, eyes glittering with gratitude and something else I can't name.

"This is awesome, I love it." He holds out his wrist. "Could you put it on for me?"

Nodding and smiling like a loon, my fingers tremble at the very touch of his warm skin as I wrap the band around his wrist, securing the clasp.

"Thank you." His eyes are warm upon me.

"You're welcome. It looks great on you."

"Yeah. I really like it. About your exam today, you don't need it but good luck. You'll kill it." He brushes his knuckles along my cheek and I don't stand a chance at stopping the electric current that runs through me at his touch.

"Thanks. I hope so."

"And I'll see you tonight?" Is it wishful thinking or do I detect a hint of a plea in his voice?

I nod and his long fingers wrap around the nape of my neck as another blinding smile steals his mouth. "Great. Until then."

He leans in, lips lightly grazing mine and he's gone before I can even open my eyes. My lips tingle from his kiss.

TRIPP

NOW

"Found you." Ry's words are a rumble in the dark, surprising me.

I hear him before I see him, turning toward his voice. The night is black and heavy with winter storm clouds, and in this part of the cemetery, there aren't any lights.

His large figure trudges up the hillside, hunched over and hands in his jacket pockets, trying to block the wind. I shiver in my spot on the frosty grass. I don't get to be warm and comfortable when my brother is six feet under in the cold ground.

"Why were you looking for me?"

The headstone is only a few feet in front of me and while too dark to see the engraving, I'm here so often that it's vivid in my mind's eye. Even when I'm not here. Even when I close my eyes at night. All the time.

And every time, it's so real that I can almost feel the etchings of the slate letters, spelling out his name—Griffin Callum Townsend—on my fingertips. He'd be thirty-two, thirty-three in about a week, to my thirty-five. But he won't be. He'll always be twenty-two.

"We need to talk." Ry looms over me, blocking my brother's grave.

I bite back a growl. Being tracked down pisses me off, especially when I come here to be alone.

"You've got a wife and kids, shouldn't you be at home in bed with them?" I don't keep the sting from my tone. "Couldn't it wait till tomorrow? It's nearly one."

This isn't the first time I've run into one of my friends here. Usually it's Carys, my childhood friend and Ry's younger sister, whom I'll find sitting in this very spot. Like me, she comes here at all hours of the day or night.

He chuckles, now on his haunches in front of me and it's then his somber gaze, almost sorry, hits me. "You weren't answering your phone and..."

Pausing, he rubs the back of his neck and releases a harsh exhale, as if carrying a hefty burden. Something has happened. Ry usually keeps an eye on me, on all of us, but this feels different.

"What is it?" I bend my knees to my chest.

"Why's the tracker off on your phone?"

My fingers curl and pull at a few tuffs of grass. "I'm off the clock."

In our line of work, the ability for any of us to be located easily is important. We all agreed to having our phones tracked. Still, I sometimes like to go off the grid.

And when not working, I do what I always do, grab a bite and come here to visit my dead brother. I didn't want to be disturbed or found.

I miss him, a lot, even after all these years. When Griff died, I lost more than a brother. A part of me died too, and no matter how much time has passed, nothing fills the void. The ache may not be as sharp or as debilitating as it used to be, it's now duller and always constant.

And even bringing those who murdered him to justice didn't fill the hollowness inside me. Peace is just a word and I doubt I'll ever find it.

"You gotta turn it back on. We talked about this." He means well but I don't appreciate being treated like a scolded child.

"Fine." I grind my teeth, holding back my frustration. "Why are you here in the middle of the night? What's wrong?"

"Come back to the office." His ominous tone confirms something happened. "Tommie found new intel while going through recordings of Ash and Taya that you're going to want to hear."

Ash Naire is a sick bastard, dead now but still a nasty asshole who was into human trafficking. And Taya Conrad is Ry's estranged mother-in-law and head of a small criminal outfit here in New York City.

We'd worked with the Feds to bring them down and had to cut a deal with Taya to get Ash. I'm still pissed that we had to leave Taya alone. She's pure evil and had a hand in my brother's death.

I leap to my feet, now more than interested; maybe Tommie found something we could use to finally nab Taya, once and for all. "Go on."

"Let's go back to the office and we'll listen to it together."

"Why can't you just tell me?"

"Tripp, we need to be in a secure location for this. C'mon, stop making this fucking difficult."

I snort, following him back to our vehicles. "I'm being difficult? That's rich coming from a stubborn bastard like you."

He chuckles, shaking his head as he gets into his car. I follow behind on my bike through the streets of the city to our office, Hart Corporation, a private firm specializing in protection, security and intelligence.

Not too long ago, we'd had to relocate to Brooklyn. Ash tried to take out the lot of us and set fire to HC. The damage to our floors of the office building was extensive.

We've only just returned to the building and everything is new and bright in the office, even at this time of night. Well, except for the surveillance room. The room is dark, lit only by computer screens and a few dim lights sporadically placed in the ceiling. Our nighttime crew are busy working at their stations.

HC is a twenty-four-hour operation. Those working overnight are monitoring active missions around the globe.

Tommie, the head of intelligence, jumps from her seat and Max, her boyfriend and Ry's brother-in-law, stands behind her.

These two helped to bring down Ash, even though Max is a doctor and has no experience with covert operations or security.

"Hey, Tripp." Tommie smiles and quickly averts her gaze, which is out of character for the straight shooter she is. "I've got it."

She holds up a flash drive, looking to Ry, and we silently follow her from the room. Each second ratchets up my nerves and even more so when we enter a conference room with Tate, Ry's wife and Max's sister, sitting at the table.

Alarm bells go off in my head. Tate and Ry have two young boys, one still a baby, and the fact that she is away from them in the middle of the night is reason enough for concern.

"Why aren't you at home with the kids?"

"Hey, Tripp, great to see you too." She's teasing but there's an unusual edge to her voice.

"Okay, take a seat, man." Ry's all business, coming to stand behind his wife, hands on her shoulders.

Van isn't here, my other childhood best friend and co-owner of HC. Even though he's on an assignment, I half expect him to walk in. There's an intense vibe and usually, when things are like this, all HC management are present.

"Fine." I drop into the seat next to Tate and watch Tommie pop the flash drive into her laptop and bring up an audio clip.

"Evan Hart and his security firm will be a problem." I instantly recognize the voice and icy fingers curl around my insides. Ash Naire. The fucker is dead but hearing his voice is unsettling.

"They might be. Let's wait. It's too early to tell. I've handled them before and will do so again, if I have to."

That's Taya Conrad, Tate and Max's mother and the only one still alive of those responsible for Griffin's death. I hate this woman.

"It's risky to wait. We need to put an end to them now. We don't need them creating any problems for us. We don't need the attention."

"Ash, relax. Should Evan, or Ry, or anyone else become a problem, I'll take care of them. I have Griffin."

My spine stiffens like steel and Tate grabs my hand, squeezing tight. I can't look at her; I'm focused on the voices.

"Isn't he the one you killed? Your daughter's college boyfriend? What does he have to do with this?" Ash sounds annoyed.

She laughs. "Griffin isn't dead but they think he is. He's my ultimate move."

I can almost see the blonde ice witch's cutting smile and want to strangle her for this vicious lie. Why does she want Ash to believe Griffin is alive?

"You're not making any sense. None of them know he's alive?" Ash asks.

"That was one thing Bobby did right."

"Bobby? Your dead son-in-law?"

Taya must nod because she continues without answering his question. "He made it look like Griffin died. He nearly did."

I stiffen, my insides burning. Why is she lying? And as for Bobby, if the man wasn't already dead, I would kill him with my bare hands.

"Why keep him alive? For what purpose?" Ash now sounds intrigued.

"Griffin Townsend was to be my last resort if my daughter didn't fall in line and marry Bobby. Tate may hate everything about me, but she's just as driven and stubborn as I am. If I had Griffin, she would obey."

Tate growls beside me, fingernails digging into my flesh, and I bite back a hiss.

"And when Bobby and my husband died, I thought about revealing Griffin, but Tate married the FBI agent and I had Max by then."

Taya's referring to how she got her son to work for her by threatening harm, or worse, to his sister. The woman is a monster and will stop at nothing to get what she wants. Ending her would be the sweetest justice.

"And now? You see Griffin as the key to controlling Hart Corporation?" Ash doesn't sound convinced.

Neither am I… about my brother being alive. I don't trust Taya. She lies, kills and will do whatever it takes to get her way.

"Yes. If needed, I could reveal him. It would be like putting the proverbial fox in a henhouse."

Unsteady breaths drag through my lungs and my heart thunders, the crazy beat pounding in my ears. She's lying. She has to be. Griffin died ten years ago. I brought his body home.

What I can't figure out is, what's her game?

"Fine. You stay on top of them. I don't care if you kill them, just make sure nothing comes back on me. Understood."

"Of course. I've got it under control. They have no idea, he's right under their noses." The recording ends.

Tate turns to look at me while I glare at her husband. I don't understand why he'd drag me into the office in the middle of the night for this bullshit.

Like we can trust Taya, even if she had no clue we'd ever hear this. That's it. She likely wanted us to find this recording. She's playing her twisted mind games.

"Where the hell did you get this?" I bolt from the chair and it wheels back with such force that it smacks against the wall.

"Zero sent it to me." Tommie stands, coming toward me with a comforting expression like she wants to put my mind at ease.

Zero is a tech wizard, like Tommie, and an asshole who worked for Ash.

"And we fucking believe him? This has got to be some kind of sick joke. This isn't real."

"Hang on." Ry's hands are out in front of him in a placating gesture. "We're gonna get it analyzed for authenticity, for sure. Let's focus as if it is real."

"If it's fucking real then it means my brother is alive." My fingers thread my hair, gripping and pulling at my scalp, hoping the pain will override the insanity brewing in my mind.

Griffin can't be alive. Shit, if he is, he's been out there for a decade. Alone. What kind of state is he in? Why hasn't he contacted us?

This is bullshit. My brother is dead.

"What does she mean by he's under our noses?" Max paces back and forth. "I've listened to it four times already and I've been racking my brain."

"Is it someone already in our lives?" Tate is now out of her seat too.

How is she dealing with this? Griffin was her first love. She saw him killed. Fuck. Or maybe she didn't. Does she believe he could be alive?

"This is crazy. She's playing with us. I picked up his body in Chicago. All those years ago. We buried him." My voice cracks as that truth sears my heart all over again.

"That's another thing. If we're going to explore this, we should examine the body." Ry is serious and my eyes bug out of my head, sweat beading under my collar.

"No way. You want to desecrate my brother's body and grave. For what? A sick joke. So she can sit back and laugh at us."

My hands wave in the air and I most probably look as incensed and unstable as I feel. Am I losing my mind?

"We should never have made a deal with that bitch. I knew this would happen. She's always messing with our heads." A growl rips through my clenched jaw.

"We're not done with Taya. We never backed off, even when we made a deal with her to get Ash." Ry locks gazes with me.

"And what exactly does that mean?" I stand still, eager to know more. Maybe something has been in the works all this time? Some way to get Taya.

"We're still working with the Feds." Ry paces. "Even as they backed off on laying any charges on Taya related to Ash and the auction, we never stopped helping them build a case. The Feds say they're close to nailing her."

"Good. At least that's one piece of good news." The burning anger deep in my core dissipates a bit. "Forget this crap."

I can't understand why they are entertaining the recording. All of this is bullshit. A waste of our time.

"What if it's true?" Tate asks.

"Don't tell me you believe this? You of all people. You were in that goddamn room when they beat Griff to death." A shot of anger flares again at the thought of what my brother went through.

Why is she even contemplating that the recording could be true? She saw Griffin die with her very own eyes.

"Your mother..." Tate flinches and I regret using that word. "Taya is a liar. Why should we believe her?"

"I know. It's hard to believe." A cry of hope carries her words. "I want to reject it. To think my mother is playing another sick joke. But what if she isn't? She doesn't know we have this recording."

"So what? What does that prove?" I point to the laptop, no more convinced than before walking in here that my brother is alive.

"What if Zero did this to help us?" Tommie slides onto the tabletop, facing me. "He's helped me before. He's just as much Ash's victim as those women were. He'd want to help."

She may trust Zero, but I can't say for sure if he helped her. She was a teenager when she formed that bond with him, and above all else, a victim. It's easy to confuse manipulation for help when your life is on the line. I don't trust Zero, and I sure as hell don't trust Taya.

"I can't ignore this." Ry holds a determined glint in his eye. "We've got to at least explore its credibility. We'll get the tape analyzed. And we should all make a list of people close to us, or even acquaintances we think could be Griffin. And also, let's take another look at Taya's people and associates for any clues."

"What are you talking about?" It's difficult not to lose my shit. They are all getting on board the crazy train. "Am I the only one who remembers what Taya Conrad is capable of? She could grab someone off the street that looks even remotely like Griff and tell us it's him. She's toying with us."

"And that's why we should exhume the body." Max's tone is wary, maybe concerned about upsetting me. "We shouldn't dismiss this. Yes, Taya is capable of anything. There's so much here we need to explore. While I've seen pictures, I didn't meet Griffin since I was in England at the time. But based on what she said, it sounds like none of you would readily recognize him."

He has a point. Taya might be doing this because she has another angle. What, I don't know, but if we don't pursue this insane claim, we'll never know.

"Let's explore this, and Tripp, I think you should sit this one out." Ry nears me, gaze intent.

"Are you fucking kidding me? There's no way I'm sitting anything out. This is my brother. And even if it's a hoax and she's playing games, I'm not taking my eye off her. I want in. She could have another play up her sleeve."

"We already have guys on her," Tommie is quick to add. "And Tripp, what do you say to exhuming the body?"

"Fuck. This is crazy." My chest aches.

I hate the idea but what Max said makes sense. If we exhume the body, we'll know one way or the other. As ridiculous as it is, what if Griff's out there? I can't turn my back on the possibility all because I'm... what the fuck am I? Scared?

Scared that all these years my brother has been alive and I was oblivious to it? Or if he is alive, why the hell hasn't he tried to contact us? Has he written us off, thinking we abandoned him? Left him for dead?

Or, if he is alive but hasn't contacted us, it could mean he's being held prisoner. I think I'm going to be sick. I need to leave.

"Fuck. Do what you need to. I'll sign whatever papers. I just need to get out of here I can't... I can't."

"Tripp." Tate lunges, grabbing my arm. "You're not alone in this. I know it feels that way, but you're not alone. So please don't shut us out. We're here for you."

She tries to hug me but I'm stiff, arms remaining at my sides. Her eyes glitter with unshed tears and I feel nothing.

Ry steps in beside her, sympathy etched in his weary countenance. "We are here for you. Don't do something you'll regret for the rest of your life."

It's as if he can read my mind. Murder fills my thoughts. "I will not regret ending that woman."

"Maybe so, but there are better ways to stop her. You could destroy your life."

"What fucking life?" I pull from his grip.

"Tripp. Promise me you'll think before you do anything."

I stare at my childhood best friend and have no words for him. This can't be true. As much as I want it to be, if it is then my brother has been out there for ten years.

"Promise me you'll talk to one of us before you do anything rash." Ry shoves his hands into his pockets.

"I'm not promising you anything."

MIA

"Fraser, this is about me, not you." My aggressive grip causes the eraser at the tip of the pencil to snap and roll off the desk. "I made this promise to myself. I said the new year. In case you need help with telling time, Thanksgiving is a week away. I still have weeks to make a decision."

The pencil rolls along the top of the desk and I toss the pinkish-red rubber pieces into the trash can. I've got to get off this call. He's only adding to my frustration.

"C'mon, St. John, just call it. What difference does a few weeks make? Come back to LA, we'll set everything up just like it was." He's so arrogant and no matter how close we've worked together, or for how many years, I never did like that about him.

"I've got a little over a month before I move anywhere, if at all. But why split hairs?" I let my sarcasm rip and roll my shoulders to lessen the mounting tension.

Why do I let him get to me?

"See, this is why you have to come back. We get along so well." My ex-business partner laughs with the odd cough thrown in.

My problem is, I care. I could lecture him about his smoking; it sounds as if he hasn't stopped, but that's what his wife's for. Besides, he's closer to sixty and doesn't appreciate a thirty-four-year-old telling him what to do.

"Mia, I gotta ask. Do you even know what it is you're waiting for?"

"Pardon?"

"I've never understood what it is you're expecting to find in New York. Why are you there? You've set this arbitrary deadline of January first to decide whether to stay or come back home. But do you know what it is you're looking for?"

I'm not going back to LA or home as he calls it. But I'm not getting into that now. His question—why—seems like a fair one, to him. He insists I left our successful entertainment law firm, one of the best in a city of hundreds, out of the blue and with barely any notice.

None of that's true.

My departure was no secret, but he was in denial. My leaving meant he had to buy me out of our firm. It's been almost a year since I left and he's still bitter. Will he ever get over it?

"We've been through this before. I told you why I needed a fresh start and you didn't want to understand."

"Look, just come home." He sighs, or maybe it's a release of smoke. "I gotta go. Talk later."

"Fine. Bye." I toss my phone onto the desk, burying my frustration. I'm glad to be done with the weekly harassment call

Time to get back to work. It isn't like I don't have enough work to keep me busy until the next millennium. And Kitty's contract for her upcoming Broadway show will not read itself.

My finger scans the lines of fine print until I hit the spot where I left off. The words blur and I blink back the water welling in my eyes.

Fraser Hinton just doesn't listen.

When I first switched legal areas of expertise, he took me in and showed me the ropes, but his firm never took off until my arrival. I hustled and worked my butt off, bringing in new clients.

And once I was established and had made a name for myself in Tinsel Town, blockbuster talent sought me out. Yet any sense of pride or accomplishment is always tainted by talking to Fraser. Guilt always overwhelms me.

A little over a year ago, I sold my home and car, needing to get away from the pain of my past. I chose New York because next to LA, it was the best city for an entertainment attorney.

And short of Alaska or Hawaii, it was farthest away from what happened. Although I'm not sure there is anywhere I could go to escape my past.

No matter how many times I told him I was leaving—he had almost nine months' notice—he tells anyone who will listen that I just up and left him with nothing. Talk about trying to trash my reputation.

I'm not sure what I'm looking for in this city. Or maybe I was never looking for something, more like running from something.

At least a dozen boxes are still stacked in the corner of my already small office. Eleven months and I still haven't unpacked everything. The boxes mock me daily.

I gave myself a year to make it work, but maybe deep down I knew it wouldn't last and that's why I never fully unpacked? On the bright side, if I leave New York, I've already got a head start on the packing.

I put down the contract and bring my laptop in front of me, pulling up the website I've been searching for weeks. Maybe Fraser is right—what am I waiting for? Is that what has me so upset?

Here I am looking up homes for sale in Nashville as if I'm moving. And maybe I am and I just haven't admitted it to myself yet. At least my office lease is month-to-month and I'd sublet my apartment, so I can afford to think this through thoroughly.

I dial the number I've called way too many times in the past couple months and dig my toes into the plush carpet under my desk. My shoes are always the first thing to go when alone in the office.

"Hey, Red, did you make up your mind?" Murray's raspy smoker's voice—now this man will *never* quit—rumbles through the phone lines.

My head plunks onto the top of the desk, exasperated. Straightening, I brush back my red locks and take a deep breath. "Hi. I haven't decided… yet. But I'm leaning toward Nashville. The one you sent me."

I glance at the online pictures of the stunning house in what's supposed to be a great area of the city. I'm trusting Murray, since I've never been there, but it's a great location for an entertainment lawyer.

"Excellent choice, and it's still on the market." He rattles off the details while I stare blankly at the computer screen.

What am I doing? Is this what I want? Moving cities changes nothing. But I'm not sure what holds me to New York and I can't go back to LA; just the thought breaks my heart.

"So how do you want to proceed? You coming out to look? You want me to make an offer?"

"Do I have to be there in person if I decide I want it?" My stomach twists at yet another upheaval.

"No, no. I can take care of it for you, I just thought… you know, the way we were talking last time."

My roiling stomach sinks at the mere mention of our conversation only days ago. I was a mess.

"No, no. I don't or I should say, can't leave right now and I trust your expertise about this place and the city."

It had been one of those rough days when for no apparent reason the memories were drowning me. My desire to get moving was something fierce. I was ready to hop on a plane to anywhere.

"Red, are you sure moving is for you?" It's the same question he asked me last time we talked. He must think I'm crazy.

"Mur, I don't know. But New York isn't what I'd hoped it would be. I'm lonely. Work is awesome. Booming." I half laugh, half cry. "Could we do a video walk-through? Take me on a virtual tour of the place before I make a decision?"

"Sure, hon. Anytime. Just let me know what works. When do you think you could move in?"

"Not until January, at the earliest. I want to keep my clients, so I need some time, and I'm thinking this place is perfect to work from home. Enough space for a home office…" I trail off, biting my bottom lip, not even sure it's what I want.

I have no social life in one of the liveliest cities in the country. I can just imagine how much of a home body I'll be if my office is in my home.

"Great idea. Send me some days and times that work for you and I'll set up the walk-through."

"Okay, I will. Bye."

I wipe at my eyes, killing any unshed tears. Murray is my real estate agent and has been with me since I first set foot in LA. While he doesn't know Nashville, he's been working with a colleague based in the city to send me listings.

My reasons for thinking about leaving New York aren't clear, even to me. I can't explain it. Other than that I don't have any friends in New York, just lots of clients. That's no one's fault but my own.

As an entertainment lawyer, all my clients are musicians, singers, actors, on the big screen, small screen and/or Broadway, producers, and performers. And most are huge successes. I don't lack for a busy life. They invite me to the latest movie premieres, film festivals, Broadway shows and parties.

While I don't accept every invitation, when I do, the parties are amazing for meeting new people and growing my business. More often than not, I'll leave those gatherings with a potential client. But that's just it. It's all business.

I close out the window on the computer screen, the beautiful house in Nashville vanishes, and I pull up my calendar. I've got a new client coming in an hour. Just enough time to finish my first pass on this contract.

The phone rings again and I groan at Fraser's name brightening the screen. I hit speaker. "Miss me so soon?"

"Funny. Listen, what's this I hear about Kitty Carmichael? She's now your client?"

My body tightens and I sit up straighter, suddenly irked that he has this information. It isn't a secret, but it also isn't any of his business.

"I'm not having this conversation with you again. My clients aren't your business and yours aren't mine." My fingers curl, wanting to crush this call.

"You know why we're talking about this. You're in breach of contract. Again. Fuck, Mia."

"I can't be in breach of my non-compete." Frustration punctures every one of my words. "Kitty was never a client of Hinton St. John. And I didn't solicit her. She came to me."

I don't bother to mention that she was a referral from another client. No, I don't say a thing because *that* client used to be with Hinton St. John and left when I did. Mentioning it will only bolster his verbal abuse.

"Don't fucking pull that shit. You know exactly what I'm getting at. I approached Kitty months ago when she was out here. She was close to signing with me. But oh no, Mia St. John can't have that. A big Broadway star signing with an LA law firm, and your ex-boss. You had to dive in with your fake compassion and charming smiles."

I'm grateful we're separated by thousands of miles. This is more than his usual bluster and his anger causes my anger to climb from a simmer to a boil.

"Fraser, we were *partners* when I left, but why let that get in the way of an *oh so sad* tale. And that's not how this went down, but I won't defend myself to you. We're done here."

I hit end and refuse to pick up when the phone rings. I rub at my temples, reminded of another reason moving to the other side of the country appealed to me—to get away from Fraser.

TRIPP

I saunter into Van's office like a delinquent teenager summoned to the principal's office. We haven't talked since before my world was upended by the recording, three days ago. Tommie cut me a copy and I've replayed it so many times, I could recite the conversation in my sleep.

Since then, I've been radio silent with the entire team, including Tate. Until today, I have answered none of their calls or texts, but I left on my phone tracker. I can be a dick but not a total one.

I needed time and space from their well-intentioned badgering, as well as to give me a chance to figure out my shit.

Even if I have my reservations about the recording, I can't walk away from it and it's only served to reignite my desire to bring Taya down. I got lazy and let my guard down. That ends now.

"We have to talk." He motions at the chair across from him and I stand, crossing my arms. "Fine, suit yourself."

Jaw clenched and gaze unamused, he shuffles papers on his desk for a few beats until finally, he turns his attention back to me. Asserting control. Nice.

My position may be among senior management at Hart Corporation, and I make my own hours, but Van is the boss.

"So I take it Ry told you about the Taya recording?" I've been tailing Taya, sticking to her like shit on the bottom of a shoe.

And when not on her, I'm looking into the people in my life and the lives of those around me. Acquaintances or individuals on the periphery who have come into our lives within the past ten years and could pass for Griff.

We're also investigating those around Taya. During our time with the Feds, Ry and I covered a lot of ground, getting to know who's who in her organization and her known associates.

Since joining HC, with our limited resources, we focused on the more suspicious and threatening individuals. We didn't come across any red flags, but that was before the possibility that Griffin could be alive.

He's right under their noses.

Her words haunt me. They are our most important lead right now, and might be the only one, unless we get more from the other avenues we're pursuing.

But so far, I've come up empty. And with the lack of urgent calls or texts, I'm guessing so have my friends.

"Yeah. How are you doing?" Van sits, pushing his chair back to bring one ankle onto his other knee.

"How do you think?"

He quirks a brow and twists his lips. "We're on it. Tommie got the autopsy report."

I nod. Tommie shares everything with me. What he doesn't say is, she's fast and will use any means necessary to get answers quickly. At the same time, she goes through official channels, should we ever need to share our findings in a court of law.

"I'm going to Chicago to speak with the medical examiner and the cops who were on the case at the time. I don't want any bullshit and face to face makes that harder." He leans forward, elbows on the edge of his desk. "If you want to come, I understand. I know Ry asked you to sit this out, but I also get why that's impossible."

I swallow past the emotions strangling me. Van's understanding is appreciated. At one time, he was dealing with horrible news about his dead father, and while sitting it out was the smart thing to do, he couldn't.

Chicago isn't something I want to be a part of. I can't do that again.

"Thanks, Van. I'm going to pass. I trust you."

I was the one to identify the body years ago and I can't relive that. While they had to rely on dental records for a conclusive identification, what if I missed something? What if I was too close to it—he was my fucking brother, the only family I had left in the world—to see that it wasn't him?

"Okay. I'll call you when I'm done."

"Thanks. Besides, I want to stay on Taya. If this is true—"

He cuts me off, quirking a brow. "You still have reservations that this isn't legit?"

"I'm not convinced. Sure the recording may be real, but this could be another one of her games." I lean forward. "I mean, think about it. How best to fuck with us than to make us believe he's alive? And once she's got us on this wild goose chase, she makes another move."

"Sure, I can see that." He nods, gaze intent on me. "But why? Why now?"

"Ry said the FBI is closing in on her. What if she knows this? We work closely with the Feds, we did so when we brought down Ash. It wouldn't be a stretch for her to think we'd help them now to put her behind bars. Look at all the chaos and pain she's caused us over the years. She needs to be stopped."

"Yeah, you're right. But how do you explain the authenticity of the recording? We got it checked and the voices are Ash and Taya. Nothing was tampered with, or remotely suspicious. Shit, Tommie's guy even gave us a rough timeframe and location of when and where it took place based on the background noise."

"I don't know. Taya and Ash most probably had the conversation but it may have been orchestrated."

My reluctance to believe is ironic and at times, frustrating. Over the years, even now, I'd give anything for Griffin to be alive. So why the fuck am I fighting the possibility?

"All right. We need more proof and we're going to get it, one way or another."

"Agreed. But Van, we have to move fast and figure this out. If Griff is alive…" My voice cracks and I clear my throat. "If he is, we need to find him before the Feds move on Taya, because if she's arrested… and he's out there, she will bargain with his life."

"Fuck." His fingers rub at his temples in a small circular motion. "I know."

"Do you know how close they are to making an arrest?"

"Nah. They won't say but they're confident. We'll keep pressing and stay close so we get the heads up before it goes down." He shuffles some papers on his desk and hands me a thin file. "I have a job for you."

"I'm on Taya." Irritation circles my words.

Griffin is priority one. How does he expect me to think about anything other than finding out if he is actually alive?

"Yeah, I know, but this shit will consume you. You need something else to focus on and I have a job that needs to get done."

Shaking my head, I open the dossier and read the case details. The assignment isn't our usual. In fact, we would normally pass on stuff like this.

Then her name hits me. Nine letters run me over like a tank.

Mia St. John.

Fuck me.

She's in New York.

Based on the details, some guy she used to work with in LA claims she breached her non-compete agreement. He's accusing her of stealing his clients and causing irreparable damage to his livelihood.

More than half the time, these agreements are drawn up to scare the person into playing it straight. There's no teeth to them. But it looks like this guy, Fraser Hinton, wants evidence to back up his claim. And he has intentions of suing her.

None of this sounds like the Mia I knew. She was honest and good to a fault. Back in college, she was always the first to help other students with notes or studying when she didn't have to, or even if it added to her workload.

Closing the folder, I look to Van. "Why would we take this case? It isn't our thing."

"I owe a buddy of mine in LAPD a favor. He helped us out on that kidnapping earlier this year and it's his brother who needs the intel."

He straightens, cracking his back and averting his gaze, long enough for me to put the pieces together.

"Look, I know it sounds like bullshit and really, it isn't enforceable. My gut tells me he's looking to cause her grief, but a debt needs to be paid and it's a fairly straightforward job. If you don't want it, I'll give it to Tango and I'll give you…" He thumbs through a few more files, looking for another case.

"No. I'll do it." I tap the folder against my leg. "You know I know her, right?"

There's a flicker in his gaze and that's all I need to confirm my suspicions that there's more to this case. This is busy work. Mia is a distraction.

"Yeah. When I saw she went to Cornell… and the name rang a bell."

I'm sure it did. Van isn't anything if not thorough with background checks before we take on any assignment. He doesn't like surprises and he would have realized the connection immediately. I talked about Mia a lot during the last two years of school, and when I first got back to New York.

"You remembered? That was twelve years ago."

"Yeah, but she's the only woman you've ever talked about."

"No, she isn't." I pause, combing my brain for another name, another woman that I've obsessed about and longed for.

Shit, he's right. There isn't another woman.

He chuckles at my realization. "Just keep it professional. While it seems like a clear-cut assignment and a short one, by my guess, it's still a job. And we have a reputation to uphold."

"Of course."

* * *

IMPULSIVE, it's the only way to explain what the hell I'm doing. Unlike all my other missions, I don't bother with any recon or research first. The case file burns my palm as I high tail it to a company SUV. Our office is close to the address of Mia's firm, and that's where I'm headed.

Entertainment law. Interesting.

The drive takes longer than it would on my bike, thanks to traffic, but I luck out and easily score a spot on the street.

Out the car window, across the street, red flashes in my vision and my stomach muscles shake. She's on the sidewalk, headed away from her office. Never have I ever had a gut-punch reaction to any woman. Until Mia.

And more than a decade since I last laid eyes on her, it's still the same. I stare at her from the street and my core clenches, heat tunneling from the base of my spine through my body.

Mia St. John.

Flaming, wavy red hair. Alabaster skin, smooth as marble. Full, bow-shaped lips that make my mouth water with thoughts of sweet strawberries. Cheekbones my fingers itch to sweep across, and her eyes. Long, dark lashes frame her soulful, big brown eyes.

My mother loved Van Morrison; I'd roll my eyes and groan whenever she played him. But after meeting Mia, every time I saw her, I'd think of "Brown-Eyed Girl" and I totally got the song.

Sha la la la la la la la la la-la te da, la te da.

She's all grown up. I mean, she was all woman back in college at the glorious age of twenty-two but now, twelve years later, at first glimpse, she's grown into herself. She walks with confidence.

Her body sways seductively down the sidewalk in her black patent high heels. She's rocking the all-white look even in late November. And with her flaming hair, it's shocking and mesmerizing, all at the same time.

Her winter coat is ankle length and open, showing she's in a white business suit. The blazer cinches at her slender waist and the pencil pants accentuate her shapely legs.

On the phone, handbag hanging off her wrist, she laughs at something whoever she's talking to says, tilting her head back. I can't hear her laugh and I want to so badly. But she's sparkling, face aglow and smile bright and wide. I must talk to her.

She opens the door to a coffee shop and I jump from the car, dashing across the street, entering only seconds after her.

And while it's nothing like the campus café where Mia worked and I hung out just to watch and talk to her, I'm taken back to our college days. The smell of coffee always makes me think of her. It always puts a smile on my face.

She's at the back of the line with the phone to her ear. Her long silky hair falls loosely down her back and her melodic laugh floats toward me. Like a tuning fork, the sound vibrates through my body, long and rhythmic, shaking me to the core.

I step in behind her in line and note that, with heels on, she's closer to my height than she ever was in college. I'm ready to make contact and this silly assignment, the reason I'm even here, is the last thing on my mind.

"I miss you too, honey," she says into the phone.

My hand is outstretched, ready to tap her on the shoulder, and with her words, it falls to my side. She's with someone, no surprise. A boyfriend? Or is it a husband? I don't see a ring.

See, this is why I put in the time and do the research and reconnaissance before ever engaging with a subject. You should always know what you're walking into. But she isn't just a subject.

This is Mia.

MIA

"Hey, Eli." I inch forward in the line and wonder if coffee is a good idea.

Eli Lansing is the lead guitar for the world-famous now-retired rock band Trojan, and also my client. I just finished speaking with Crystal, his seven-, soon to be eight-year-old daughter. I absolutely love talking to her but every time I do, I end up wanting to cry.

Maybe water or tea is a better idea. Something to hydrate me or soothe my soul. If it were later in the day, I could go straight to a cocktail. A good vodka martini would be great to drown my sorrows.

"Did she make you feel guilty?" Eli's welcomed voice warms my inside.

"Not intentionally, but yeah. She was tugging on my heartstrings pretty hard."

"Don't feel guilty. Mia, you're doing what's right for you and your sanity. I'll talk to her again to help her understand why you're there and we're here. She just misses you like crazy. I do too."

"Oh, Eli." I lower my voice, remembering I'm in public and can't cry. "I miss you too."

We are more than client and lawyer. He's also my friend and soon will be living in New York City. While I love the idea, I'm not so sure it's enough to keep me here as his close presence also comes with its pitfalls.

"Hey, hang on a sec." I'm now at the counter and I smile at the cashier. "Hi, I'll have a mint green tea, extra large."

I scan the display case, my gaze snagging on the lemon pound cake. My weakness. Just the right balance of sweet and tart. But I've got snacks back at the office and dinner isn't too far off.

"Anything else?" the girl behind the counter asks.

"No, thanks. That's it."

She rings me up and Eli asks, "Where are you?"

"Oh, I'm out to shake off my afternoon funk." He laughs and I can't help but smile.

I've not once regretted sharing with him my silly ritual of needing a pick me up around two or three in the afternoon.

"Oh, I miss those. Remember that one time, we took off to Pacific Park and rode the Ferris wheel?"

"Oh my God, yes. That was a fun afternoon." I can almost smell the sea salt air and feel the sand in my toes.

"So when are you coming out?" I'm referring to his move across the country for his new acting job. "Have you told Crystal yet?"

I slide out of the way, waiting for my order with a small group of people doing the same thing. Head down, I fumble with my purse, trying to slip my wallet back inside with the phone to my ear.

"Soon, and yeah, she knows. She's going to miss her friends but understands it's my job. Besides, she's excited about being close to you."

Guilt for thinking about leaving New York when they will be here soon tugs at my heart.

"That'll be fun." I feel like a fraud knowing I might leave.

"That's one thing she's looking forward to. Listen, I know this is me sticking my nose in where it doesn't belong… but don't be so hard on yourself. It always takes time to adjust to a new city. A new life."

"I know." I cringe at the unintended defensiveness to my tone.

Adjusting to the city isn't the problem. It's longing, wishing I could change things and make what happened never exist. No such chance.

"Do you? It just seems to me you aren't allowing yourself to live your life."

"What does that mean?" I curl in on myself, feeling exposed and self-conscious with having this kind of conversation in public.

"Well, you up-end your life and move to New York for a fresh start, which I totally get. Melanie's been gone six years..." His pain and remorse fill his pause.

Melanie is Crystal's mother. A one-night stand and groupie that Eli got pregnant. He took full responsibility and their plan was to raise their daughter together, even if there was no future for them as a couple.

She was a heavy drug user and despite being clean for the pregnancy, she started using again six months after giving birth and overdosed when Crystal was two.

"Hey, that wasn't your fault either," I say.

"I know, and this isn't about me." He clears this throat. "What I mean is, you're already talking about moving. Your one-year rule never made sense. These things take time. Give yourself time."

My eyes flutter closed, concentrating on his words of wisdom. He isn't too far off the mark. I still don't know why I'm twisting myself in knots for answers or searching for peace when I can't help thinking, I just need to stand still.

"Fair enough." My eyes pop open when the barista calls my order. "I've got to go. We'll talk soon."

"Okay. Take care. Bye."

My fingers wrap around the hot beverage and I thank the barista.

"Mia." Behind me, a deep throaty voice gives me pause. It's familiar but I can't place it.

I turn, drink in hand, to see the only man ever featured in my dreams. Patrick Townsend stands before me and I blink several times, making sure I'm not dreaming.

Tightening my grip on the cup, I step away from the counter, toward him. "Patrick?"

Still as handsome as ever.

Still as intense as ever.

A mess of blond hair, dramatic blue eyes. His tall, lean body wears his dark jeans, a white tee and leather jacket perfectly.

"Yeah, it's me. Hi, I thought that was you." His piercing eyes cause my heart to flutter wildly. "How are you?"

"Oh, my." My fingers cover my mouth, trembling, and I quickly lower my hand from his vision. "What are you doing here?"

"I came in for a drink." He holds up a bottle of water and a white paper bag. "And I saw you. I could hardly believe it. How long has it been?"

Twelve years.

And not a day goes by without thinking about him.

"Years. I live in New York now. My office is just up the street." I point in the wrong direction and fumble to course correct. "And you?"

"Me too. Born and raised and still living in New York. I'll never leave this city. Where were you before?"

His hands slide into his front jeans pockets and my gaze follows every one of his sexy, self-assured moves. Suddenly, my throat is parched.

I'm thirsty for something I can't have. In my lustful daze, I take a gulp of the tea, forgetting it's steaming hot until it's too late.

"Ow." I quickly pull the cup away, wincing at the burning on not only my lips and tongue but also down my throat.

Way to go, Mia.

"You okay?" He steps into my personal space.

I'm reminded of how much of a man he is. His build. Broad and muscled. His scent. Masculine and citrusy. His fingers, warm and comforting, curling around my arm to steady me.

A jolt of electricity—that familiar but never old spark—dances down my spine at his touch.

"Yes, that wasn't smart." I'm making a mess of this and if I stay too much longer, one of us will wear this hot beverage. "Patrick, um, I've got a client call in about fifteen minutes. I'd love to catch up, but I have very little time right now."

"Of course." Backing up, his hold falls from me and I feel the loss like a jerk to my chest. "Let me walk with you. We can get in a few more minutes and make plans."

I falter halfway to the exit of the shop, my steps stuttering as I peer over my shoulder at him. "Plans?"

He nods and his lips twitch upward at the corners. It isn't quite a smile, but it's no less inviting. "Yeah. You don't think I'm going to let you get away so easily. I want to set a time to catch up." He walks around me to hold open the door. "Let's go."

Brushing past him, I'm immediately hit with the chill of outside. Just what I need to clear my muddled brain.

"So, you never did say. Where were you living before New York?" Now beside me, he inches nearer, close enough that our arms brush occasionally as we walk.

Even through the layers of our clothes, his touch is electric and a temptation I can't deny.

One of his arms slides behind me in what feels like a protective or possessive gesture, and his hand hovers at my lower back. The heat of him, so close, is dizzying and all I can think about. Will he touch me? Take me in his arms?

Okay, Mia, stop this insane fantasy and focus on what he's saying. Or more like, I'm up and he's waiting for my response.

"I lived in LA for many years."

"Wow, the opposite end of the country. Talk about extremes. What made you pick up roots and come over to the dark side?"

His eyes twinkle with mischief and I laugh, but it's more nervous than lighthearted. If he only knew why I'm here.

"I needed a change." Glancing up the street, I wish we were at my office. But there are still a few more buildings to go.

"I get that. And what is it you do? Are you practicing law?"

"Yes. I'm an entertainment lawyer." I wonder what field he specializes in and hope by divulging this about myself, he'll offer up more about himself.

"Entertainment law. Hmmm… I always figured you'd work for the PD's office or work with not-for-profits or the like, to take down corporate America."

I don't know why but his comment causes heat to rise within me and not in a good way. Almost as if I'm embarrassed by my chosen area of law, and while he's right, it wasn't my first choice, there's nothing wrong with it.

"Things change. I ended up in LA and it made the most sense, even if at the time I was one of many lawyers in that field. I've been at it now for a little over six years and I love it."

"That's great." He slows as if knowing we're near, but how could he know it's my office?

"Well, this is me." I stop at the next door over.

He gazes up at the building and then back at me. "Mia."

Warmth floods my body at the same time goosebumps pop along my skin from the sound of my name tumbling from his lips. His gaze drops to my mouth and then to the concrete.

His unsure move, or more like avoidance, incites a strange feeling in my stomach. Not quite butterflies, more churning and confusion.

Clearing his throat, he looks up at me. "It was great to run into you. Can I drop by your office some time?"

"Ah, sure. But maybe call first. I've got appointments and deadlines so it's best if I know when you're coming by. Otherwise, it could be a wasted trip for you."

"Never." He shakes his head and his golden locks fall onto his forehead. "Even just to see you for a few minutes would be worth it."

Why is my heart racing? And of course, now I blush. *Stop.*

"Give me your phone." He puts his hand out, palm up.

I pass him my drink so I can grab my phone from my purse. We then trade, cup for phone, and I watch him enter his number. Will I call him? I could. I want to. But what good will come of it?

His jacket then vibrates and I'm guessing it's a text he just sent. He hands my phone back to me.

"Now we have each other's numbers. I'll call you or text soon."

Butterflies swoop and twirl in my stomach. I can hardly believe Patrick's in front of me, let alone that he's going to call me.

"Great. And it was great to see you again." My hand grasps his hard forearm in a friendly gesture.

We both look to where we are touching before his gaze captures mine. "I almost forgot. This is for you."

He holds up the small white paper bag from the coffee shop. Curious, I take it and open it. An unrestrained grin steals my face.

"How did you..." I bury my nose in the opening and sniff. Delicious notes of lemon and icing sugar fill my senses. "Ah, lemon pound cake. How did you know I'd love this?"

"Lemon is your favorite." He's smiling, warm and attentive. "I could never forget that, and I must confess, I saw you eyeing the slices in the coffee shop."

Now butterflies are alive in my stomach with the knowledge he remembered how much I love lemon anything. Followed by another blush and I shake my head as my smile continues to grow. My cheeks ache but I can't, nor do I want to, stop myself.

"This is very sweet of you. Thank you."

"You're welcome."

"Bye." I turn before I lose my willpower and stay rooted to the spot.

My office is on the second floor, and while I sometimes take the elevator if I'm with clients or have my hands full, most times I take the stairs. I push the stairwell door open when the sound of my name—coming from Patrick—stills my heart, stopping me in my tracks.

"Mia." He's outside with his foot holding the door open. "Dinner tonight?"

The butterflies are in a frenzy now.

"Ah, sure," I say without even thinking to check my calendar.

"Is Italian still your favorite?"

Leaning on the open stairwell door more for support than anything else, I cock my head to one side and smile.

"You don't need to ask that question. Italian is absolutely, and always will be, my favorite."

"Awesome. Text me your home address and I'll pick you up at seven thirty."

"Okay." I no sooner say it than he's gone.

Feeling every bit the college girl I once was, crazy about Patrick

Townsend, I let out a squeal, quickly followed by the clamping of my lips. I've got to stifle this giddiness until I'm within the confines of my office. I don't need any of the other tenants coming out to see who's making a ruckus.

My foot is on the first step when I remember he sent a text to himself and I want to see it. While I'm at it, I might as well send him my address. I find my phone and pull up the text.

A warm, rich peal of laughter erupts from within me at what he typed but sent from me to him.

Mia: I've missed you.

TRIPP

I have a light bounce to my step as I leave Mia's office building, and a goofy grin that I can't seem to curb. And truth be told, I don't want to dim this feeling, not even a bit.

Mia St. John. She's in New York and we're going to dinner.

I meant what I wrote in the text. I've missed her and didn't realize just how much until now. And I'm not wild to admit it, and think the saying is such a cliché, but Mia is the one that got away.

In my defense, at the time, I didn't realize losing her was a risk. I was filled with hope when I asked her to the end of school party and had truly believed we had a chance even if I was graduating. Nothing was impossible and I was motivated. I'd wasted too much time and should have made my interest known sooner.

Our mutual attraction was undeniable. Still is. And she'd be hard pressed or a liar to negate our electrifying chemistry. Not after that brief but charged encounter.

I hop into my car, lean back against the headrest and close my eyes. On the way to her office, there had been just a few inches of space between us, close enough to smell the provocative floral and woody notes of her on the light wind. Her feminine scent still lingers as if she's next to me.

Tonight can't come soon enough. I can't wait to see her again.

Dinner isn't about the bogus case. That's what the whole thing is, bogus. I still have to do my due diligence, and I will. But dinner is about Mia.

More than anything, I want to get to know her again. Reconnect. Maybe have more. While we can't pick up where things ended—shit, they didn't end. They were severed.

The past is the past, best to leave it where it belongs. My assignment aside, I want to see what's possible with Mia.

This is a second chance for both of us. I only hope this time she doesn't try to run, because I'll be ready.

* * *

WE WIND through the tables and chairs of the Italian restaurant, only a few blocks from her place. When I picked her up, she was outside her apartment door by the time I got to her floor. We walked over since it was close and it made for a brisk, chilly stroll.

The server leads the way to our table, with Mia in front of me. Every few steps, she glances over her shoulder as if checking to make sure I'm still there. What does she think? I'm going to vanish? She's the one who took off back in college.

At the table, I remove her coat and she's more casual than earlier today in dark denim jeans that accentuate her lean, toned legs, and a glittery blue blouse.

"You look great."

"Thank you." A flush steals down the curve of her neck and a wild fluttering ripples through her slender body.

Fuuuck, I love how responsive she still is to me after all these years. I used to take too much pleasure in flirting with her when she worked at the coffee shop on campus.

She slides into the booth and I follow right behind her, maybe a little too eager. Our thighs brush against each other while moving along the vinyl, and she sucks in a sharp breath as her cheeks flush.

We make idle conversation while perusing the menu. As if in

unspoken understanding, we broach nothing of significance until we've ordered our food and wine.

"So tell me what you've been doing since you left Cornell." She groans and rolls her eyes. "Shit. I told myself to stay away from talking about school. About..."

She's referring to our last night, all those years ago. I'd invited her to an end of school party and we spent one mind-blowing night together, only for her to take off before I woke up.

"Let's ease into that." I wouldn't say I'm still angry about her disappearing act, but the wound is still sore. "I do want to talk about it and we will." My gaze is pointed, ensuring she gets that the topic is unavoidable. "But let's save that for later."

"Okay." She forces a tight smile.

Maybe nervous? An uncontrolled grin stretches across my face. I can't deny I like how easily I affect her.

"I'll start. I graduated, then joined the FBI, and now I work for my friend's security and intelligence firm. And that's about it."

She laughs, eyes sparkling. "Well, if that's how we're going to cover the past twelve years, we might run out of things to talk about."

"Never." My gaze is intent on her. "Let's see. I came back to the city that summer with plans of law school in the fall and the FBI approached me."

"You never went to Columbia?"

"Nope. I'd expressed my interest to the FBI the summer before, and it paid off. Working for the Bureau had always been my goal."

Some days it's hard to believe I no longer work for them. It was my choice and I'm glad I left, yet when I first started out, I saw myself retiring with the Bureau. Funny how life things usually don't work out the way you had anticipated.

"I don't think I knew that. So how did you end up working for them sooner than expected?" She lifts her wine glass to her mouth.

"They were working on a case and needed someone to go in undercover. A certain someone, and I fit the bill. I jumped at the chance. I'd always wanted to be part of something bigger. To do my part in stopping the injustices in the world."

I shift on the bench, placing my hand flat on the seat for leverage. My fingertips lightly graze her knee, and there's a pregnant pause, everything suspended as a rush of heat washes through me.

"Go on," she says, her voice low and breathy.

For a second, I'm not sure if she's encouraging me to continue touching her, inching my hand up her silky thigh, or keep telling my story.

I clear my throat and remove my hand, not needing the temptation. It's hard enough as it is to keep my hands to myself.

"When I was eleven, my best friends lost their fathers. Actually, one of them lost both of his parents—all three of them violently murdered. I rechanneled my grief and anger into doing something good."

"I'm so sorry. That's horrible, but your goal is noble."

"No, it isn't. I'm a guy and need to blow off my aggression somehow. I could have just as easily ended up in a life of crime." I chuckle, once again fidgeting, and feeling exposed.

"You? A drug lord or killer? Not possible." Her tone is light and she laughs. "You're a good guy through and through."

Perhaps sensing my unease, or wanting to steer us from the dark topic, she says, "Tell me about working undercover. That sounds exciting and dangerous. Did you like it?"

"Yeah, mostly. In the beginning it was hard, adjusting to being someone else. You have a legend and it's your cover. It's critical to know it inside and out."

"I can't imagine. It would be hard to keep stories straight."

"You don't have a choice. It's the difference between life and death. There's no room for error. You have to stick to your story. Your name, where you were born, your parents… it was hard at first, but after Griffin…"

I abruptly stop, swallowing thickly, and my insides twist. My brother is another topic I should steer clear of.

"Griffin? He's your younger brother, right? What about him?"

Licking my lips, I verbally shove the past aside, getting it out of the way in a rush. "Yeah, after he died, it got easier to be someone else. The job, being undercover, was an escape, and I welcomed it."

My fingers curl around my glass and I bring it to my mouth for something to do. Anything to mentally regroup.

Fuck, why did I go there? I don't talk about Griffin like this with anyone.

But why am I surprised? It's always been this way when I'm around Mia. I would tell her more than I tell anyone else.

Shit, one time at the coffee shop, I told her all about my mother dying of cancer and my father drinking himself to death. I didn't talk about shit like that. Never.

Well, obviously not true, but only with Mia.

I hadn't planned on mentioning Griffin, yet here I am spilling my fucking guts.

"I'm sorry about your brother. What happened?" She twists the base of her wine glass.

Well, so much for staying away from dark topics. Death isn't easy to talk about, and I'm sensing her unease. There's no delicate way to tell his story.

I take a minute to gather my thoughts, choose my words carefully, and to collect the steam to push through those difficult memories.

"He was murdered, beaten beyond recognition, and his body was found in a dumpster in Chicago." My words rush from my throat as one long word.

My lips twist and tighten as the taste of anger—or is it regret?—sours in my mouth. I don't even know if it's true. What if Griffin is alive?

She sucks in a breath, dropping her fork onto her plate. "Oh, Patrick."

Words fail me. I'm a jumbled mess of ugly emotions and my stomach pitches. The urge to tell her is overwhelming and I fear once I start, I won't stop.

"The autopsy said the cause of death was blunt force trauma to his skull. Likely from a baseball bat or something similar."

Mia turns green and I force myself to keep my mouth shut, stopping just before I add that later, Tate confirmed those details. Her father and soon-to-be husband had kidnapped Griffin and Tate. They made her watch while they beat him to death.

I harshly rub a hand down my face, clenching my jaw. This conversation needs to stop. "Shit, Mia. If this is too much..."

Her hand flies to mine on the table, fingers curling around my fist, and my body begins to thrum. Her tenderness quiets my burning rage and sorrow.

"Please continue." She lightly rubs her hand over my knuckles.

"I get the feeling this will be our last date thanks to this conversation," I jest but the tone of my voice is all wrong, hollow.

Tonight was supposed to be a good time, not a funeral procession. If she runs after this, I have no one to blame but myself.

"Is this a date?" Her fingers twitch, tighten on top of mine.

"I'd like it to be." Yeah, but it can't. I need to maintain some kind of distance while I investigate her. I'm putting the assignment at risk, even if it's bullshit.

She glances down at the tablecloth, her cheeks turning a light shade of pink. "Me too. Please go on. You're not ruining anything. I want to hear this. I asked."

My heart squeezes at her genuine encouragement, and while I should stop, I can't deny the strange sense of relief I get from talking to her. I'll tread carefully.

"I flew to Chicago to identify the body and couldn't. It was the same height. Same build. Same blond hair. All resembling Griff, but I couldn't say for sure. I hadn't seen him in close to a year at that point."

I toss back a glass of water. I've shifted my tone, telling her the details, not all but enough. And because it's Mia. She's calm and patient, encouraging even. She gives me the time to tell this tale, her hand still warm upon mine.

"I couldn't even say if the clothes were his. They had to rely on dental records to prove it was him. The medical officials had told me as much before I even got on a plane, but I insisted. I had to see him."

Fuck. I'd been undercover, on a case, when the call came in. Aside from his driver's license, which was found on him, there was no way to tell by looking at the body that it was my brother.

I was in and out of the city in a day. His body shipped back to New York. Carys, Griffin's best friend, handled all the arrangements for the funeral and service after, and I wasn't there for that. I had to go under again, and I wanted to, unable to deal with the death of my brother.

Thoughts of Van going to Chicago to talk to those who worked on the case come back to me. What if I missed something? Something that would have showed it wasn't Griff?

I won't tell Mia about Griff being potentially alive. I could be putting her at risk; there's so much we don't know. And I'm not sure I could say the words.

"Oh my God, Patrick. That's horrible." Her voice is unsteady, filled with emotion.

It's hard to believe I'm a trained professional because I'm rambling like an idiot. Until now, I didn't realize just how much I needed to talk to someone.

No, not just someone. Her.

"I'm so sorry. I can't even imagine." She worries her bottom lip.

I remove my hand from hers and regret ever falling down this rabbit hole. Baring my soul to her. What a fucking great way to ruin a date. Dammit, this isn't a date. I'm not even being honest about why or how I knew she was in the city.

"I'm the one who should be sorry for even bringing this up. So much for fun, light conversation." My chuckle is brittle.

With my appetite gone, I slide my plate with bruschetta to the side and push up my sleeves before resting my forearms back on the table.

"Oh my, you still have it." Her fingers land on my wrist and her touch is an electric jolt.

She grips the band around my wrist. The worn brown leather band she made for me many years ago. Her chest rises and falls, unsteady with her shallow breaths.

So much passes between us with just a look and it feels as if a hand has ripped through my chest, holding my heart in its clutches. I'm the first to break the connection, desperately seeking a reprieve from the ache.

"Yeah, I still have it. I only ever take it off when I'm undercover. Otherwise it's on me at all times."

"I don't know what to say. To tell you the truth, I never thought you'd wear it and now, I'm just blown away to see it on you." Her breath shudders, chest heaving.

"It means a lot to me. You gave it to me." My chest tightens. "Made it with your own hands. It was perfect for me, still is."

Fuck. I cannot believe what I'm saying. All of it is true and from the fucking heart, but I rarely do this. This isn't me, or maybe this *is* me, with Mia.

"Patrick." My name is almost strangled in the way she says it.

This woman has always cut me open, seen way more than others do and gotten me in a way that very few have. She's easy to talk to and I don't feel judged or self-conscious sharing with her how I feel.

In fact, it's liberating in a strange way to tell her most of it. I haven't done so in a long time. Sure, I have Carys and Tate, and both are easy to talk to about Griff, but not like this.

"You wear it well." Her fingers release the band and she rests her hand beside my arm. "And it's held up, really."

"Yup, and now that we've reconnected, should I need a new one, I've got you." I lighten the mood and her eyes widen, getting the message I want to keep seeing her. "Are you still making them?"

"Yes, and no. I don't make them anymore, but I still have the business." Her demeanor shifts, a look I'm unable to decipher flitting across her features.

"We've changed with the times, but it was a godsend when money was tight. As I focused on becoming a lawyer and other priorities, I could no longer give it the attention it needed. So I took on business students, giving them an opportunity to apply what they were learning, and eventually found two awesome and very talented women—business-savvy and creative. They invested in the company and we're partners."

She's beaming with all this talk of her flourishing homemade venture, but there's still wariness or something guarded about her.

"What about your sister? Wasn't she part owner? Is she still involved?"

I'm surprised it's possible with her already pale skin tone, but she blanches, staring down into her lap.

"Like you with your brother, she died."

My stomach drops, free-falling at her experience of a similar loss.

"What happened?" I kick out my legs, restless.

"Um, it was an accident involving a tractor trailer. She died on impact, about six years ago. And I miss her every day." She blinks and one fat tear slides down her cheek.

My fingers curl, stopping myself from wiping away the wetness. The need to soothe, caress her soft skin, is overwhelming.

She aggressively swipes her fingers across her cheek, shaking her head and forcing a smile. "I'm sorry. Now it's my turn to feel bad for veering the conversation into such sad and dark territory. I didn't plan on crying in front of you."

"It's okay." Her grief cuts through my chest.

Our waiter removes our plates and we sit in silence, both of us trapped in our heads.

"This was great." Mia folds her napkin, resting it on the table. "It was great seeing you."

"Yeah it was, but you're talking like it's over. Don't you want dessert?" I want more time with her, even though I have things that need my attention tonight.

And the longer we stay in each other's company, the more I risk doing something I'll regret. I'm investigating her. I need to get that straight.

"Oh, no. Dinner was amazing. I couldn't eat another bite." Her hand lies flat on her stomach and she glances at me. "Well, unless we share something."

"Now you're talking. They make fantastic gelato. Do you like gelato?" I pick up the dessert menu and she nods. "You'll love the lemon."

She laughs, bumping shoulders. "Now how can I say no to that?"

"How about a coffee? Cappuccino?"

"Cappuccino, please."

"Yeah." I motion to the waiter and give him our order.

It's also time for the one thing that we can't table until next time. Her expression sobers, suggesting she realizes it too.

"Okay, I gotta ask, what happened that night?"

A panicky glint swims in her wide brown eyes. "I suppose this conversation was inevitable. Long overdue. But before that, I can't help but think this is more than a coincidence."

"What do you mean?" I'm a bastard.

She's no fool and I should just tell her the truth about her ex-business partner and the assignment. But now isn't the time.

Tonight was about catching up, and if I say anything, it could be the end before we even begin.

"You running into me in New York City of all places, in a coffee shop just steps from my office. Why haven't we seen each other before now?" She eyes me warily.

Despite her suspicion, I get the feeling she's also hiding something.

"How long have you been living in New York?"

I already know. After meeting her earlier today, I looked into her background and did my usual pre-work for an assignment.

I also have the feeling if I hadn't gotten this case, we may never have crossed paths. And the *why* of that nags at me. She would have known I'd be here. New York is my home. I told her as much at school.

"Just one month shy of a year. But this dinner… it feels weird."

A heavy, sludge-like sensation runs through my gut.

"That's my fault. This evening hasn't exactly been a barrel of laughs. We've talked about dead siblings." I try to keep my tone light but it falls flat.

"No, that isn't it. I don't know how to explain it, but it feels like..." She grapples for the right words, and I'm overwhelmed with the sense that she's evading the unresolved issue between us.

"What's weird is how everything was left between us." I'm a shit.

Now I'm deflecting her question and manipulating her by playing on any guilt or remorse she may still have since college. I want to be honest, I do, and will as soon as I talk to some of the clients named in the folder.

"Yes." She's slightly panicked.

"It's one of life's mysteries for me. Tell me." I tense, gut clenching, and anxious for what she'll say.

I've gone over our last encounter countless times and I always end up with the same conclusion. She wasn't that into me. Not to sound arrogant or cocky, but I'm good in bed, giving more than taking, so it wasn't the sex. That only leaves me. She changed her mind about me, no longer interested, and got the hell out of Dodge.

"I don't have a good answer." Her response is frustrating.

"Try me. Why did you just up and leave that morning? Or did you leave in the middle of the night, I don't know?"

"I freaked." Her gaze darts around the restaurant—it's busy, loud even, yet she lowers her voice. "I'd just had sex for the first time with a guy I was crazy about and I knew it could go nowhere. I was confused. I'd wanted my first time to be special, with someone that there was potential for a future. That wasn't us."

"It wasn't special?" Dread rolls through me. "Do you feel like I pressured you?"

Maybe I'm not as good in bed as I thought. Fuck, who am I kidding? Sleeping with Mia, all those years ago, was about more than sex. I'd wanted it to be special. Being with her had been mind-blowing, everything I'd ever fantasized and more. Shit, it doesn't sound like it was for her.

"Oh, God. No. Not at all. I wanted it. I made that choice." A wonderful blush spreads across her cheeks. "I wouldn't have gone to the party otherwise. It wasn't until the next morning, when I think the reality of it hit me… and I kind of freaked."

She traces the red and white blocks of the checkered tablecloth and finally raises her head to meet my eyes.

"That's when I left. It wasn't my finest moment. And by the time I cooled off, which was several days later, I was already home and working for the summer at a law firm."

"In Michigan?" I was heading back to New York, trying to figure out how to find her.

She nods and we pause while the waiter places our coffees and a bowl with scoops of creamy yellow gelato with two spoons on the table.

"I talked myself out of contacting you." She grabs onto her cup, looking down into the frothy white liquid.

"What do you mean?"

"You weren't coming back. There wasn't a future for us."

"Wow. You knew that we had no future?" I don't bother hiding my sarcasm. "What if I told you I was prepared to make visits, when I could, to Ithaca?"

"You would have?" She's surprised, eyebrows rising.

"I don't know. I'd wasted my time and regretted not making a move sooner. I wanted a chance with you. I was open to anything." I take her hand in mine and her fingers curl around my palm. "But we didn't get a chance to have that kind of conversation. That's my point."

"Fair enough."

"Let's back up a bit. You said that was your first time. I guessed afterward, but why didn't you say anything before?"

"I should have. It was foolish." Now I see some of the shy woman from college in her uncertain expression.

She has no clue how beautiful she is, even when shy or unsure. And it was because of that I decided to go slow with her.

I'd wanted her from the moment we met but at first, the timing wasn't right—I was dating someone else, and then there was the fact that Mia was timid and quiet.

Going slow and getting her to open up had been fun, but we ran out of time. I was taking my time, enjoying her and trying to figure her out. In retrospect, I took too much time and moved too slow. By the time my last exam rolled around, it hit me. I was graduating, and I'd never even gone out with Mia.

Talk about foolish.

The invitation to the party was my last shot. And even at that, with the benefit of hindsight, I was too late.

"I was foolish too. I should have told you from the get-go that I was crazy about you."

MIA

"I was foolish too. I should have told you from the get-go that I was crazy about you." His eyes strip every ounce of my confidence.

It's like I'm back at the cafe in college, reeking of coffee, hair a mess, and this gorgeous man is flirting with me, to the point where I'll do whatever he asks of me.

"The feeling was mutual."

He holds up a spoonful of gelato to my mouth and I willingly open. His eyes smolder as he watches my tongue dart out for a taste before my lips ensnare the creamy goodness.

"Mmm, that is amazing." I release the now-empty spoon and wipe at the corner of my mouth.

"You're amazing." He winks and puts the next spoonful in his mouth.

"It's a good thing I'm sitting down, or I'd be a puddle on the floor." I fan myself, blushing, despite the nerves still churning inside me given the topic of conversation.

He places the spoon in the bowl. "When I woke up alone in the bed, I hoped I'd find you in the bathroom or downstairs even though I knew better."

I swallow past the lump of guilt in my throat and take his hand once more. Hoping he can feel how sorry I am, how I also wish I could change what I did that night.

"By the time I got my ass in gear and hustled to your place, you were gone. I didn't even have your fucking number. I was kicking myself. I went to the coffee shop and your friend, the barista..."

"Kylie?"

"Yeah, her. She refused to give me your number. I respected her for not readily giving it out, but I was pissed. I had no way of contacting you. So I gave her my number and asked her to pass it on. All I knew was you lived in Michigan, but you'd never said where and I didn't have your parents' names."

I angle my head to the side, wrinkling my brow. "Kylie didn't give me your number."

"Yeah, I found out later. She figured, if you left me without word then you had good reason."

"Patrick—"

"Please let me finish. When school started that September, I contacted Cornell. Of course, they wouldn't tell me anything so the first chance I got, I went up there."

"You did?" Melancholy creeps into my throat and stings the back of my eyes. He tried to contact me. If he'd found me, maybe it could have changed everything.

"Yeah. That's how I found out you were no longer a student. You didn't come back. I went to the café and Kylie still worked there. She told me she'd never passed on my number, not knowing why you'd just left.

"This time, she gave me your number but said that it was no longer in service. I think she took pity on me and she was bummed you'd never returned. I tried to find you but eventually, I stopped. I got the picture—you didn't want to be found."

"It wasn't like that." I shake my head as he offers the last bit of gelato. "I tried to look for you. After that night, I was confused but once home and with time…"

I struggle with what to say and what to leave out. Now isn't the time or place for the full story. And a small voice in my head asks whether I should ever tell him everything? Telling him won't change anything.

"You did?" He frowns, skeptical with a hint of surprise.

"Yeah, I remembered you said you lived in New York City. I called every single Patrick or P. Townsend in the tri-state area. It was a lot of calls, and I came up empty."

I leave out that I tried several months later with Columbia University and that was also a dead end, and then almost a year after that. I even tried again, many years after, when I had more money and means, but I struck out every time. Telling him this just sounds desperate and it could lead in a direction I don't want to go. Not now, at least.

"Shit. I wasn't listed and was undercover for a long period of time. That first case was nearly eighteen months." Regret clouds his expression.

"It sounds like we both tried to connect with each other. I'm sorry for my part in that. I shouldn't have freaked out and run. If I could go back and change it, I would."

His knuckles caress my cheek and I shiver. "Tell me about you. How did you end up in LA from Michigan?"

"That's a story for another day." I'm saved from saying more when our server comes to the table with the check.

The restaurant is still fairly busy when we leave and this time, once outside, he takes hold of my hand, pulling me into him.

"Did you have an enjoyable dinner?" His nose brushes my cheek and his touch is like fire. I may combust.

"It was awesome. And you're right, this place is amazing. I wish I'd known all these many months it was right in my backyard."

"Well, it isn't going anywhere." He wraps his arm around me, and I snuggle into him, feeling as if I'm home. "Now what do you feel like doing? I could take you home or I could show you around some more. There are lots of great places in your neighborhood."

"I'll take a rain check on the tour. It's been a long day, and an amazing night, but I've got an early start."

My mind and heart are all over the place. I want to spend more time with him and yet I also need some space. I'm still not sure this is real or if I should even be indulging all my wild and crazy feelings for this man.

"Home it is." He's the picture of disappointed and my heart climbs up my throat, wanting to leap into his arms.

It's cold and the wind has picked up, but I'm warm and comfortable in his embrace. Too comfortable. My dreams of him pale compared to the real thing. I could get used to this.

I glance up at him. "I'm glad that we ran into each other."

Something flickers in his eyes and again, I wonder just how much of a coincidence our reunion really was. His fleeting expression looks a lot like guilt. Did he stage the coffee shop run-in?

I really don't care. So what if he looked me up or saw me on the street at another point in time and deliberately bumped into me? I'm flattered.

Yet the thought also pains me because feelings aside, I can't pursue anything with this man for so many reasons. Even if every fiber of my being wants him.

This can't happen.

We can't happen.

There's so much I still need to tell him, and I don't even know if I should. I might leave for Nashville in a month, so what's the point?

If I do leave, I likely won't come back, and he said so himself, New York is his home. I don't see him uprooting his life for me, no matter how much he says he might have years ago.

His voice pulls me from my rambling thoughts. "Sorry. What did you say?"

"We're here. I could take you up to your place, but something tells me we should call it a night. You need time and I have work."

"Work? You're not done for the night?"

"I'm working on a case. I've got some things I need to check in on."

"I see. Do you want company? I could go with you." Why am I asking? I just told him I was tired. This evening is like a dream I don't want to end.

"No, it's okay. It isn't safe, but thank you." He turns me to face him, his hands on my upper arms.

"Okay. Well, you be safe. And thank you for tonight. Maybe we'll see each other again?"

His fingers cup the side of my face. "There're no maybes about it, we will for sure."

My silly heart does a happy dance and a smile blooms on my face. "Good night, Patrick."

"Good night, Mia." His fingers thread through my hair and he bends his head, planting his lips on mine.

The pressure of his kiss is light, slow and sweet, and my hands clasp at the back of his neck, fingers sliding through his locks.

He deepens the kiss, his tongue fierce and possessive, and I tighten my fingers, curling around his thick hair. I love the feel, the softness. The sensations coursing through me, through my veins, nerves and muscles, are almost overwhelming. Almost new.

But that isn't true. I've felt this before.

This intensity.

This desire.

I've felt all of this before with this very man.

I break our connection, briefly staring into his eyes, but that makes me feel even more vulnerable. Turning away, I push through the double doors of my building.

"Mia."

I stop at the sound of his voice, peering over my shoulder, and he's now at a safer distance, on the sidewalk in front of the door, bathed in the streetlight. Earlier today comes to mind when he did something similar outside my office building.

Snow falls gently around him. The flakes are weightless and delicate, and I can tell it won't stay. Yet with the light upon him and the night as the backdrop, he looks like an angel. A sexy, confident one, if there is such a thing, and I want to weep.

"Yes?" I'm mesmerized and I blink to stave off the prickling at the back of my eyes.

"Do you have plans for Thanksgiving?"

"Uh, no." I didn't see that coming and wish I'd answered differently. I want to be with him, always have, but things are different. There's so much he doesn't know.

"Good friends of mine always put together a great spread. Football, awesome food, and company. I'd like you to come."

"Oh, that's nice of you to think of me. But…"

"Hey, don't say no. Think about it."

"But you'll have to tell your friend if you're bringing a guest, so they know what to plan for and prepare."

"Nah, Carys always has enough to feed an army. We can talk about it some more. Think about it. Night, Mia."

"Okay. Good night."

Turning on my heel, I pick up the pace, nodding to greet the man at the front desk before pushing through the door to the stairwell.

My insides are like a loot bag full of goodies, jostled and spilled upon the floor. I don't even know where to start to pick up the pieces.

Once I'm in my apartment, I undress, remove my makeup and undertake my night routine. Thoughts of Patrick, dinner and our conversation swim in my head.

I slide under the covers, turn off the light and hope for sleep even if it's futile. Lying in the darkness, I replay the night and the many conversations we had during our time in college.

The kiss.

Our one night together.

His smile… he doesn't smile like he used to. And I suppose that's understandable. I can appreciate all too well how loss, the vast aching grief, can weigh heavy on any joy.

Tonight makes me smile. A genuine smile, and not just on the outside. Inside too. My heart is happy. Even now, a few hours after our dinner and it's still bashing around inside my chest.

Patrick Townsend is here, in my life again. I don't really know what to do with that buoyant feeling inside me.

So many times I'd wished for him, especially in those years right after college. I would have done anything for that man to come back to me. I dreamed he was looking for me and that we found each other.

I chalked them up to silly dreams because we were friends. Yes, friends that hoped for more but for our own reasons never acted on it. Or waited too long… but I had strong feelings for him. Still do.

And I tried. I really tried to find him. After tonight's conversation, it explains why I wasn't successful in my search.

While I scoured New York State for him, he was working for the FBI, undercover most of the time. I thought I was insane. There were moments when I questioned if he'd lied to me about going to Columbia University or if I'd imagined him. But I had proof he was real and yet there was no trace of him.

Patrick Townsend of New York City didn't exist.

Even knowing now why I couldn't find him, I'm saddened and angry. Maybe I should have tried harder. Maybe I should have flipped my thinking and pushed the possibilities.

Instead of cold-calling all the Townsends in the state and surrounding areas and even calling law firms, which proved to be time-consuming, exhausting, and fruitless, why didn't I think about a change in career?

Dammit, this is crazy.

I'll always wonder maybe… just maybe, I could have found him. I wish I could have told him and given him a chance.

Dammit, I tried.

With my face in the pillow, a sob shoots from my throat like a bullet, ripping through me.

My failed attempt no longer matters.

It's too late.

It's too late for us.

It was always too late for us.

TRIPP

Mia's words from our dinner conversation echo through my mind on my way to HC. She tried to find me. That reality is both painful and maddening—to think my job, being undercover, kept us apart—but it also settles all of my disturbing thoughts about why she left.

Our connection—this crazy attraction—isn't all in my head or one-sided, no matter how we both try to downplay it.

All the more reason to wrap up this stupid Hinton assignment and come clean. I requested contact information on the clients named in the report so I can confirm or dismiss his outlandish claim.

I park the car and stroll toward the HC building. Barely restrained anger surges through me, blanketing the dark street and weighing down my steps. I'm checking in to get a report on Taya. I'll be on her for a shift tomorrow.

Griffin and that recording are never too far from my mind. Why does it feel like the universe is conspiring against me?

I'm not one to wallow, I'm a fucking fighter but sometimes it feels like too much. There's Griffin and the insane possibility he might be alive, and if so, how do we find him? And there's having to deal with the likes of Taya, and finally, why can't things just be easy and straightforward with Mia?

There's no doubt about it, this is our time. I feel it in my bones.

Mia and I are happening. And she may be pissed when she hears about the investigation and my part in it, but I won't walk away. And she won't be running. Not a chance in hell.

* * *

THE NEXT SEVERAL days are spent on Taya, even with Mia and our dinner never too far from my thoughts.

Taya Conrad will pay for her sins, for her part in my brother's death. Van's trip to Chicago was a dead end. The medical examiner at the time of Griffin's death is deceased and no one working there now knew anything about the case.

Of course, the files on record were all in order and showed the dental records match the body. No red flags, and the same goes for the police. So we're back to square one. We always seem to wind up here and it infuriates me.

Last night, Tommie, Van and I spent the better part of it narrowing down individuals who might be Griffin. We looked at anyone and everyone who came into our lives and Taya's within the past ten years. There's a lot of ground to cover even with the entire team working on this.

We ended the hours of work with four potential individuals to investigate. It's a stretch and feels like a game. None of these guys look like Griff, but they have the basics: blond or light brown hair, similar build and blue eyes. That's it.

We're also working under the assumption that Griffin doesn't look like he used to. And that's based solely on what Taya said in the recording. Because there's no way he could be out in the open, and none of us have come across him.

And all of this could be in vain. It could be a lie. Although I'm cautiously warming to the idea of Taya having Griff, even if there are more questions than answers.

The other scenario is Griff is alive but being held captive somewhere close by. Right under our noses. This is more likely and if so, more dire because we'd be searching for the proverbial needle in a haystack.

And then there's the other possible scenario that we've only entertained once and then shelved it because… I'm not sure how we'd deal with it. There's the possibility he's alive and knows where we are but doesn't want to come forward for whatever reason.

More than likely because he's done with us, because he feels we abandoned him and he can't forgive that. I like to think this outcome isn't plausible. Because if so, it means I've already lost any chance at getting my brother back.

And then finally, there's the ultimate question that I still toy with even if the others dare not think it—is he even alive?

We divvied up the four subjects and Van took one, Tommie took another, and I've taken the remaining two. We each have research to do to make sure the timeline fits. We don't want to get too far down the path with any of them if the years don't add up. There has to be a slim chance they could be Griffin for us to further pursue.

Then we make contact and ask questions. But ultimately, it comes down to DNA. That's what's going to give us our answer. And in many ways, I just want to go in for the kill. Let's cut to the chase and let science do the talking.

And on top of all that, I'm still watching Taya when I can. I don't want to miss anything. Like she said, he's right under our noses.

It's morning, a little past eight, and Taya is still in her apartment. I'm on my way to relieve Tango who is on her right now, and from the latest report, everything's normal.

Again, I'd like to just get in her face and confront her. Force her to tell us. But I don't think she'll tell us the truth and then we'd lose our advantage. And then there's the FBI. They are moving in on her, soon, and like Van said, it's looking good.

Without a doubt, Taya will use any information on my brother to bargain if arrested, but the Feds might not care. And then what?

She gets put away with a secret she isn't willing to divulge.

Fuck!

My hand slams on the steering wheel and there's a rustling in the back of the vehicle. My aggravation getting the better of me and I'm reminded she's back there. She doesn't know that I know.

Parking the car, I push my shades up the bridge of my nose, searching for my cool. Then I text Tango, letting him know I'm in position and he's relieved of his duty.

A few minutes later, his car merges into traffic about a block up the street. In the rearview mirror, nothing moves in the back but she's there. This girl, from the second she could walk, she always did things her way.

"You can come out now." I turn off the engine, gaze glued to the back seat.

Nothing. She's sticking to this game of hide and seek, and a smile spreads across my lips.

"Fine, don't come out, but it's a lot more interesting up here than back there. And even at that, it's pretty fucking boring."

A black head of hair pops up. Carys rests her arms along the top of the seat and grins. "How did you know I was here?"

"I saw you climb into the car."

"You did? Shoot, and I thought I was being so stealthy." Pushing onto the cushion, she climbs to the front seat.

"Why didn't you say something sooner or kick me out?"

"I find you amusing."

"Whatever." She snuggles into the seat, looking out the window. "So what are we doing?"

"We're watching Taya Conrad's apartment."

"And?"

"And nothing. That's it. We wait until she comes out and we follow."

"Wow, that sounds boring."

"Yeah, it can be, but it can also be informative. You never know until it happens."

"Okay." Turning to face me, she pulls her legs up onto the seat. "How are you?"

"Fine." I'm fixed on the building entrance.

Taya is usually out by nine in the morning and once her driver arrives, it's an excellent indication she'll be making an appearance. So far, there's no sign of him.

"I haven't talked to you since the news. You've been ignoring my calls." She quirks a brow, her gaze unrelenting.

A pang of guilt hits me in the chest. I can't deny I've been ignoring her. She's Van's wife, Ry's younger sister and like a sister to me.

We grew up together, all five of us—Ry, Van, Griff, Carys and me—and since my brother's death, I have grown even closer to her. Carys and Griff were best friends, and she's become an extension of him in some ways.

"Don't you have children who need their mother? Particularly at this time of the morning?" I peer at her over the top of my sunglasses.

I'm a jerk, pulling this chauvinistic crap, like only a mother can take care of her kids. Van's a great father and is often doing all the things a parent needs to do.

She quirks a dark brow and purses her lips. "I don't even bring that gender crap into our conversation. Evan's with the kids and he knows I'm here, bugging your ass. So let's talk. How've you been?"

"Asked and answered. Fine." My jaw tightens, not wanting to be mothered even if she means well.

"Have you talked to Tate since you all listened to the recording?"

"Did you hear it?"

I'm not deflecting, more curious, since I hadn't even thought about how she would have reacted to the conversation between Taya and Ash. I've been too wrapped up in myself to think about anyone else.

"Yes."

"And?" I remove my glasses, looking directly in her eyes.

"It's shocking. Almost unbelievable." Wide expressive eyes, the color of the ocean, speak of the impossible. "But… but I want to believe he's alive. Is that stupid?"

"No." *Fuck, I feel the same way even if I can't say the words.*

"How do you think Ry and Tate are dealing with this?"

"What do you mean?" Why does she keep coming back to Tate?

"Well, Griff was her first love, and now she's married to Ry. Things could get sticky if, I mean, *when* we find Griff."

"I haven't given it any thought but no, they won't. Tate and Ry have a life, a family. That was ten years ago."

I'm quick to dismiss her concern but then pause to give it more thought. What if Griff is stuck mentally back then? It could cause some tension, but Tate is with Ry. That's all there is to it.

"I suppose it's none of our business. I've tried talking to my brother, but he refuses to even talk about it. He wants Griff to be alive."

"There's your answer. Stop sticking your nose where it doesn't belong." My tone is light, playful, despite needing her to catch my drift.

This situation is rife with pitfalls, and we don't need to be borrowing trouble. We have enough to deal with and so many things could go wrong. First and foremost, all of this could be for nothing. Griff may be gone.

And if not, we may never find him. If we do, we may not be able to get to him safely, or Taya could catch wind that we know and move him. And I could go on. My head hurts just thinking about it.

"I think you should talk to her. She could use someone and I'm not safe seeing as her husband is my brother."

She's given this a lot of thought, and once again I'm reminded how thoughtful and caring she is. Her presence today is all about checking on me. She will not allow me to dodge her like I'm doing with everyone else so I can brood over this latest development.

I could talk to Tate. Shit, I *should* talk to her. She's been there for me more times than I care to admit, and while the topic of my brother and her husband isn't something I want to delve into, I should for her. She'd do it for me.

Taya's driver pulls up in front of the building and hops out of the car. I straighten, my heart rate kicking up a notch. He runs a hand through his blond hair, checks the entrance of the building, most probably for Taya, before pulling out a pack of cigarettes.

With his lower back against the front of the car, he bends one leg, resting the sole of his dress shoe against the front tire. He tilts his head and cups one hand around the lighter and cigarette.

He takes a long drag, and I rack my brain trying to remember his name and what we know about him. He's been a staple in her organization, like Tiny, one of her henchmen, and there's another guy, Franz.

Carys slices through my musings. "So Evan mentioned you're on an assignment involving an old flame?"

Mother of Christ. Van.

This is why working with friends can be a terrible idea. A pain in the ass. They know too much about everything.

My fingers curl around the steering wheel, gripping the leather. I don't want to talk about Mia with Carys. It's too soon. And besides, I don't know what I'd say.

She's the only bright spot in my life right now. Shit, not just right now, she's always been a bright spot even when she was only a memory.

We've talked and texted a few times since our dinner. Light and flirty banter, nothing serious. I even gave her the address to Carys and Van's, coaxing her to come for Thanksgiving. While she'd initially accepted the invitation, it was clear she had reservations. I even told her she could meet me at their place if it made things easier.

During our back and forth, we also talked about another date, but we haven't been able to find time. From the sound of things, she's swamped with work and that suits me since I need to be honest the next time we see each other.

"Van needs to keep his mouth shut."

She snickers. "C'mon, tell me."

"She's a friend from college, and I'm investigating a claim made against her which is total bullshit."

I should drop by her office after this. I've talked to all the clients she allegedly "stole." Time to come clean. I have to tell her I orchestrated our "chance" meeting at the coffee shop and why. I only hope she understands.

"What's she being accused of?"

"Can't say, you know that." I give her a wry expression, and then out the window of the car, we watch the driver straighten.

He's very attuned to his employer's presence even with his back to the entrance. He must sense her arrival, or maybe they have a predetermined time. While this is routine—I've sat here before and watched this very thing unfold—I can't help but hope for something extraordinary.

Like Taya to walk out of the building with Griffin at her side. *Fuck, I'm an idiot.*

The driver dashes around the hood of the car, opening the back passenger door as Taya exits the building. She pauses before getting in to say something to him. He nods, and she runs a hand down the front lapel of his coat, then gets into the car.

"Okay, look alive." No matter how many times I do this, the chase still gets the adrenaline flooding my body. "Are you coming along for the ride or do you need to go?"

Carys whips her head in the direction of the building—until now, oblivious to the surveillance—in time to see the driver get into the front.

"Oh, did she come down?"

I nod, starting the engine and she pouts. "Darn, I missed it. Yeah, I can stay. Let's do this."

Smirking, I pull out onto the road. Carys isn't going to like surveillance. More times than not, there's nothing exciting about it.

We tail Taya for the better part of three hours as she goes about her business around the city. For all of it, we're either driving or parked at a safe distance watching.

And like I called it, Carys is cool with some of the waiting but for most of it, she makes my ears bleed with her incessant chatter.

I love her but she doesn't know how to stay quiet, and to share my pain, I blow up Van's phone with texts. It backfires because the bastard is busting a gut, loving how his wife is torturing me and he refuses to come get her. Carys isn't aware of my SOS to her husband.

My replacement arrives while we're parked and I don't even tell her I'm taking her home, I just do.

"Okay, this is you." The car idles in front of her house.

"I'd like to say this was fun, but it was worse than watching paint dry. But I loved hanging with you." She leans in and kisses my cheek.

"Me too." Not a lie, bleeding ears aside.

"Listen, if you want to talk or help with this, please call me. I'll do anything."

"I will, and thanks." I won't be calling her for another stakeout or tail.

Even if I was insane enough to consider it, Van would kill me first because it's too risky. I'm surprised he was okay with her tagging along today.

The drive to Mia's office is blissfully silent and in complete contrast to my pulse pounding with apprehension. Mia could tell me to get lost and never want to speak to me again. I don't give myself the chance to second guess what I'm about to do.

It's a little after midday; there's a light dusting of freshly fallen snow and the ground looks clean and pure. For the time being anyway. My jacket is open, unbuttoned, and I tighten the front around me to stave off the cold and cross the street into her building.

The door to her office is shut and when I step into the vestibule, the receptionist isn't at the front desk and no one is waiting. On the wall above a sleek leather couch is a simple silver logo: St. John & Co.

Pride warms my insides and pushes up the corners of my mouth. She's achieved all of her career dreams and from what I researched and those I've talked to, she's well respected and very good at what she does. All of those I spoke to—well, with the exception of Hinton himself—had nothing but high praise for Mia.

Muffled sounds of someone talking come from behind a closed door. It's the only other door in this small space. From what I can tell, there's only one person in there. It must be Mia. I lightly tap on the door and poke my head in.

The stunning redhead, the woman in my dreams, turns from the screen with a slight crease forming between her brows.

"One second." She holds up a finger and I nod, slipping from the room.

Guilt burrows its way into my chest. Not only am I here to admit I lied to her—fuck—I also dropped in unannounced, which is against what she asked of me.

"Patrick, come on in." She brushes past me, stopping to scribble a note on a piece of paper at the front desk.

Her fiery locks are piled high on her head in a messy bun and a few wispy tendrils fall loosely around her face. She's wearing a high-waisted black pencil skirt and an ocean blue top.

A pair of gold high heels with shimmering straps crisscross her feet to knot at her ankles, showing off her toned calves perfectly. The entire outfit is subtle but suggestive of her slender curves and does screwy things to my blood pressure.

"Hey, I should have called. I hadn't planned on visiting." I stand in the doorway to her office, watching her. "It was kind of spur of the moment."

She really isn't focused on me, sticking the note to her receptionist's computer screen. Preoccupied.

Maybe this is a bad time, as she often mentioned how busy she was in our calls and texts. Or is she stalling?

All those times I delayed setting up another date because I wasn't near to closing the case come at me in a different light. Maybe she was stalling too, for her own reasons?

"Okay. I don't have a lot of time though."

I turn into the office with her behind me but grab at her hand as she walks by. "Hey, you okay?"

Her slender fingers entwine with mine and her head drops to look at our hands before shifting her gaze back at me.

"Sorry, I'm just thinking about the last call I had. The work I have to get started on."

I tug her hand toward me and the rest of her comes too. "I should have called, and I won't take up too much of your time, but..."

Pausing, my eyes are stuck on her mouth and a rush of heat slams into me. My craving mingles with a deeper, unspoken desire. I want this woman. The yearning is more intense than ever. I want to touch her freely. I want to kiss her.

Fuck this.

My mouth covers hers in one smooth move and all the tension seeps from my body. I'm getting what I want and she melts into me.

She widens her mouth and releases a breathy moan. She wants this too and I'm on the verge of losing all control.

Suddenly insatiable, my demanding tongue strokes her and my teeth sink into her plump bottom lip. I need all of her.

"Patrick." She pulls her hand from mine and rests her forehead on my chest.

We stand like that for a few beats, and I feed on her alluring scent. I wish I didn't have to ruin this moment with my bullshit. Why didn't I just tell her the truth in the coffee shop?

I know why. Because I didn't want to reconnect like that. And I also wanted to do my job *and* indulge in Mia. Selfish bastard.

"You don't make this easy." She looks up at me with a sexy grin playing on her lips.

Before I can take her lips once more, she turns to sit behind her desk. I shove my hands into my pockets to stop from going after her, and I rock on my heels.

"So what's up? I've got another call in ten minutes."

"Two things. One, I want to go out with you again and Thanksgiving doesn't count."

It's true, I want to see her again and being here only makes that need more critical, but I'm also testing where she stands. Does she want to see me again? I fucking hate this troubled feeling gnawing at my insides.

Her smile widens, her cheeks heating. "You won't take no for an answer, will you?"

"Not a chance. So we're good for Thanksgiving? I'll pick you up at say, noon." This could all change once I say what I have to say but I'm not giving up.

"Noon?"

"Yeah, it's for lunch and then we watch the game. I want you to meet and hang with my friends."

Her protest takes shape in her hardening expression. I wait with anticipation and something shifts in her features. She merely exhales and shakes her head.

"Fine. That sounds good. Was that it?" She picks up a folder from a pile on her desk and I take a seat across from her.

"No, this one's trickier." I have her attention and she stops what she's doing.

"Patrick, I should tell you, I may not stay in New York." She motions to the boxes in the corner, the ones I noticed when I walked in.

She's thrown me for a loop, and why? Am I getting too close? Moving too fast? And why the hell is she leaving?

"What do you mean?"

"I'm not sure if this move was the right thing. I gave myself a year and January first will be just that. I might go to Nashville."

"Why? What's there?" My next breath catches in my chest and my words carry a hint of fear. *Fuck.*

"I-I…" She stumbles over her words. "It's a great city. Good for my business. I don't really have a lot keeping me here. No social life to speak of." There's a faint flush to her neck. "And that's my fault. I haven't really put myself out there. The change might be good."

All of it sounds like excuses, but why, it isn't clear.

"Well, you have me now so there's a reason to stay."

"Do I?"

"Absolutely."

Silence falls upon us. It isn't awkward, rather meaningful. She's the first to break away. Again.

"Okay. That's good to know. I'm just not sure… you said there was another reason you were here?"

"Yeah. I have something to tell you. And you're not going to like it." I feel nauseous and light-headed. What is my problem?

But this is Mia.

I could be shattering our chance before it's even born.

"What?" She shuts the file folder and straightens. "Are you married?"

"What? No. Not married. Single. And in case you haven't noticed, very interested in pursuing something with you. Picking up where we left off twelve years ago."

"What? You mean one night of hot sex?" She's trying to be funny but there's a flash of something almost painful in her features.

"No, well, yes to sex but I want a lot more than that with you." I move to the edge of the chair, now resting my elbows on the desk.

Every word is shrapnel cutting up my throat. "You were right about our meeting each other in the coffee shop being more planned than happenstance."

"I knew it." She sits back in her chair, crossing her arms over her chest.

She purses her lips, her features and body language shuttering.

"Remember when I mentioned that I work for Hart Corporation? HC. Well, we do security, surveillance and investigations."

She nods and I'm losing the battle against this sinking feeling as if she's slipping away before I even get the words out.

"And while typically not our kind of work, we were hired to look into you."

"Into me?" Her eyes widen and my heart flips.

"Yes, Fraser Hinton hired us."

"Fraser. Are you serious?" I nod and she frowns. "What on earth for? Are you a private investigator?"

"No. This kind of thing… well, it's more for the courts, if anything at all."

"What is he accusing me of?"

"He claims you are in breach of your non-compete."

"You've got to…" She jumps from her seat, arms waving in the air. "That's ridiculous. We argue weekly about him wanting me to come back but he knows I didn't take any clients. This is bullshit."

She paces, stopping to stare at me. "What exactly did he ask your firm to do?"

"He claims you stole three of his biggest clients—Eli Lansing, Gigi Sommers and Jonas Chambers." I'm telling her more than I should but I don't give a fuck. I'm fighting for Mia, for a chance.

"Oh my God, I can't believe he did this. I didn't steal anyone."

"I believe you. I looked into it and spoke to all of them."

"You spoke to my clients about me, about this, without even telling me?" She fixes me with a hostile glare and distress jerks at my heart.

"I'm not obligated to tell you. Fraser is our client." My tone is flat, needing her to understand I was just doing my job.

"You've got to be kidding me. And you came here claiming to be my friend. But meanwhile, you're investigating me. Why didn't you just ask me?"

"I'm not faking." I sound testy, almost offended. "I am your friend but I couldn't say anything. You'd say you were innocent."

"I am innocent."

"Yes, but I needed to come to that conclusion on my own." I work to rid my voice of any defense. "You didn't take those clients with you. They all admitted to leaving Hinton of their own accord and that, at first, you refused to take them on as clients. I even have proof of that."

She nods, folding her arms over her middle. She's still closed off, even more so now and I'm not so sure if I still have a chance to be with her.

"I'm closing the assignment."

"What does that mean?"

"It means he'll get a report stating his claims are unfounded. We could not substantiate any of it and he doesn't have a case."

She glances to her screen and then back at me, expression unreadable. "I need you to go. I've got a call coming in any minute now."

"Mia." My voice cracks and I clear my throat, while inching toward her, only to stop at the hard gleam in her eyes. "Do you understand it was just work?"

"Sure." She shrugs without conviction and my chest deflates. "Just let me think about this."

Her phone rings and she glances to the screen. "I have to get this. Just give me some time. I'll call you."

Everything about her is lifeless and dismissive.

"Will you?" I'm not so sure. What she doesn't know is, this isn't the end. I won't accept we are over.

"Yes. I've got to get this."

"Okay, call me anytime, night or day. Mia..." I wait while she answers the call, not moving, and eventually she puts them on hold.

Exasperated or on the verge of tears, I can't really tell, she pinches her mouth. "Yes?"

"Call me."

My eyes bore into hers, needing her to understand I will see her again. She's the first to look away, still stiff and neutral.

"Fine. Goodbye, Patrick."

MIA

I'm vibrating with rage.

By the time my final meeting, a two-hour conference call, comes to an end, I'm shaking. Since Patrick left, I've had back-to-back meetings and I've kept it together for the most part. But as the last meeting of my day nears the end, his words play in my head and I need to speak to Fraser.

"Larry, this was a productive call. I think we landed in a great spot. Send me the contract once you have it completed and I'll go over it, have Jonas sign it."

The call wraps up, and I hit end when there's a knock on the outer door to my office. It's past six in the evening and I'm not expecting anyone.

Please don't be Patrick. I'm exhausted and on the verge of tears. If I see him right now, I'll break down and sob.

I open the door to the hallway and a guy in jeans and a bomber jacket, maybe a college student, stands there with an envelope in his hand. A knot forms between my shoulder blades, taut and growing.

"Mia St. John?" The young man plasters on an obligatory smile.

"Yes."

"Here you go." He hands me the packet with my typed name on the front. "You've been served."

He turns on his heel, hastily retreating.

Wonderful.

I rip open the envelope, noting the return address in the top left-hand corner, one I'm familiar with in LA. My phone rings and it's in my office.

I jog as best as is possible in heels toward the phone. "Mia St. John."

I'm half-listening to the voice on the other end, eager to see more of what I'm holding in my hand.

"Hey, it's Eli. I've got great news."

His cheerful tone causes me to interject with "Can you just hang on a sec?" While at the same time, he says, "We've booked our tickets."

With the phone still to my ear, I pull the pages from the envelope, scanning the contents. Everything fades away as the words on the page consume me. My eyes must be playing tricks on me. This can't be true.

"Unbelievable," slips from my mouth.

"What's wrong? Mia, what's going on?" Eli's worried tone pulls me from the dark space in my mind.

"What? Sorry, I'm..." My gaze is glued to the legal documents in my hand. "It's Fraser."

"What's he done now?" His dislike of my ex-partner is clear in his tone.

"He's suing me for breach of contract. He's saying I broke the terms of my non-compete."

"What? Is this related to the call I got from this guy?"

"What guy?"

I slump into my chair and twirl around to look out the only window in my tiny office. He must mean Patrick.

"Um, I was going to tell you, I got a call from a guy. He said he was based in New York. Let me just check, I wrote his name down. Oh, here it is... Patrick Townsend, Hart Corporation."

The knot between my shoulders doubles in size and an inkling of a headache forms at my temples. I wish Eli had called me right away, or Patrick had been honest with me in the café. Although I'm not sure it would have changed anything.

"Yes, it's related. Fraser claims I stole you and some other clients from him."

"Fucker. That's bullshit."

"The guy, Patrick, who called you… Fraser hired his firm to investigate me. To prove his claim. Do you believe that?"

"Are you kidding me? I wondered what it was all about. Townsend wouldn't say. I'm sorry, Mia, I should have called you sooner. I've been preoccupied with the move—"

"Eli, this isn't on you. It's all right." I didn't mean to make him feel guilty. He's caught in the middle of the mess.

"I'm going to talk to Fraser, right now."

"No. Don't. Thank you, but I can handle this. I just… I thought we were more than business partners. I thought we were friends, but obviously, I was wrong."

"You already know this but I hate that guy. He's a weasel, and you were always too good for him. I was so happy when you said you were leaving—well, not happy that you were leaving LA, but cutting ties with him."

This isn't news to me and nothing I haven't heard from other clients. Why did I try so hard with Fraser when so many saw him for what he obviously really is—a selfish jerk.

"Eli, sorry but I've got to go. I need to call Fraser. Figure something out."

"Yeah, sure. But don't fucking give him anything. You did nothing wrong."

"I don't intend to give him anything but a piece of my mind."

He chuckles. "Listen, Crystal isn't here, but she's going to call later. Talk then?"

"Yes, later. Bye." Ending the call, I drop my head into my hands and let out an exasperated moan.

Standing, I shake off my mini freak-out and pick up my phone again. He answers on the third ring.

"Hi, Mia. How are you?" His voice is no different from any other time we're spoken. He mustn't know I have been served.

"Something interesting happened today."

"Oh?" Now I hear it, the trepidation in his tone.

"You don't have a case. Breach of contract? Really, Fraser? Is this your idea of a joke?"

"I'm not joking." He pauses and neither of us rushes to fill the dead air, each of us waiting the other out.

He's the first to crack. I was always a better lawyer than him, but never treated him as if I was better. Never.

"For fuck's sake, Mia, this can't be a surprise. What did you think, you could leave me high and dry? Fuck me over and I'd just take it?"

It's as if he's punched me in the gut.

"None of that is true. You're rewriting history. My decision to leave wasn't made overnight. I'd been struggling for months. Years even. Every day in LA got harder, especially once I'd gotten into a groove with work and I didn't have to hustle anymore."

I don't want to be vulnerable with him. I didn't intend to and talking about the reasons I left, the internal struggle and the demons I battle, causes me such pain. If he had been a true friend, he would know this.

He doesn't get to see my pain. Not anymore.

"I was honest with you every step of the way. I told you I was looking at other cities and I'd need a buy-out."

I pause, hoping he'll jump in and agree with me. Tell me he was wrong, he takes it back and let's forget this ever happened.

"I thought you were fucking joking. Or it was just more of your whining like you normally do. How was I to know you were serious?"

His words hurt. Selfish bastard. And now, it's plain to see he understood none of what I was going through. Or more likely, he never cared.

"We've known each other for many years now, and I've been nothing but a partner to you."

"You ruined me when you left." His voice rises and his face is likely growing redder by the second. "I had to buy you out, do you know what that did to me? Angela is leaving me. The business is a mess. I've had no new business for a fucking year."

All of this is news to me, and while it saddens me, none of this is my fault.

"My leaving had nothing to do with your marriage failing or the business crumbling. That isn't on me. It's on you."

"Of course you'd say that. You have no clue, do you?"

"What, Fraser? All this tells me is that you were riding my coattails. I was the one bringing in new business, growing the firm, and had been for a while, we both know that. And guess what? You were just reaping the rewards." Something thick clogs my throat.

"You know, I used to think of you as a mentor. A friend. And now this lawsuit... it's bullshit. You won't win. So I suggest you drop it."

"Mia, you aren't in a position to threaten me." He releases a lengthy sigh. "Look, you're overreacting. This will all go away if you come back to LA. Let's patch things up and open Hinton St. John again. Just think of the reopening party we could have. We were awesome together. We could be again."

I twist my lips, wishing he could see me right now. Then I wouldn't need any words to tell him how I feel.

"Even if I came back to LA, it wouldn't solve your problems. We are done. I'll never go into business with you again. Goodbye."

I toss the phone onto my desk and drop back into my chair, exhausted and on the verge of tears.

Over the years, there had been a few clients who refused to work with him and I heard the rumblings among some in the industry. Fraser could be difficult, but I ignored it. We got along okay and he'd given me a shot when I needed it the most.

But now, maybe they saw something I didn't. Or maybe I was the one choosing not to see what was right in front of me all along. Just how selfish and smarmy Fraser could be.

I needed a job and, just as importantly, a distraction when I'd first met him. I was broken and desperate, but I didn't miss the fact that Hinton and Associates was a nobody firm.

I contemplated continuing the job search, but I'd taken too much time away from work and needed the money. I wondered if there would be enough business to keep me busy.

That's when I made it my mission to grow the business. Lose myself in my work. Even before my name was on the wall or the business cards, I treated the firm like it was my own.

I busted my ass and delivered in spades. I brought in stars he could only dream of, and every new client and every signed contract lined his pockets. I figured Fraser recognized my contribution, but now it seems I became his competition.

There's a knock at my door and my head snaps up. Patrick stands in the doorway. "Hey, I'm back."

"I can see that." I push to my feet, straightening the front of my outfit. "I said I'd call."

"I didn't want to leave things the way we did."

I close my eyes and take a deep breath. I feel him edge closer to my side, within touching distance, but he doesn't reach for me. I don't know if I'm grateful or disappointed.

"What's wrong?"

"Your client." I don't resist the urge to make a dig. "Fraser Hinton is suing me."

"What? Back up." His tone has a shocked edge to it.

"He's taking me to court." I hold up the papers, my fingers curling so tight that the pages crinkle. "Breach of my non-compete. I guess your report didn't change his mind."

It isn't likely that Fraser has the report from HC yet, but I don't really care about the details. He lied to me, that's all that matters. I slap the document down on my desk and step from behind it, brushing past him.

"I'll get him to see things more clearly." He grabs for my hand, curling his fingers around my palm.

His gesture is consoling, and I fear I may cry. I can't. Not in front of him. If I start, I may never stop.

And this isn't just about my ex-business partner. It's the fact that this man from my past, who holds such a huge place in my heart… he is here. And he wants to offer me support. Comfort me.

"I can handle this on my own. I did nothing wrong. He doesn't have a case."

"I know you've got this, and he might drop it once he sees in our report that he has nothing to use. But you don't have to manage it on your own. Let me take care of it for you."

His fingers pinch a wisp of my hair, softly sliding down to its end. "I didn't want this assignment from the beginning. The only reason I took it was because I saw your name."

My lips twitch and a small smile breaches my sadness. "That's why you took the case?"

"Yeah. I figured it was bogus and wanted to clear your name. We may not have seen each other in more than a decade but I believed you were innocent. And this Hinton guy is an asshole. And the more I looked into it, the more I was glad I took the case."

"You know, even if we go to court, apart from the wasted time and money, this won't hurt me. My clients, the ones he's named—they know the situation and if any of my other clients hear about it, I can explain. I'm not worried. I'm just hurt."

He nods, curling his arm around me and bringing me into his solid chest. I want to melt into him, lose myself in his body, but things aren't that easy.

"Sure, but there's a better way. I'll get him to back off."

"Okay." I rest my head on his collarbone and my hand curls into his shirt.

"You want to grab some dinner?" he mumbles into the mass of hair atop my head.

"As much as I'd like to, I'm waiting on a contract that I need completed tonight. I was just on my way home and have some work to do while I wait. If we eat..." Heat creeps into my cheeks. "I'm not going to get any work done."

"All right. Get your things and I'll take you home." He releases me, wearing a small yet understanding smile.

I wish I could just forget about work and everything else.

Just be with Patrick.

But I do the grown-up thing and gather my files, slip on my coat and boots, and lock up the office for the night.

He's parked outside the building and we get into a black SUV, a company car that he drives. Like me, he explains that he doesn't own a vehicle because he has no need for one in the city. But he has a motorcycle and promises to take me for a ride when the weather is better.

My heart does a flip-flop at the thought. I may not be here too long after the new year and yet he's talking as if I will. And for the first time in months, the idea of staying in New York, of really giving it a try, is appealing.

The reality is I put a lot of work into this past year, endless hours building my business, and I was run ragged. No time for a social life and, truthfully, no time to think. And that's what I'm chasing. The distraction. Something to fill my mind, my days and nights, so I don't have to stop and sit with my own thoughts.

"Thanks for the ride, I'll talk to you later." I lean over the console and give him a quick kiss.

I want more but don't trust myself to indulge and leave. And even at that, I marvel at how, in such a short period of time, I feel like we're together.

He takes hold of my hand and the simple touch sends a shock wave through my body. "Mia. About Thanksgiving..."

It's the day after tomorrow and while I did agree to go, I'm unsure if it's a good idea. I edge out of the car, his hold still on me, and plant my feet firmly on the sidewalk.

I need to be grounded. His hands on me cause a hot tight coil of excitement, low in my belly.

"I won't take no for an answer." He squeezes my fingers.

"Fine. Pick me up at my place."

For the first time since we reconnected, he smiles, and it's brilliant. Beautiful even. His joy tugs at my heart, tangling with my conflicted emotions when I think about what we're doing.

Maybe we will be good for each other.

Maybe we will mend each other's broken hearts.

Maybe... I know better than that.

He doesn't know everything and when he does, none of this—us—may be possible.

TRIPP

It's Thanksgiving and I choose to spend the first part of it working. Tailing Taya as usual. The big lumbering idiot known as Tiny, what a joke, leads the way to the car with Taya Conrad several feet behind. The driver stands with the back door open, wearing a bored expression.

I know how he feels. My ass is numb from sitting here for the better part of three hours. I watch as Tiny, one of her right-hand men, gets in the car and she follows.

During the time I spent watching and waiting, I called Fraser Hinton. I didn't give a fuck that it was seven in the morning on the west coast.

My call and the timing was deliberate. The guy is a jerk and I don't know how or why Mia partnered with him. He spoke like she took advantage of him and all her success is thanks to him. I warned him against pursuing his lawsuit.

It's unfounded and he will lose. Not to mention, I hinted that more trouble would find him if he didn't heed my advice.

Asshole.

The black sedan drives through the streets of the city, and lately, this is how I seem to fill my days, tailing Taya Conrad, thinking of Mia. She's never far from my mind.

We're no closer to finding out if Griffin is alive, and if he is, where the fuck is he? Taya has done nothing even remotely interesting or suspicious related to the possibility of Griffin. And none of our potential leads panned out. We checked all four guys we'd shortlisted and came up empty.

Three of them weren't even possible once we looked into their backgrounds and the timeline. Nothing meshed.

One came close on paper, some guy Taya keeps hidden for random jobs. But his DNA wasn't a match.

We've been scraping the barrel for possibilities and coming up empty. We're no closer to finding him and still have no answers. And meanwhile, the Feds are getting closer.

Despite it being Thanksgiving, this woman has no one who cares to break bread with her. I volunteered for the first shift and have spent the morning driving around town.

The sedan pulls up to her apartment and I glance over at my phone, lying on the passenger seat. Fuck. It's twelve thirty. I'm late to pick up Mia.

I've been so wrapped up in watching Taya that I lost track of time. I call into HC and request relief. I'm already over my shift but told them I'd stay on her until I had to go.

Then I call Mia and the phone rings and rings without an answer. Maybe she's in the shower or working. I send her a text.

Me: Sorry, running late. I should be there in about 30.

Backup arrives shortly after and in no time flat, I'm in front of her apartment, double parking. I might get a ticket but hopefully, I'll be quick.

I race up the stairs, not bothering with the elevator, and check my phone once more. No reply to my text.

Striding with purpose, I'm quickly at her door and knocking. No answer. It's several more knocks until the sound of a muffled voice comes through the door.

"Coming."

The door swings open and Mia stands before me in a pair of shorts and a tank top. Her hair is in a high ponytail and she seems scattered and breathless. I feel the heat coming from her apartment or maybe it's me.

"Patrick." She's surprised to see me, and right behind her is a young girl.

The child now stands beside Mia, and she looks to be around eight or nine, with blonde hair and a blinding smile of innocence.

"Who is he?" she asks, peering up at Mia and then at me.

"Oh my God, I completely forgot." Her hand covers her mouth and her eyes widen.

"Hey, sorry I'm late." Uneasy, I can't help but feel as if I've stepped into an alternate universe. "I called and sent a text to let you know I was on my way."

"Oh, my phone, I don't even know where it is." She glances back into the apartment and then at me. "I lost track… it's been… it's been crazy. I haven't been that focused… work and…"

I try to string her rambling together, and a tall, familiar-looking guy joins us.

Brown hair. Muscles. T-shirt and shorts.

My chest spasms, aching as if a knife is ripping through my heart.

Who the hell is this?

"Hey, Mia, where's the—" He stops in his tracks and I'm completely off kilter.

Am I in the Twilight Zone? She lives with a guy and a kid. When all this time she made it sound like it was just her.

The guy she was speaking to on the phone in the coffee shop comes to mind. I'm an idiot. Was I totally blinded by my feelings for her that I missed the signs? And why the hell didn't she say something?

"Oh." Confusion swims in her brown eyes and she whips her head from me to the guy to the kid.

"Is this a bad time?" I don't hide the irritation in my stupid question.

I am supposed to be here. What about them? Who the fuck are they?

"No, Patrick, no. Eli. Crystal." She glances at both of them in turn. "This is my friend, Patrick Townsend. And Patrick, this is Eli Lansing and Crystal Lansing."

Lansing? It's the same name as one of the clients I called. The musician turned actor that Hinton accused her of stealing. That's why he looks familiar. He was the lead guitarist for Trojan, a now-retired rock band.

I thought he was her client yet this appears to be more than business. And the girl is his daughter. Is she Mia's too? She could be, with her light dusting of freckles and brown eyes just like Mia.

"Hey, Patrick. Are you the same guy I talked to over the phone?" Eli leans forward, brushing Mia's shoulder as he stretches his hand out to me.

I don't like how close he is to her. He's very familiar with her, too comfortable for my liking. I don't take his hand. It's childish but I don't even acknowledge it.

My gaze is fixed on Mia, and she swallows with difficulty. Her cheeks turn red and the tension mounts among us.

He drops his hand and straightens, fixed to her side, his hand still on her shoulder. He brings his daughter to stand behind him, almost as if I may be a threat and he feels the need to protect her from me.

"Are you okay, Mia?" His fingers curl into her flesh.

"Yes. Can you guys just give us a minute?" Her gaze is pleading at the two of them, and he nods, taking his daughter's hand.

"Daddy, who is that guy?" They turn, walking away from us. "What's going on?"

He lowers his voice so I'm unable to hear his response and they disappear into another room.

"Patrick, I'm sorry, I forgot. I even forgot Eli and Crystal were coming. They came in last night."

"So what are you saying?" There's a bite to my tone.

Is this just an excuse?

"I'm going to have to pass on Thanksgiving. I'm so sorry to do this at the last minute. They just got here, and we had a late start to the day. We were just getting ready to make breakfast… I mean, brunch."

I cross my arms over my torso. Each word is a jab to my chest and maybe I'm protecting myself from the miserable sensation growing within me.

Numb I can deal with. Numb I'm used to. I don't know what to say, and right now, I feel like shit. And I'm not too happy with Mia.

"Fine." I turn to leave, at a loss for words that won't hurt her.

She grabs my shoulder. "Can we maybe go out tomorrow? And I'll explain more to you. This just isn't a good time."

It feels like she's just trying to placate me and it burns my gut.

"Fine."

The drive to Carys and Van's is a blur. And I'm not in much of a mood to celebrate once I get there. And sure enough, as to be expected, because of my arrival without my guest, the questions fly.

More so from the women than the guys. And after our meal, both Tate and Carys crowd me in the kitchen.

"So what happened to Mia?" Carys wipes down the counter even though her husband just did it like five minutes ago.

As is tradition, the guys usually clean up after these kinds of gatherings. We just finished and while Ry and Van escaped, I wasn't so lucky.

"I told you, she couldn't make it." I don't even know what to think about what she's doing.

"Really? I so wanted to meet her. Doesn't she have her own law firm? Couldn't she take one day off?" Carys asks.

"It has nothing to do with her business. She has guests and forgot they were coming in." Even as I say the words, I have a hard time believing them.

Did I miss her cues? Maybe she wanted to give me the kiss-off and this was her way of doing it. That doesn't feel like the Mia I know but maybe that's it. It has been over twelve years, maybe I don't know her at all.

"Look, I think I'm gonna cut out." I point toward the front door.

"No, stay. Go watch the game with the guys. Take a drink with you. What would you like?" Tate opens the fridge for me to scan the various beverages lining the shelf.

We haven't talked since the news of Griffin. And while that isn't too unusual, we bonded because of my brother. I'm usually the last guy to want to have a chat but I should.

"Hey, how you holding up? Do you want to talk?" Guilt is a toxic beast.

I have been meaning to reach out to Tate since I spoke with Carys. But I haven't. Too caught up in Taya, Griff, Mia and not wanting to scratch too deep on how I'm dealing, or not, with all that's going on.

Tate smiles and nods while Carys says, "Oh, I can be here for this?"

She's teasing and I plant my palm on her face, gently pushing her away. "This is none of your business, kid."

Her fingers curl around my wrist and she shoves my hand to the side. "Whatever."

Despite her interest in sticking around, Carys leaves and I head up to the den with Tate. My gut churns, gearing up for this heart to heart.

"How are you doing?" I sit on the couch, patting the space beside me.

"Okay. And you?"

"I should have reached out sooner. You've been on my mind since we heard the recording."

"Hey, don't sweat it. You've been dealing with a lot. Me, I've just been going crazy." She releases a hollow laugh. "I wish we had something to go on. This is so frustrating. We've been going through potential people and nothing. Is he even alive?"

"Yeah, if only we knew for sure."

"I just want to ask my mother point blank."

"Don't go to Taya." I've been tempted to but that woman can't be trusted.

I'm not immune to her and Tate is even more vulnerable. The monster is her mother and she finally cut ties with her nearly six years ago. It would have been way longer than that, if her parents hadn't kidnapped her and forced her to marry into the mafia.

"Why not?"

"Because she won't tell us. Whether he's dead or alive, she'll get nothing but joy from your question. She won't hand him over unless it's to her benefit."

Her shoulders deflate and she nods. "Ry and I are racking our brains for other ways to find out more without tipping our hand but..."

"How's he doing?" At first, I couldn't imagine what Ry is going through but after seeing Mia with another guy, *fuck*, I feel for him. He's likely in even more turmoil because Griffin isn't just some guy.

"He's like the rest of us. He wants Griffin to be alive. He wants answers. A lead."

"Yeah, but how are you two doing with this possibility?"

Tate was with Griffin when he was murdered. They met at school in Chicago and none of the rest of us met Tate until after my brother had been killed. Ry was her handler when she was a confidential informant to the FBI.

They fought their attraction for many reasons and Griffin was front and center among them. Both were guilt-ridden to think they could be together while my brother was dead.

"Nothing changes for us if Griffin is alive. If this had been years ago, when we'd just met... well, that would be different. But Ry is my heart. He's my home and family. None of that changes if what my mother said is true. And I want it to be true."

"Yeah, me too." In a rare moment, I admit what I wish for.

Perhaps it's because I'm raw from what happened with Mia or because Tate and I have never lied to each other.

"If he is alive, why hasn't he tried to contact any of us?" Tate nibbles on her bottom lip, worry lining her forehead.

"Maybe he can't. He could be held captive." I'm offering up theories for her sake as much as mine. "It goes against what Taya said but anything is possible."

"Tripp, look who's here." Carys stands at the entrance to the room with Mia at her side.

A wild longing strikes me square in the chest and the iron band constricting my lungs, the one I never knew was there, snaps. Damn, my heart is banging around in my chest at the sight of her in a pair of jeans and a white sweater with her hair braided to the side.

She's here.

Her expression is sheepish, almost remorseful. "Hi, I'm sorry for just crashing like this."

"Hey, I told you, you're not crashing. You were invited, and we're so glad that you could make it." Carys points toward us. "This is Tate. Remember my brother you met downstairs? This is his wife."

"Hi, nice to meet you." Tate stands, going to Mia. "I'm not a big hugger but I feel like I should. Our Tripp doesn't bring other friends around so you must be special."

She is... special, that is. Tate pulls her in for a quick hug and my insides cartwheel. My worlds collide. A strange mess of confusion and solace drifts through my chest at the sight.

Mia, the woman I've crushed on hard since college, the only one I ever dreamed of having more with, is here. With my family—the people closest to me. I could get used to this. To us.

But I've got questions. Am I special to her? Is that why she's here? Or is she here to explain things to me? Like why her client and his child are living with her. Things I don't want to hear.

MIA

Tate surprises me with her warm embrace and I pull back to see a glimmer of a smile flit over Patrick's lips before he hides it behind his usual cool stare.

My body quivers, both excited and anxious to be here. These people care about him, a lot. It's clear to see they are his family.

"And I think you know this guy." Carys hooks a thumb at him, winking.

"Such a funny girl." He strides toward us, eyes on Carys as if he's going to make her pay.

She laughs, they take fake shots at each other, and then she and Tate excuse themselves, leaving us alone. I'm a mess, still upset for completely forgetting about today, and my nerves kick into overdrive at the thought of trying to explain this to him.

This time of year is always an emotional rollercoaster, chaos on my heart and soul, leaving me scattered and lost.

"I'm glad to see you." His eyes gleam with amusement and something deeper, more vulnerable.

"I'm so sorry for earlier. I don't have a good excuse for my scrambled brain. First it was Fraser, then I was thrown for a loop when Eli showed up. He says he told me the flight info and that he was coming a day ago. I swear, I don't remember."

I'm babbling, one hand waving about and the other clutching at the side of my head, afraid I may lose it. My nerves tingle and spark. I am driven to fix my blunder.

"I was going to bed when they knocked on my door last night. Talk about embarrassing." I let out a jittery laugh. "Today is my mistake and I feel rotten—"

His hands grab hold of mine, securing them in his, sure and steady. "It's okay."

His deep soothing voice settles things inside me, making breathing easier.

But it's short-lived. He's got something on his mind and as if unable to keep it to himself, he forges ahead in a gruff voice.

"Eli Lansing. He's the same one I spoke to, right? The one Fraser claims you stole."

"I didn't steal him," I unintentionally snap, still raw from Fraser's dick move.

"Relax. Eli's a client, but he's living with you?"

I suppose it looked like that to him, but doesn't he think I'd have said something sooner if that was the case?

"He isn't living with me. He's moving to New York for work and is here to complete a few things for the move. You know, school for Crystal, to sign some paperwork for HBO."

"So what? You were together and not anymore?" His gaze narrows, assessing me. "Is Crystal yours?"

Like a bomb detonating internally, everything seizes and then explodes. Air is locked in my lungs, my heart stutters and I struggle to find the words.

"Whoa. No. Hang on."

Needing space but not wanting to let him go, I pull him further into the room, still holding his hand. I sit on the sofa and he takes the seat next to me.

"I met Eli at a party. One of those Hollywood things where it's just as much about being seen as it is about schmoozing, drumming up new business. He was the lead guitarist for Trojan."

"Yeah. I know."

"Since the band is no longer, he was looking for his own lawyer—one to look out for his personal interests." I run my fingers through my hair, frustrated because I get where he's coming from but also don't like feeling like I have to defend my actions.

I inhale a deep breath. "Anyway, we hit it off, and I made a pitch for his business. He was interested."

"I bet he was," he mutters gruffly under his breath.

"What do you mean by that?"

"Nothing."

I scowl and soften my features. I'm the one who needs to explain, not him. "We arranged a meeting and the day of, his babysitter was sick. So I suggested meeting him at his house."

My gaze drops to my lap and my shoulders curl inward as if protecting myself from the ache. He tenses beside me, leaning in to grab my gaze.

"I met *his* daughter that day. She isn't mine, but Crystal stole my heart. So that's why he's more than just a client. I care for his daughter, for him. I'd help him out. If he didn't have someone to watch her, I would. We became friends."

I clasp my hands together, folding and unfolding them for something to do with this unbearable anxious energy inside of me. I could keep talking, tell him everything, no matter how difficult it would be. But now isn't the right time.

"I have another lawyer I consult where Eli is concerned because the lines are blurred, but he refuses to get another lawyer."

"Hey, I understand." His expression is neutral and I'm not so sure he does.

"I can be objective where his business interests are concerned."

"I'm sure you can. Sounds like you've had this battle with yourself?" He raises a brow and offers a droll grin.

"You figured that out, eh?"

"I get it."

"Do you? Today's mix-up wasn't deliberate and I'm sorry."

"It's cool. Forget about it." His solid bicep flexes beneath my head as his arms settle around me. I sigh, sinking into him, relieved we're okay.

"So how long are they here for?" he asks.

"Two weeks."

Eli deliberately chose this time to come visit. There's so much more I could tell Patrick and he deserves to know some, if not all. But how do I tell him I'm days away from the time of year when I experienced my greatest loss?

Not a day goes by that I don't remember but the anniversary is always the hardest.

At this time of year, the throbbing in my chest is extreme when I think of a special moment we shared. The tears are hotter, falling faster and harder, when I look at pictures of us. The strangle in my throat is stronger and it's relentless when I say her name.

And I am distracted and emotional. Nothing stops the debilitating ache from coming for me. Not even work, my escape, can save me.

Usually, I'm best when I'm head down and knee deep, toiling away at building my business and growing my client base. But not at this time of year.

My New York practice hasn't given me the diversion I once had. The firm is thriving. I'm established and clients come to me, not like when I was first starting out in LA. And now, the reward is a steady stream of income, fewer hours and time on my hands.

I've always hated that saying. Time on my hands. Most people would kill for more free time. Not me. I want to crush it.

Idle time eats at me, drags me into the darkness, and how on earth do I explain this without telling him everything?

If I stay in New York, if we want a relationship, I must tell him. And the irony is, when I tell him, I could lose him.

"What's going on in there?" His finger lightly taps against my head. "You're quiet."

"Sorry. It's the holidays. This time of year is hard for me. That's kind of why I was hesitant to accept this invitation."

"Because of your sister?"

"Yes, that's some of it." I'm going to hell. My heart spasms guiltily for not being fully honest.

"What about your parents?"

"My parents." The deep-seated anguish of their abandonment unfurls in my stomach.

His quizzical stare causes me to shrink inwardly. I love my parents despite everything.

"My mother died two years ago, and my father… well, let's just say we're estranged. He isn't doing too well, from what I hear, but I would be the last person he'd want to see."

"Really? I thought you had a tight family."

"I did… but that was a long time ago." The familiar and unwanted seesaw of resignation and denial starts to pick up speed. "A lot has changed. That summer changed so much for me."

"What summer?" He looks at me, confused.

"The one when I didn't go back to school."

He shifts, twisting to face me fully. "You never told me what happened. Why didn't you go back to Cornell?"

And there it is. One question I've been dreading, not knowing how I'd respond without taking us down a certain road.

"Money was tight, tighter than normal, and I needed to take time off before completing my undergrad to make some money."

"Even with your grades? And what about loans?"

"I had a partial scholarship, but it wasn't enough. And loans weren't an option."

There's no point going into all the additional expenses that came at me, the many I had never counted on. I wonder if there's any point in any of this.

His touch, a stroke along my cheek, sends a shiver down my spine and I'm pulled from my futile thoughts. I melt into him, shutting my eyes and savoring his caress and nearness.

His breath fans at my ear. "I'm fucking thrilled you're here."

I angle my head backward, getting a better look at him. "Me too."

He dips his head, lightly brushing his lips across mine in a gentle kiss. But he doesn't stop there. The tip of his tongue darts out to slide along the seam of my lips, teasing me, and he draws back, our eyes tangling before he dives in again, crushing his mouth to mine.

The kiss is possessive, owning me. His tongue delves into my mouth, teeth clashing, lips sucking, and I release a whimpering moan that slips down his throat.

"So glad you're here," he murmurs against my swollen lips.

Pulling back, he breaks our kiss and tucks loose strands of my hair behind my ear. A palm cradles the back of my head and he bends to kiss my forehead.

I nip at his earlobe and in response, his fingers dig into my sides. I feel as if we're on the verge of something. Something playful or serious. It's hard to tell which way we'll go.

We stare at each other. Our bodies are close, breaths mingling, and an interminable silence grows between us. Uncertain if I can handle whatever this is. Right now. And anyone could walk in on us, so I drag us back to more neutral, safe territory.

"How come they all call you Tripp?"

His fingers weave into my hair and he studies me. "It's a nickname. Few people call me Patrick."

"Oh. Would you prefer I call you Tripp?"

"No," he says in his blunt way. "I like it."

"Okay." I blush and heat spreads from the center of my chest. "But why Tripp?"

A tiny grin struggles to break free from his flat lips. "My brother."

"What about him?" It feels like I'm in the wrong profession and should have been a dentist. This is like pulling teeth.

"We were young. I think I was six, or nah, must have been seven, and we thought it'd be cool to come up with nicknames. Ry had a ready-made one and came up with Twinkie for Carys."

"What?" I laugh, unable to imagine the woman I met minutes ago, so in charge, as a Twinkie.

"Yeah, she hates it. Still, to this day he'll use it once in a while. Then for Evan, we decided on Van. I wanted Trick." His gem-like eyes shimmer with nostalgia.

"I get it. So what happened? How come you ended up with Tripp?"

"Griff couldn't say Trick. Whenever he tried, it came out as Tripp. The guys thought it was hilarious and started calling me Tripp too. They refused to call me Trick. So Tripp just stuck."

"That's cute." His yearning for his lost brother tugs at my heart.

Patrick runs a hand roughly through his hair and stands. I try not to take his departure as rejection. I get to my feet as well and shiver, rubbing my hands along my arms, suddenly cold.

"You're not alone. You know that, right?"

"I know." His arms wrap around me and I rest my head against his chest.

His steady heartbeat is comforting, and yet a sadness I know all too well swells around me. He didn't understand my meaning.

When I said he wasn't alone, I wasn't talking about me. I was referring to the room full of people downstairs. His family.

In the brief minutes I had with them earlier when I arrived, it's clear he isn't alone. As for me, I don't know if I'll be here.

We spend the rest of the day with his friends and he drops me home well after nine in the evening.

We stand outside my apartment door and I step into him, sliding my arms around his neck.

"Thank you for such a wonderful day."

His hands wrap around my hips, pulling me against him. "You're welcome. I should be thanking you for making today amazing."

There's fire in his eyes. Angling his head, he crushes his mouth to mine. Lips strong and firm, demanding. I open for him and his tongue surges forward. A growl, low and feral, vibrates from his throat.

He strokes my mouth, tasting and playing. I'm dizzy with madness. My blood simmers, burning through me, along with a shiver.

The ding of the elevator and the murmur of voices somehow gets through to me and I break the kiss, pressing my forehead against his hot lips before I pull away.

His sultry stare wanders down my body and back up again. Almost imperceptibly, his blue irises darken. One corner of his lips edges up and his tongue darts out to lick his bottom lip.

"So sweet."

A flush spreads like wildfire up my neck and into my face. "You're naughty."

"I'd like to be with you."

"Okay, I have to go in before I do something that could get me arrested for indecent exposure." I laugh and his eyebrows arch.

"Now that I want to see."

"Maybe another time." I wink, surprised at my bold flirting. I've gotten better at it with age.

I press onto my toes and lightly kiss his lips once more, quick to pull away before he draws me in for a longer, deeper kiss. I may never leave his arms if he does.

"We'll talk soon." I slide the key into the door and turn back to him.

"Definitely. When can we see each other again?" His voice is deep and husky and my core quivers with need.

"Soon, hopefully. For the next little bit, I'm going to be very busy. There's a lot going on at work. So maybe week after next?"

Impulsively, I give him another hug and then nuzzle my face into the crook of his neck. I can't face him, knowing I'm not telling him the truth.

I will be out of town, and while simple to say, it will invite too many questions that I'm not prepared to answer.

"Not sure I can wait that long." He tightens his hold, kissing the top of my head. "Let's try for sooner."

I nod into his chest and pull away. One more kiss and I slip into my dark apartment. It looks like Eli and Crystal are in bed. Thank goodness. I can be alone with my thoughts.

With each passing minute I spend with Patrick, it's harder to think about walking away. And I'm not so sure I can destroy him with the truth. It might be better for all if I leave. He's already lost so much, his parents and his brother, and I don't want to be the one to tear down the little he has left.

It might be best to not start anything with him, even though it feels like we already have. I should move to Nashville and never look back.

TRIPP

The early December sun is high and bright, almost blinding, in the sky. There's a sharp crispness in the air and despite the chill, I've got the window rolled down to keep me alert.

It's Griffin's birthday. He would be thirty-three.

My phone rings. It's Van and I pick up on the first ring. "Yeah."

"Hey, where are you?"

"Columbus Circle. Taya's having lunch with Cavallo."

"Bruno?" Van asks and I grunt in response. "Interesting. I wonder what that's about."

His curiosity has no bite. HC isn't big enough to take on La Cosa Nostra, nor would we want to.

We had our dance with the devil when his sister, Anna, was in the mob's clutches. Once she was free, we agreed, if at all possible, we wouldn't tangle with those guys again.

Bruno Cavallo is the don of the most powerful mob family in New York City and Conrad has done business with them over the years. These two together isn't surprising, but the fact that Cavallo is out in broad daylight is.

Now nearing his late sixties, the man is somewhat of a recluse and conducts most of his business behind closed doors.

"What's up?" I flip through the music channels, not interested in music or any conversation.

"Can you come in? We need to talk."

"No, can't. There's no one else on Taya for another two hours. I'm not leaving." I don't want to miss anything and a meeting with the Cavallo Don, out in public like this, is virtually unheard of. There's no way I'm stepping away.

"Tripp, I want to do this in person."

"Ain't gonna happen. Just say it." I drum my fingers impatiently on the leather steering wheel. Why is he dragging this out?

"We got the DNA results from the body."

I can tell by his grave tone what the outcome is. "It isn't him, is it?"

"No."

Griffin is alive.

A chill curls deep into my chest and my throat constricts. The past ten years, all the days and nights I visited that grave site, flash before my eyes.

I thought I was talking to my brother. I felt closer to him there than anywhere else and it wasn't even him.

"Who the fuck did we bury?"

"We don't know," Van says sharply. "They're running the results through ViCAP. Maybe we'll get lucky and whoever the guy was has a record or someone's been looking for him. We're not giving up. When we find out who it is, that might be a lead." His tone is hopeful, and it only pisses me off.

"This doesn't mean he's alive. Just that he's still fucking dead but we may never find his body." A raw, savage need to hurt something tunnels through me.

I'm beyond frustrated. Every time we unearth something new or close a possible avenue, we're left with more questions and no closer to finding Griffin.

"Yeah, but let's not get ahead of ourselves." He uses his detached professional voice on me. "For now, we're operating on the assumption he's alive."

"Fuck." I slam my palm against the wheel and a lady on the sidewalk jumps back from the car, glaring at me. "And what about the Feds, where are they with arresting Taya?"

"They're ready. Any day now."

"Van, we're fucked." I don't even bother to hide my never-ending irritation at the fucked-up situation we're in. "They're not going to let us make a deal with her."

He's silent. He knows I'm right, but he doesn't want to admit it. Typically, we might be able to negotiate. For instance, drop one of the charges or offer a reduced sentence in exchange for information on where or who Griffin is.

It isn't likely the Feds will agree to that this time. They did once before on our ask, when we were working with them to bring down Ash Naire, and that didn't end so well for us.

Taya had ties to the sick fuck, and we thought we could use that. Instead, we were left empty-handed, and she evaded human trafficking charges. She'd already be rotting in jail if not for that deal.

"I'll ask. No promises but it's worth the ask." I release a growl and he barrels over me. "We'll move faster. It feels like it's time to have a talk with some of her men. Put the screws to Tiny, Franz or whoever was around back then."

We've talked about this before, but the chances of more intel from her men are slim. To pull off what she did, falsifying dental records and finding a body similar to my brother's, she couldn't do it on her own.

She'd want to keep it to her tight-knit group and might have outsourced so as not to have anyone in her inner circle blackmail her at a future date.

"And what if only Warren, Taya and Bobby knew the truth? Two of them are dead and she'll be behind bars. What then?"

"Tripp—" Van starts, and I can already hear his placating response.

I hang up. It's a dick move but I'm not in the mood for him to mollify me. I'm not swallowing any shit right now.

Not to be a total asshole, I text him to explain I need time. If only we had more of it.

We're fucked unless we get a lead.

Out the windshield, I stare at the entrance of the restaurant as Taya exits with Bruno Cavallo behind her. Four guys, in addition to the three that came out ahead of Taya, follow the mob boss.

They aren't easy to dismiss. Beefy men, Italian suits, sunglasses, and all of them are alert, constantly scanning their surroundings. They reek of mafia.

A woman headed toward them causes me to pause on her slender form. I can't see much of her because of the mob of men but from the bit I can see, there's something familiar about her.

It isn't only her appearance, with the long blonde hair and fashionable clothes, but the way she walks that holds my attention. There's definitely something that sends a tingling like pins and needles lighting up my spine.

Taya separates from the group and her men follow toward the idling car parked along the curb, several feet from the restaurant. Her driver is waiting with the back door open.

It's only when one of Cavallo's goons steps onto the road to round the vehicle that I get a good look at the other woman.

Shit.

I grab the binoculars on the passenger seat and stare through the lenses. The blonde is now past Cavallo's men and her lips are moving, her gaze ahead. She's calling to Taya and fuck me, it's Tate.

Her mother stops mid-slide into the car and straightens, peering over at her daughter marching along the sidewalk toward her. Taya puts on a sinister smile and I unbuckle my seat belt. I've got to get over there.

What the hell is Tate doing here? Ry will lose his shit when he hears about this, because I'd bet my life he doesn't know his wife is about to face off with her psycho mother.

She hasn't seen me and I rush across the busy street, eyes trained on the two women. Taya's men are alert, forming a human barricade around them.

Tate stops mid-stride, only feet from her mother's car. Something is wrong. She stumbles, one hand outstretched as if looking for something to steady her and the other wraps around her middle.

She falters again, and my steps stutter, watching and waiting. Shit, I need to get over there. I pick up the pace as Tate's hand now covers her mouth and her features morph as if she's in pain or about to faint.

What the hell? I'm now on the sidewalk, gunning for her when I shift my gaze onto what, or more accurately whom, she's fixed on. The driver.

He glowers at her, almost annoyed but also assessing for any potential threat. Then I see it. I nearly tumble over my own feet as an alarming comprehension slices through me.

The driver. Blond hair. Blue eyes.

Griffin.

He looks nothing like Griffin. But the eyes and something else, something I can't describe. The man is about the same height as my brother. A similar build, maybe more muscled than before. And the hair, while shorter, it's the same shade of blond.

Why the hell didn't I *see* him before? We should have looked into him.

Fuck. Tate sobs, her body trembles and her mother's lips twist into a satisfied sneer as her hand lands on her driver's forearm. I'm finally at Tate's side.

"It's okay," I whisper, bringing her into my side and stabbing Taya with a glare.

"It's… it's him." Tate's voice cracks, so low I can barely hear her over the sounds of cars and people on the street.

She's transfixed on the driver, and I regard him, pushing aside the physical similarities. He looks nothing like my brother.

Just another mob guy with muscles and a stone-cold poker face. Not a twitch or a blink of recognition from him. He glares, looking right through me.

This can't be Griffin. I rack my brain, trying to think what information we have on Taya's driver. Not even his name comes to mind and yet, I've heard it before. I should know it. I want to say it starts with an R, but that's a guess. I'm coming up blank.

"What the fuck do you want?" Tiny asks, standing on the street like the thug he is.

"What's wrong, Tate, darling?" Taya's words are laced with venomous joy.

And that's when my doubt is erased. Her joy gives it away. Even if I can't see Griffin in his features, she confirms it with her smugness.

Only to solidify it further when she says, "I knew if anyone would figure it out that it would be you."

She starts toward her daughter and I step in front of Tate. In a flash, things go sideways. Like rats rising from the sewers, the FBI descends upon us. Tate and I are hauled out of the way and I'm quick to identify ourselves.

Shaking, Tate curls into my side and we watch her mother being handcuffed. Relief at the sight of the woman being hauled off battles with uncertainty for the driver. Is he going to be arrested too?

The Feds also handcuff Cavallo and some are forced to contend with the enforcers who are kicking up a stink. But interestingly enough, the driver is the first to get out of the fray. He's quick to high-tail it up the street, away from it all. But he doesn't leave.

He stops about a hundred, hundred and twenty feet from it all, watching. Tate's sharp shallow breaths pull my attention away from him. She's pale, eyes glued to the guy we think is Griffin.

"Just breathe." I don't want her to have a panic attack or pass out. "Focus on your breathing. You're going to be okay."

"We've got to talk to him," she says, digging her nails into the arm of my jacket, gaze still on him.

I nod and head us in his direction, leading her the long way around the confusion of fists and shouting.

As we near him, he narrows his gaze. "Back off."

This guy may have similarities to my brother, but we don't know for sure. And he works for Taya. He could have a gun.

Before I can get my wits about me, to properly assess if he's a threat, Tate breaks free of my hold and is quick to grab at his arm, not willing to let him walk away.

It happens so fast that I can barely grab hold of her before he rips his arm from her grasp. "Don't touch me."

"I'm sorry. It's just that..." Her lips wobble, eyes glittering with unshed tears.

"What?" He straightens to his full height, balling his hands into fists at his sides.

I straighten my spine, poised to react if I have to. Her tears do nothing to soften his cold exterior. He doesn't know who she is or care at all.

"You don't need to be a dick." I step into his face and he presses his hand into my chest to keep me at a safe distance.

Normally I wouldn't back down, but this could be my brother. I will not hurt him or make this any more difficult or awkward unless he forces me by threatening Tate or me.

"What do you want? Who are you?" The voice is familiar, or is it wishful thinking?

"You don't know who we are?" She stands beside me, sounding more confident.

"No. Why should I?"

Many emotions streak through me in an instant. Shocked to anxious to puzzled. If this is Griffin, fuck, what did Taya do to him?

The driver glances over to the commotion and I follow his gaze. Things are dying down and most of the mob men are gone. Either they've been arrested for interfering or they've chosen to leave. None of Taya's men are around.

Tate's still focused on him. "We think you're... no, no."

She shakes her head, looking to me with a silent plea. She doesn't know how to do this and neither do I.

"Who are you?" I figure that's as good a place to start as any, and it buys us some time.

"Riff Stevens, and who are you?"

Riff. Of course, now it's coming back to me. If my memory serves me right, he came on the scene as part of Taya's crew—her driver—about four or five years ago. He looks to be about the right age. Shit, if he *is* Griff, today's his birthday.

"How old are you?"

"What? I asked you, who the fuck are you?" His eyes narrow, squinting with the glare of the afternoon sun.

"I'm Patrick Townsend, and this is Tate Wolfe. Taya is her mother."

He studies the blonde beside me and his examination is likely more to do with her connection to Taya than anything else.

"Max is your brother." His hard gaze is fixed on her. "You're twins, right?"

She nods and shivers, pulling her coat tighter around her. "When's your birthday?"

He tilts his head to the side, staring at her puzzled, and my lungs constrict.

"What's with all the questions?" He's defensive.

"Can we go inside and talk?" I tip my head toward a restaurant and tighten my arm around Tate. Maybe if we get off the street and away from the bust not too far away, it might settle his nerves a bit. Not only his, Tate's and mine as well.

"I'm not going anywhere with you. I'm out." He turns on his heel but she grabs at his shoulder.

He stills and snarls, whipping around to face us. "Look lady, don't fucking touch me."

Leaning into her face, he sets his features into a menacing glare. She tenses, as do I, and finally, he exhales harshly. "I don't care if you're the boss's daughter. Hands off. Got it?"

"I'm sorry. It's just that we think we know who you are."

"Who I am?" He straightens. "I fucking know who I am."

"And so do I." My conviction is an act because I don't know for sure. "You were born right here, in New York. And in fact, today's your birthday."

"So what? You could have found that out any number of ways. That proves nothing." Something akin to doubt creeps into his hard gaze.

I TRY NOT to react to the fact he didn't refute anything I said. Does he know he is Griffin?

"What about your parents? Siblings?" I ask.

He pauses, opening his mouth and then clamping his mouth shut, his lips now a firm line. Confusion or panic flickers in his gaze. It appears that he doesn't know the answer to my questions.

"I don't have time for this bullshit." He turns again and this time Tate is smart enough not to touch him.

But she bolts from my arms, hurrying to keep pace, get in front of him. "Wait. Riff?"

"Yeah." He pauses and twists to look at her.

"Happy birthday." She offers a small, genuine smile, and a tear slips from her eye. "Before you go, if you don't mind me asking, how old are you?"

"Thirty-three." His shoulders relax a little.

That many coincidences—his birthday, age, born here—knock us both back a step. With any assumed identity, it is always best to stick as close as possible to the facts, but usually it's so you don't forget. So you don't get caught in a lie.

I'm convinced he isn't lying. He doesn't remember us or Griffin. These details, the ones that match Griffin's, are likely for Taya's benefit. It's easier for her to remember the truth.

Many questions swim in my head and yet, I can't move or think or do anything but stare at him.

"We done?" He steps around us and it's my turn to grab at him, even knowing it isn't the smartest move.

"Fucking hands off." He's quick, in my face, pushing me against the wall of a building.

"Easy." I hold my hands out to the side as if in surrender. "We're not done."

"Yes. We are. I'm not sticking around for the Feds to decide they want to question or arrest me too."

Releasing me, he pushes at my chest and strides away in the same direction as before.

"Hey, Griffin." I'm looking for a reaction.

"Name's not Griffin." He stops and squares his shoulders, now facing us. He tries for a menacing glare, but it looks more agitated than anything else.

"We know this is hard to believe, and you might think we're crazy…" Tate whips her head from him to me. "We think you're his brother."

She points to me and he cocks his head to one side, regarding me with newfound interest. It's clear to see when things click and he's too late to cover it up.

If you really look, the resemblance is easy to spot even with what I'm guessing is his plastic surgery. He tears his gaze from mine as if it hurts to look my way.

I'd fucking love to get him to a doctor and have some tests done—DNA, for sure, among others. Parts of his face, on their own, look like Griffin but not when put together.

He had surgery, no doubt, and I'd wager we'll find scars to prove it. I wonder what story he was told to explain any markings or scars on his body. I want to ask but won't spook him any more than he already is.

"You're fucking lunatics." His scorn is a little too harsh, a little too much as if he's covering because he might be entertaining the notion.

"Think about it." I shove my hands into my pockets and try to relax my stance. "You don't have to say anything but I'm guessing your past isn't clear, is it? You have questions? We're here to talk. We may be wrong… or we may be right."

"This is my number." Tate thrusts her business card at him, and he hesitates to accept it. "Call me anytime."

"Or me." I whip out a crumpled HC card from my jacket. "How do we reach you?"

"You don't."

He turns on his heel and neither of us hustle after him. We've dumped a lot on him. He needs to digest this.

Tate's the first to move, stepping in front of me as people walk around us on the busy sidewalk. Clear blue eyes glitter with confidence, maybe even hope.

"Tripp, he's been right under our noses."

TRIPP

We meet the gang at Ry and Tate's place. Our texts are vague but enough to get them all there by the time we arrive. Tate needed to get home for her boys.

Tension takes up residence in the space. Everyone is seated around the room, bombarding us with eager stares and unspoken questions.

Tate clears her throat, her fingers fumbling with the edges of her blouse. Instead of starting this, she flips her gaze in my direction, silently urging me to do the talking.

There's no easy way to get to the point, and I've always been blunt, if nothing else.

"We found Griffin."

As soon as his name leaves my lips, Ry and Van speak over each other, demanding more details.

Carys jumps to her feet, stunned and spinning around the room as if expecting to see my brother among us. Tommie and Max both wear similar relieved expressions. They were the ones to start this wild goose chase and I suppose I get where they're coming from.

The recording has caused a lot of angst and turmoil. At least now we have something, or more accurately, some*one* to go on. A way to find more answers and maybe even a resolution.

"How? Where is he?" Ry's terse voice cuts through the noise.

I look to his wife, more as a warning or heads up. Once I retell the tale, he isn't going to be pleased to hear about her involvement.

She nods and I start at Columbus Circle after my conversation with Van. As expected, Ry's now on his feet when I get to the part where I noticed Tate on the street.

"What the hell?" He glares at her. "Why didn't you tell me?"

"Ry." She nears, reaching for his hand.

Both of them are in turmoil and neither of them have it easy. I can see both sides of this, why Tate felt the need to get answers and why Ry is shocked, worried she did this on her own. If only I could help.

"Guys, focus. Questions after." Van takes charge before we get off track.

Ry brings his wife to his side, an arm loose around her waist, and Van gives the go-ahead to continue.

They listen with rapt attention, no one interrupting despite a few silent reactions at various parts of the story. Van and Ry tense at the arrival of the FBI, Max growls at his mother's comment aimed at his sister. The comment we could assume confirms her driver is Griffin.

"He doesn't know who he is? He didn't recognize you?" Carys stands at my side, eyes damp.

Even having considered that scenario, the ache of my twisted heart isn't any less.

"No, he doesn't know me or Tate, and we don't know what happened to him, why it's like that. He could have lost his memory with the beating..."

I hate thinking about what he might have endured all these years. Was the beating in Chicago the only time he was tortured or was there more? Rage crawls out of the darkness, coiling around my heart.

"And you really think it's Griffin?" She clings to my arm, hopeful.

"I think so. It was the eyes. If he'd been wearing sunglasses, I doubt I would have given him a second look. Tate saw it first."

Everyone looks to her, and she swallows with difficulty, still shaken from our encounter and nodding. "His voice is the same too."

"Yeah. I'd say it's him." My jaw tenses, angry. Why the fuck didn't I see it sooner?

"Could he be faking?" Van asks.

"What do you mean?" Tate is first to respond.

"Is there any way he remembers… knows who he is, but he's been conditioned by Taya or too afraid to admit it?"

"Nah." I shake my head. "He didn't believe us and even though I got the sense he has gaps in his history, he was quick to dismiss our claim."

"If we could only talk to him some more, tell him more about his past, find out what he thinks his life has been…" Tate slumps backward, leaning into Ry.

"I'll start looking into Riff Stevens, find out all we can on him, and now that we have more to go on, I'll have another look at Taya, Warren and Bobby from back then." Tommie reaches into her bag and pulls out a tablet. "I should get back to the office."

"Sounds good." Van runs a hand through his hair, pacing to the window and back in thought.

"How did you leave it with him?" Ry shifts Tate to one side, still holding her close.

"He's got our numbers." She looks up at him. "We gave him our cards."

"Yeah, but I think we give him a few days to sit with this and then we make contact again." I pick up my jacket, now itching to leave.

To go to Mia.

I have this sudden need to tell her. She may think of something none of us have and I just need… need her.

"What are you thinking?" Max raises his head from staring over Tommie's shoulder at her screen.

"I doubt he will reach out to us and, with Taya arrested and things not looking good for her, he could see it as an opportunity to leave." I shrug on my jacket.

"Leave?" Carys asks, frantic.

I place a hand on her shoulder. "Relax. We won't let it get to that.

Today, we planted a few questions in his head. Let's just give him a day or two."

"What we need is a DNA test." Van places his hands on his hips. "Any chance he'd agree to it?"

"No. It's too soon." I head for the door. "You know how to reach me."

Ry strides after me, grabbing at my arm. His expression is solemn, mirroring my mood. "Hey, Tripp, this is good news."

"Yeah, it is. But it's feeling like it might be a long road."

"Sure, but we'll get there." He claps my back, pushing out a smile, and I leave.

My first thought is Mia once I'm alone. We've both been busy. I've been wrapped up in finding Griffin, so much so we've mostly talked and texted. And when I tried to see her, the timing never worked.

If I had a free moment, she had a client meeting or dinner or was working toward a deadline. This time, I don't call or text her that I'm coming over. I just need to see her.

It's Saturday and when Eli answers the door, disappointment dampens my need. The burning need to see her, touch her and tell her my brother is alive fizzles.

"Hey, Patrick, right?" Eli rests one arm above his head on the doorjamb.

"Is Mia here?" I look past him into the apartment, where I find Crystal on the floor with papers and crayons strewn about.

"Ah, no, she isn't."

I take several steps one way and then the other, peering into some of the other rooms, looking for Mia, and the little girl stops drawing. "Hi, mister, what's your name?"

"Patrick." I force my lips upward into a tight, most probably pathetic, smile.

"I'm Crystal. Do you want to color with me? Daddy's on a call and Mia's gone."

"Gone?" I nail her father with my agitation. "Is she at her office?"

"No, she isn't here. In the city." With a furtive look to his daughter, he motions for us to move into the hall. "Honey, I'll be back in a second. Daddy's gonna be right here outside. Okay?"

"All right." Her head is down, engrossed in her art.

He strides to the front door, speaking into his mobile, which I hadn't noticed before. "Hey, Gray, let me call you back."

With one last examination of the room, I stall on a painting. It's the only thing adorning the white walls. The only personal touch to the room, and clearly, the art is a child's work.

Did Crystal do it? And if so, why is it hanging on her wall like it's the Mona Lisa? Treasured.

The canvas isn't big, maybe ten by fourteen inches, and painted an ocean blue. A misshapen heart is off center, and two flowers are hanging out in the sky. The images are big and bright.

Eli clears his throat and I twist to see him shove his phone into the back pocket of his jeans. He's standing at the doorway, waiting for me to follow.

Once we're out in the hall, he smiles sheepishly. "Sorry about that. Listen..."

"What aren't you telling me?"

"She's taken off for a few days."

"What do you mean, taken off? Where is she?"

Did she decide to move to Nashville, and if so, why the hell didn't she say something?

"No, she rented a car." He hesitates, dropping his gaze to his bare feet, and I want to shake the words out of him.

Why didn't she tell me she was getting out of town? She's had chances to tell me during our calls and texts.

"You know, this time of year is hard for her."

"Yeah, she told me." I nod, recalling our conversation at Thanksgiving, over a week ago.

And all this time, she has been lonely, missing her sister. I saw her for less than five minutes, a few days ago now. I dropped by with coffee, hoping I'd be more successful with an impromptu visit, even if it went against her wishes. No such luck; she was preoccupied with work, or so I thought.

Now that I think about it, something was off about her. I had been too focused on my shit and I pushed it to the back of my mind. Fuck. What did I miss?

I seem to be missing a lot of shit right in front of my eyes. I fucking missed that the body in Chicago ten years ago wasn't my brother. And shit, Taya's driver. I've seen him almost every day for weeks.

"Well, then you know she needs to be alone right now." His grave expression intensifies the churning in my gut. "That's one reason we're visiting. I didn't want her to be alone. She needs her space but… if I'd known about you, I wouldn't have intruded."

"Well, yeah, she has me." I'm a possessive asshole.

He clearly knows a fuck of a lot more about Mia and what she's dealing with than I do, and it pisses me off.

"Look, I'm not here to get in the way. It's obvious you care about her and she's told me you have a history. We'll be gone soon, but in the meantime, I'll let you know if she comes back. I've got your number."

"Did something happen?" It's hard to make sense of this. I'm not being insensitive. I get missing your sibling but it sounds like she could be gone for a while.

"No, just what you'd expect."

He's talking in riddles, or more like, I'm in the dark and if I give away I don't understand, he might clam up.

"She's got her phone. She promised to check messages at least once a day. You could call her."

"Fine." I turn, more frustrated than anything else and not wanting to take it out on this guy. He's trying to help.

I can feel his stare at my back and halfway to the elevator, I glance over my shoulder. "Hey, Eli, thanks."

"No problem."

She has her phone. I could get Tommie on this, to trace her phone, and then I'd know where Mia is in no time at all. But I can't and won't do that. It sounds like she doesn't want to be found.

Is she running again?

What the hell? First Griffin and now Mia. I can't lose her, not when I've only just found her.

Once in the car, I call her and as Eli predicted, it goes straight to voicemail.

"Hey, Mia. It's Patrick. I just went by your place. Eli said you're out of town. Call me when you can. I've got news." I pause but quickly rush past any lingering doubt. "I miss you."

MIA

"I miss you." Patrick's deep, velvety voice pierces my already aching chest.

Checked out and bag in the back seat of the rental car, I stroll down to the sandy shores of the Atlantic one last time.

Early December in Montauk isn't balmy, but it's quieter, a sleepy nautical town. A sharp contrast to the crowds and activities in the summer, and just what I needed.

At the water's edge, the wind has multiplied in speed and ferocity. Now it's violent and feral, ripping through my body.

I tighten my scarf and pull my hat further down on my head—both purchased on the drive out to Long Island's easternmost point.

Despite the chill, there's something wild and freeing about being here. These past five days were rough but also needed and at first, when I left the city, I had no destination in mind. Only the driving desire to move. Get out. Be alone.

I felt awful for leaving my guests but my need had nothing to do with getting away from Eli and Crystal. Even if they hadn't been here, I would have left. I always do at this time of year.

The anniversary of my daughter's death.

Lucy would be twelve now and every day, all the time, I wonder who she would be. What would she be like on the cusp of being a teenager?

Would she still be an adventurous girl? Fearless in all pursuits? Or would she have become more practical like me, weighing her options before making a move?

She's always with me, never far from my thoughts, yet the ocean makes me feel closer to her. Especially right now.

Her ashes were scattered in the Pacific, just off the coast of her favorite beach. It doesn't matter that now I'm staring out at the Atlantic.

The ocean is the ocean.

The sharp whitecaps, cresting and falling, are mesmerizing as the choppy waves crash upon the shore.

Lucy loved the water. She loved to surf and swim. I can't even count how many days we'd spent all our free time at the beach.

I blink and one small, frozen tear sticks to my lashes. I've cried more tears in these past six years than any other time in my life.

I've cried until I have no more tears left in my body.

Arms sliding around my middle, I hug myself, wishing I could just hug her one more time. Wishing I could spend one more day with her. And Emily.

I wish I could see them both, one more time.

God, I miss them both so much.

And now, reconnecting with Patrick is like losing her all over again. How do I tell him? How do I give him the gift of fatherhood, only to take it away in the next breath?

I can't.

Maybe leaving is the best, but that's cowardly. I'm not a coward.

Lucy wouldn't want me to do it this way. And even if she's gone, he deserves to know her. Even if through memories, he deserves to know this beautiful person we created.

She is his as much as she is mine.

The wind whips around me and with one last look, I return to the parking lot and get in the car.

I turn the heat on full blast and find my phone. Patrick answers on the first ring.

"Mia?"

"Hi."

"Where are you? Are you okay?"

Guilt curls like a tight grip around my throat. "Montauk. I'm heading back."

"Montauk? What are you doing there? Are you okay?"

"I'm fine. I just needed to get away. I'll explain later."

An explanation is long overdue. A cold sweat courses through me at the thought of that conversation. I don't want to hurt him, destroy him.

"I need to see you. Can you meet me somewhere?"

"Sure." My foolish heart somersaults at hearing he wants to see me. "I've got the drive back. It'll be three hours or more. I have to return the car."

"That's fine. Are you dressed warm? Where I want to meet is outside."

"I'm good."

He rattles off an address and I enter it into my phone's maps. It's a cemetery. Griffin.

"Patrick, are you okay?"

"Yeah. I'll be better when I see you. Text me when you're close."

"Okay."

"And Mia, drive safe."

His concern widens the crack to my heart. I'm going to break him when he hears what I have to say. I both long to and dread seeing him.

"I will. See you soon."

TRIPP

My lips twitch with the hint of a smile and I shove my phone into my pocket. Finally hearing Mia's voice brings calm to the disorder of my heart and mind. It's been way too long since I've seen her.

I want to tell her about Griffin, need to share that with her, and most of all, I just want to see her. My chest tightens at the thought of her.

But she has a long drive ahead of her and I have a call to make. A conversation I'm not too eager to have, thanks to my meddling friends. I told Riff I'd give him space, but that didn't mean I'd let too much time pass. It's only been a few days and I need to keep the pressure on.

If we're going to get to the bottom of this, confirm he is in fact Griffin, we need his cooperation. And I've got a ton of questions I'm just itching to ask.

Out the windshield of the car, I stare at the bleak winter day. The streets are wet and slushy from the snowfall and the sky is cloudy and gray. I'm stalling.

It's unrealistic to think or wish for things to be easier. This situation, a dead brother winding up alive, is all-around rare, and to complicate matters, he has no memory of who he is. *Fuck Taya.*

If she wasn't behind bars, I'd want to kill her. What else is new? At least on that front, something worked in our favor. She tried to get bail, but it was denied and she's stuck in jail until the trial. No date has been set yet.

Time to get the conversation over with. Instead of using the phone, I start the car, wanting to warm up my body, and call from the Bluetooth with the number Tate and Carys pried out of him.

"Hello." Riff answers on the third ring and I can almost see his wary expression, matching his tone.

"Hi, it's Tripp."

A growl rumbles through the phone line followed by a mutter, which I'm pretty sure was a curse. "What do you want?"

"I'd like to meet and talk."

"Not interested. Why can't you assholes leave me alone? First those two meddling women show up and now you."

He's talking about Carys and Tate, who couldn't leave well enough alone and give him space after we'd all confronted him. They had to find out where he lived and pay him a visit.

"Well, it could be worse. I could be at your front door."

"Fuck, tell me you're not."

"I'm not." My chuckle is hollow because there isn't anything amusing about this. "C'mon, you know we have to talk—"

"I don't have to do anything." His anger, or maybe it's fear, is fierce.

"Fair enough, but you know we can get to the bottom of this a lot quicker if we work together."

We're all in a tough spot and there's no easy or right way to do this. I can't blame him for his suspicious nature, but isn't he the least bit curious?

"Look, let's meet somewhere neutral to talk. Get to know each other better."

I try for casual, less threatening, I hope. But for my efforts, all I get in return is more pissed-off Riff.

"And what if I don't want to get to know you?"

My heart slams against my ribs and my ire stirs in my belly. He's trying my patience.

"Look. I'm no longer asking…" I wait and he doesn't respond but I can hear his breathing on the other end. At least he hasn't hung up. That's got to be a good sign.

"You pick the place," I offer, hoping it feels like a concession.

We get a few more rounds of his grunts and curses before he relents, rattling off a restaurant in the city. I had thought about telling him about Mia. I want her there.

It isn't rational and I'm not fully able to explain it to myself, but she might be able to help defray the tension. I don't say anything to him, leaving it as a surprise.

MIA

A man stands at the top of a small hill with his back to me. Patrick. I make my way through the headstones. It's a cold day, but the sun is brilliant and the sky, a startling blue.

Less than five feet from where he stands is a mound of dirt piled high, well over seven feet. It looks fresh. Who died? My stomach clenches

On the phone, he'd asked me to meet him at Griffin's grave. The hole in the earth is cordoned off with yellow tape, and Patrick is at one end of the hole. Is this a plot next to his brother's?

His head is hung low. This must be torture for him, even all these years later. I understand his loss, all too well.

. I clear my throat, letting him know I'm here and he turns, immediately reaching for me, and draws me into his sturdy arms. A small sob slips past my lips and I'm startled at how unchecked my emotions are. I thought the drive had afforded me the time to bury my grief.

My loss, tears and anger have been running free with abandon these past few days. It was a struggle to tame them on the drive back to reality and obviously, I failed.

A welling of sadness rises in my throat and I bury my head into his chest, hoping to muffle my anguish.

"Hey, I'm glad to see you. Are you okay?" He pulls back, studying my features.

I try to keep my expression neutral, nodding despite the maelstrom of feelings rushing through me.

"Hi." I inhale the smell of him.

There's so much I have to say to him. And he has news, too, that's why he has asked me here. He can go first.

"Sorry I disappeared without calling. I got your message. Is this Griffin's grave?" I inspect the deep hole in the ground.

"Yeah. You were gone for a while."

"Five days. I thought I'd only take a few..."

"I want to hear about you but first, Griffin is alive." He pushes back a strand of hair falling into his eyes.

"What?" My eyebrows shoot to my hairline and a ringing fills my ears. I can't have heard right. "What are you talking about."

"I know, it sounds crazy, right?" There's a cautiously optimistic lilt to his voice.

"It sounds like a miracle. It's one of those things you wish for when you lose someone, but how is this possible?" Tears clog my throat, confusion swirling in my mind.

"We got our hands on a recording suggesting his death was staged. We've been investigating, not only the validity of the recording, but all of the events around his death, and any possible leads. Van went to Chicago to review the police and medical examiner's reports and we had the body exhumed for DNA testing." His expression sobers as he turns to the hole and pile of dirt.

"Oh my God." My hand covers my mouth, incredulous. "You've been dealing with this all this time?"

"Yeah."

"How? Patrick, this would be difficult. I can't imagine how you'd even begin to handle this... Griffin alive, but not knowing where or how to find him. All those unanswered questions, the waiting..."

Tears and confusion crawl their way up my throat, mixing with my own loss, and imagining what it would be like to get similar same news.

"It's been crazy and I've wanted to tell you but it was too soon. We'd just reconnected, I didn't know if Griff was even alive or if it was some sick joke. I could have been putting you at risk if the recording was all part of something bigger."

His gaze slides to the ground and back to me. "It still could be but I needed to tell you."

I close my eyes while his last words echo in my brain. His need for me is overwhelming, drowning me with both joy and dread.

The power to cause him great suffering isn't what I want. I wish… I wish I could cast aside this burden. Help him deal with this news about his brother and forget the rest.

"Hey, I understand and I'm… I'm just so grateful that you told me. That you wanted to tell me. Are you any closer to getting answers?"

"Yeah. The body buried here isn't Griffin." He pauses and my stomach drops like a stone to my toes. "And we think we may have found him."

"Oh my God." Tears spring free and there's no chance of holding them back. "This is good news, right?"

He lifts me off the ground, surprising me as a smile springs to his face. He twirls us around and I cling to him, trying to find some laughter, anything to let him know how happy I am for him.

My mind spins like my body. I came here to talk to him, tell him. That's changed because of this news. I can't tell him. Not now. Not when this is a moment of celebration.

Fingers clasped tightly at the back of his neck, I bury my face into his throat, and we continue to spin. It's almost as if he wants to be dizzy, to make the world, and us in it, a blur. I can understand that. Nothing making sense is sometimes just what you need.

Finally he stops and I stay like that, still holding on to him, needing his steady heartbeat and solid body.

"Tell me more." My voice comes out like a rasp.

Slowly, he plants me onto the ground, and we stand on the hill, in front of the place where he believed his brother was buried for more than a decade. My eyes are trained ahead, giving him the privacy, without scrutiny, I'm sensing he needs to make it easier to tell me everything.

The story is surreal and feels like just that, a story. While hard to believe, there's also hope. Words tumble from his mouth, and emotion fills his voice, blanketing his body, and I wonder if he feels any fear.

"Yeah, it's just the beginning. Who knows if he'll want anything to do with us." He kicks the ground with the toe of his boot, causing clumps of dirt to fly in all directions. "Carys and Tate couldn't leave well enough alone."

"What?"

"They worked fast, enlisting Tommie's help in finding out where he lived. They took a box of pictures, ticket stubs and shit like that from our childhood. All things Griffin would have been part of, known about. And showed up at his doorstep only a day after we told him we think he's Griff." His look is incredulous and irritated. "They thought they'd take him down memory lane."

"Oh no."

"Yeah." He shoves his hands into his pockets. "It didn't go so well."

My gaze lands on the tombstone with his brother's name and date of birth... I suck in a breath.

December third.

That day is indelibly etched in my heart. What are the chances? It can't be.

"What's wrong?" His hand rests on my back.

"He just had a birthday?"

"Yeah. That's the day I found out he was alive. He just turned thirty-three."

Shaking my head and hoping to shake off this strange coincidence of dates, I focus on our conversation. "Have you spoken to him since Carys and Tate went over there?"

"No. I wanted to give him some time. I contacted him today."

"That's good."

"We're meeting for dinner and I'd like you to come with me."

"What?"

"Please. I'd like you to be there when I meet with Griffin."

I can't explain it but panic bubbles inside of me. Can I meet his supposedly dead brother? Can I handle this?

He doesn't fully understand what he's asking. And if I turn him down, I have to give him an explanation. I can't dump even more on him and I won't lie.

"What? Me? But you've got so much to talk about. Are you sure I should be there?"

"Of course. Why?"

"Throwing me into the mix, well, that might not be the best way to go, but it..." A stiff wind tosses around my long hair and I wrestle to bring it all into my hand.

"I need you." He takes hold of my other hand and the sincerity in his jewel-like blue eyes slays me. "You help me focus."

"Okay." I can't deny him. I won't. Hearing he needs me just as much as I need him brings me both turmoil and peace. No matter what I have to do—the right thing—I will do my best to lessen his pain and suffering.

"Thank you." His gaze is a mixture of gratitude and resignation. "I might scare him away. You won't."

"I don't know about that."

TRIPP

We enter the restaurant and Griffin's waiting for us, looking like he may bolt. But he hasn't so I'll take that as a win.

"Hi. Thanks for meeting us." I try for a smile, something to put him at ease, but he only narrows his gaze in return. "This is Mia."

"Hi." She smiles, warm and wide.

"Are you a shrink?" His expression darkens.

"No, not at all. I'm a lawyer, which you might think is worse." She laughs, adding quickly, "But it's entertainment law. Completely unrelated to why I'm here. Patrick and I are friends and he asked me to come."

"Patrick?" He eyes her warily and then me.

"That's me. Tripp's a nickname. You actually gave it to me when we were kids."

He flinches, knitting his brow and backing away from us. I curse under my breath. I'm already blowing it and we haven't even sat down.

"Shall we go to our table?" Mia motions to the hostess and we follow her to a booth at the back of the restaurant.

It's private, as I requested. Griff slides into one side of the table, and Mia and I sit on the other. Things are awkward and tense, the conversation stilted, and even Mia is nervous.

Maybe this is too much for her?

Relief lines his face every time the server interrupts us to take our order and bring our drinks. So far our conversation has been superficial and useless.

Our food arrives and I figure now is as good a time as any to dive right in. Our next interruption shouldn't be for a while.

"So, you've had some time to think about what we said the other day."

He edges away from the table, his back pressed into the booth, and folds his arms over his chest. He's already closed off to anything I have to say and I can't deny it burns.

He may be Griffin, but I still miss my brother. If only I could just shake some sense into this man, make him see who I am, what we used to mean to each other.

"Yeah, so? I don't know what you want."

"Don't you want to know about your life? Who you are?" Frustration coats my words. "Why don't I just tell you."

He tenses and Mia echoes his body language, her gaze trained on my brother. She's right, I'm coming on too strong.

"Your full name is Griffin Townsend. You're thirty-three, born and raised in New York City to Callum and Lucy, both dead. You have an older brother, me. Your birthday is December third."

Judging from his disgusted expression, each word spills from my mouth like sewage but I can't stop myself.

"What I think Patrick is trying to say is, what's your story?" She's friendly and calm. "Who are you? Tell us about your family and how you came to work for—"

"Taya Conrad." I fill in her mental gap and am suddenly overwhelmingly grateful Mia is here.

She's doing exactly what I hoped she'd do. Saving me from myself. He relaxes a bit, loosening his arms.

"My parents were Tim and Kathy Stevens. I don't remember them at all and they're both dead. They were killed in a boating accident years before I lost my memory. I don't have any brothers or sisters." Anger burns in his blue eyes, so much like mine, grilling me. "I was born in New York and you're right about my birthday, but we already went over that."

"What do you remember?" She places a hand on his forearm, drawing his attention back to her. "Do you know why you don't have any recollection of your past?"

"My earliest memory is about ten years ago. I woke up in a hospital and I was in a lot of pain. I didn't know who I was or where I was. Taya Conrad was there."

I lean in, forcing myself to keep my mouth shut and let him talk. I've got so many questions.

"She filled in the blanks. Despite not knowing her, there wasn't anyone else to ask. She told me she'd found me beaten on the streets. My name is Mark Stevens."

A lot of this isn't new to me. Tommie has shared anything and everything she's been able to find, including interviews she's had with people from Mark's past.

This guy across from me may not be Griffin, but he isn't Mark. I'm sure of it.

My hunch is based on what Tommie's learned, and because of that, we're not only testing the body in the grave for a match to Griffin, but also to Mark. My gut tells me we buried Stevens.

"Why do you go by Riff?" So much for keeping my mouth shut. Mia looks at me, eyes wide in a *what are you doing?* kind of look.

"Don't know." He shrugs. "She called me that."

"Who? Taya?"

He nods. "Yeah, and the guys who work for her did too. I never asked."

It's a fucking easy leap to why she did it. Griffin. Griff. Riff. Just drop the G.

Right under our noses.

"Did you find out who assaulted you?" Mia asks.

"No. It looked like I was mugged. Only my licence was on me. There's a police report, and even an article in the newspaper. I almost didn't survive. I had to have several surgeries and I have a pin in my jaw." He points to the left side of his face. "One in my hip. Scars."

He lifts his sleeve to reveal tattoos. "I've gotten ink to cover most of them. Taya paid for all of it. The surgeries, the ink... she was the only one there. Whoever the fuckers were, they certainly had a blast on me."

Mia winces and vengeance burns in my belly. I still remember the day Tate recounted his beating and, at the time, what we all thought had killed him.

And now here he is, singing the praises of Taya Conrad as if she was his savior when she had a hand in his beating.

"Didn't it strike you as odd that this stranger, who is from New York, just happens to be in Chicago and then stays with you for however many days or weeks, or even months, while you recovered?"

"She was there on business when I was attacked." He's quick to defend. "And while I said she was there, at the hospital, she did leave for days at a time. She had work. And then she flew me to New York once I was able to and arranged for the best medical care. I also had several surgeries here. She was the only one who gave a damn."

Even if he had, or still has, doubts or questions about Taya's motives, he was vulnerable. Alone without any memory.

She fucking duped him, but there's no point saying so right now. He has no allegiance to me, and his lack of trust for anything I say is clear.

"Has any of your memory come back?" I ask.

"What, since you talked to me?" His lip curls with disdain. "No. And it won't. There's permanent damage to my brain, to my memory."

"That's horrible." Mia fidgets beside me.

"I went back to my neighborhood, looking for people who might know me. But that didn't help."

"How so?" She tilts her head to the side.

"No one recognized me. No surprise." He gestures to his face. "People knew Mark Stevens, but nothing about a beating or where I went. Some said they hadn't seen me in months before the beating took place. And I had no fixed address... that still bothers me."

He gazes down at his food, avoiding eye contact again. He has touched none of it and I doubt he will.

"That is strange." She looks to me. "What did you do without a place to live?"

"Taya offered me a job, a steady paycheck, and a place to live. I wasn't stupid. I had no other choice. I took it and that's how I'm here today."

"Do you know a Megan Earle?" I really don't know how to keep my mouth shut.

But I can't. This is my chance to make him see what's right in front of him. He is Griffin, or at the very least, he isn't Mark.

"Who?"

"She dated Mark Stevens throughout high school and she says you aren't him. She thinks he's dead. After his parents died, he had some kind of mental break and took to the streets." I watch him for any twitch or sign from him that suggests he knows he isn't Mark, and that he might be Griffin. "He'd been missing for close to three months before you were supposedly beaten and left for dead."

Something akin to recognition flashes in his troubled stare. "Oh, Megan... yeah, I talked to her and I'm aware of what she thinks. I can't explain that."

"How about because you aren't Mark?" My confidence gets the better of me.

"That proves nothing. For all I know, she has some kind of grudge."

"Maybe. But she isn't the only one to say that you aren't him. We talked to several people who knew Mark Stevens, and all had similar things to say. Some even said they think Mark left the state."

"Again, I don't know. In case you fucking missed it, I can't remember and never will." His jaw tightens and fingers curl to the point that his knuckles turn white.

There's no point pushing the Mark Stevens angle. My guess is, Taya found some random guy on the street who could pass for Griff. She killed him, cooked the dental records or paid someone off to have him pass as my dead brother. The poor guy didn't stand a chance.

Switching angles, I continue to push him like he's a suspect I think is guilty. "So you're fine working for Conrad? How do you stomach what she does?"

I can't help myself.

Something needs to knock some sense into him. At least get him to be open to the idea that he could be Griffin. Right now, he's closed off to any suggestion of it.

"I keep my mouth shut and do my job. I'm paid to look the other way. Stick to my business."

"And you're—"

"You're her driver?" Mia interjects, glaring at me.

"Yeah. But I've been looking for a change. I wanted out and Taya caught wind of my plans. She wasn't too happy about that. Her arrest comes at a good time."

"What do you mean?" She pushes her plate to the edge of the table, barely having eaten anything, and he does the same.

"I know nothing else but this life. I'm a driver and also trained to be an enforcer. When needed, I'm used as extra muscle, but I don't want to be in this life forever."

Well this is at least a ray of hope. He does need to get the hell out of that life.

"That's good." She smiles. "I could help you figure out what you want to do."

I shove a fry into my mouth, not hungry but to keep down my warring emotions at how well he's responding to Mia.

"You must have seen things in your job." I push again. "Would you tell us about it?"

He may not want to entertain the idea of being my brother but maybe he'll help strengthen the case against Taya. She needs to stay in prison for the rest of her life, and if he can give us more that we can use to bolster the prosecution's case, all the better.

"What do you mean?"

"You must have seen and heard things. You drove her around."

"I'm not a snitch and I didn't pay attention to her business." He's lying, averting his gaze. "Like I said, I kept my head down. I never wanted to be involved in any of her dealings. I didn't want any blowback."

"But you must've—" I say, and Mia places a hand on my arm, giving me a look that screams *back off*.

"That's okay." She turns to him. "You don't have to tell us anything you don't want to. We're here to listen to your story and try to understand."

"I don't like to think about what I've seen. Sure, Taya helped me and sometimes, I got the feeling she never wanted the balance of power to shift. She needed to keep me where I was."

"Where you were?" she probes.

"In the dark. Unsure of who I am and what future I have." This time he looks directly at me and my chest squeezes.

For a split second, I *see* Griffin. It isn't something tangible or even visible, more like a feeling. "I work for a security and intelligence firm. We could always use a guy like you."

He raises a brow. "Working with you?"

"Why not?" I tap my fingers on the tabletop and stop, realizing I'm nervous.

"You don't know me from that guy." He points to a man walking toward the restrooms. "Or any other person. I'm a stranger to you and yet you're willing to give me a job?"

"Yeah, you're..." I stop before I stick my foot in my mouth again by calling him my brother.

"And I don't know you. You're a stranger to me. I could be going from one disaster to another."

"You think of working for Conrad as disastrous?"

"Yeah. It's only a matter of time before shit blows up. I just never knew if I would go down with it or not. Now's my chance to leave."

"What do you mean by leave?" There's something to the way he says it that irks me, as if he's talking about more than just leaving a job.

"I don't know. Find a new job. Leave the city. I don't know yet, but what I do know is, I've got nothing keeping me here."

Nausea swirls in my stomach, disappointed with how he sees

things. He couldn't be more wrong, but again, I keep my mouth shut. He thinks he's alone. He isn't.

He has a family—Ry, Van, Carys, Tate. Yet he doesn't know any of us, and from the sound of it, he doesn't want to. And it isn't as if he's going to one day remember us.

"Look, I gotta go." He slides from the booth. "Mia, it was nice to meet you."

"It was lovely to meet you too." She stands and wraps her arms around him.

He doesn't flinch, growl or pull away. In fact, he hugs her for longer than I like and there's a serenity that slides over his features in Mia's arms.

"I'm actually glad you were here." He chuckles, running a hand through his hair.

"Good. I'm glad." She reaches into her pocket. "Here's my number if you ever want to talk."

She hands him her card and surprisingly, he takes it, smiling. "Thanks."

A strange sensation coils tight around my heart and I'm not sure why. I asked her to help me reach Griffin, and she's done just that. But seeing her bond with him, how easily they have connected doesn't sit well with me.

And I don't like my reaction. Is it because she's already made headway with my brother in only one visit? Or is it because Griffin seems so comfortable with my woman?

Without so much as a backward glance, he leaves, and I hang my head, exhaling long and hard.

"You okay?" She slides back into the booth.

"Fuck, I messed that up." My fingers rake through my hair.

"You pushed a little too hard, but it's understandable. Don't beat yourself up."

"I just want him to remember but that's impossible. Or maybe, I just want him to…" I can't finish the sentence but she does it for me.

"You want him to *want* to be your brother."

"Yeah."

"Give him time. This is a lot to take in. And he's also dealing with not knowing who he is. The only identity he has is Riff Stevens. Like any of us would, he's resisting the loss of that too. He's lost a lot already."

I reach for her hand, entwining my fingers with hers. Her warm brown eyes greet mine and she looks tired. Why didn't I notice sooner? I'm a fucking tool for missing it.

Shadowed circles lie beneath her eyes and her hair, while windswept, is more disheveled than I'm used to seeing.

"Tell me about your trip."

"I just needed to get away." She nibbles on her bottom lip. "All this stuff with Fraser and the holidays… I don't want to talk about it right now but I will tell you. Soon."

Something isn't as it seems and I can't put my finger on it. I want to push but I've done enough for one night.

"Okay." My fingers slide under her chin, tilting her head to look at me. "You can tell me anything. Whenever you're ready, I'm here."

MIA

I'm here.

He's here.

Words I wished to hear for so many years. Countless dark and lonely nights, what I would have given to have Patrick by my side. And now, knowing this, having him here sits heavy, like a ball of lead in the pit of my stomach.

My entire world ground to a halt with Lucy's death, and for the first time in a long time, it's starting to feel like things are budding, pushing and fighting against the darkness toward the light.

I've been hopeful with the reappearance of Patrick in my life and I've resisted it, fighting the gravitational pull and the natural instinct to run to him. Embrace all he has to give and don't look back.

But I can't do that. Not to him. So I'm faced with knowing I'm about to pull out the roots of whatever we're nurturing. Rip them from the ground and ruin any chance of a future.

But I have no choice.

He deserves to know.

"Can we go to your place to talk?" I'd prefer mine since I have a feeling he'll kick me out once I tell him, but Eli and Crystal are still here.

"Sure."

He pays the bill and we take a cab to his townhouse in Greenwich Village. It's a three-story townhouse in the West Village with its own private garden. It's the first thing to catch my attention through the large French doors. The inside is modest and barely furnished, with a mixture of modern fixtures and historical charm.

"Oh my goodness, this place is magnificent." I'm blown away and can't even begin to understand how he can afford something like this.

"Let me take you on a tour." He grabs my hand. "Before you start wondering which bank I robbed, my parents bought this place for a song when they came from Ireland. It was a dump. The owner went bankrupt, and it needed a lot of work."

He leads me through the rooms with ten-foot-high ceiling, exposed beams and bricks, and many levels.

"It's beautiful."

"This is the original wood flooring." He taps his foot on the wide, pine planks. "As you can see, I'm slowly renovating floor by floor and will probably be done by the time I die."

"Don't say that." I bat at his arm, backing out of the bathroom on the second floor. It's in the mid-stages of renovation, with the tiles on one wall completely removed and the other halfway done.

"This is a treasure. Five bedrooms and six baths. Five fireplaces. Wow. I don't even want to think what it would be worth today despite the work still to be done."

My mind fills with so many thoughts. This home is only further proof that he'll never leave the city. New York is home, and this is the perfect place to have a family. I swallow past the lump in my throat.

We settle in what looks to be the most lived-in room, with a couch, a couple armchairs, TV and fireplace.

"And then there's my shoebox," I add lamely, suddenly feeling a little overwhelmed and out of place in his lovely home.

"From the little I've seen, I love your shoebox. Most of all because you're there." From behind, he wraps his arms around me and brushes my hair to one side.

His hot breath and stubbled jaw cause my skin to pucker, and he buries his face into the crook of my neck. I shiver, all my nerve endings tingling.

"You cold?" His soft lips press feathery kisses at my nape, warming me further.

"No."

It isn't a lie. While the house is a bit drafty with the lack of furniture and carpet, being in his arms ignites a passionate need low in my core.

"Let me start a fire."

Lips, arms and his chest fall away from me and my stomach dips with the loss.

I snuggle into the corner of the sofa, pulling a blanket over me while he gets to work piling scraps of newspaper and blocks of wood into the brick fireplace.

The surroundings, being here with him, are perfect. The perfect night, and I'm about to ruin it. My blood pounds in my head.

Slowly, orange-yellow flames crackle and pop in the hearth and the smoky, inviting scent fills the room. Patrick slides in beside me, one arm sliding around my shoulders, and his fingers stroke seductively down my arm.

My pulse triples at the nearness of him and my anxiety of how or when to tell him. Us, together, here, is too good to be true. How do I wreck this?

Eyes heavy-lidded and molten, he kisses me slow and gentle. Almost sweet. Chipping away at my nerves. Then his kisses shift to long and deep. Endless. I love all his kisses. Every kiss makes my head swim and body ache for him.

My fingers burrow into the hair at the back of his neck and my body molds to his, drawing him closer. His lips stray from mine, trailing down the column of my neck, and I slant my head to the side, reveling in every lick of his tongue or press of his lips against my now-scorching skin.

Teeth nip at the flesh of my collarbone. I feel as if I may explode. Before things go too far, so far I chicken out and don't say what I set out to, I try to get a hold of my senses.

I need to walk away from this maddening pleasure, but I'm not even able to put up a fight when his mouth covers mine again, kissing me over and over. He is driving me mad with his mouth.

"Patrick." I pull my head back and whip the blanket from me, hotter than hell.

"What's wrong?"

Everything.

I want to be with him. To forget the past and the present. Forget that I owe him the truth. How I thought I could leave the past buried is beyond comprehension.

Deep down it would always come to this.

I spring from the couch, brushing out of his reach, and twist to face him once in the middle of the room. The now-roaring fire is at my back and heating me up.

"I don't know how to say this without breaking your heart."

Both eyebrows climb to his hairline and his mouth mashes into a grim line as he now stands. "Just say it."

"That night back in college." I edge my way to the side of the room, seeking support from the wall.

This is hell. The words jam in the back of my throat, choking me, as something tangles around my heart into tight, painful knots.

He tracks my moves, and I stand feet from him, preparing to rip the proverbial Band-Aid off.

"I got pregnant." I try to breathe.

"What?" His eyes narrow and he steps toward me, but I hold up a hand, needing the distance if I'm to tell him everything.

"I know. Go figure. A virgin one minute and about to be a mother the next." My brittle chuckle, filled with so much pain, hurts my ears and he flinches. "Sorry, I shouldn't make light of it. There was nothing funny about it."

"Why didn't you tell me?" The hard lines and defined muscles of his well-built body are on edge, wired and taut.

"I'm getting there. Please just listen. I'll tell you everything." My throat narrows on my promise, a familiar burn tickling my nose.

Now inching away from me, he stops when his legs hit the back of the couch. Nodding, brow scrunched, he perches on the edge of the furniture, sure to plant his feet firmly on the floor. His eyes are stuck on me.

I draw in a ragged breath, needing the air or energy for what I have to say. Like the rush of a waterfall, my words spill from my mouth.

"I didn't know I was pregnant until almost my third month. I know it sounds crazy, hard to believe, but I was used to missing periods or being late. My cycle isn't steady or predictable. I've skipped periods before."

My gaze falls to the floor, past my flat stomach where I once carried my beautiful baby girl.

"I was stressed. I was feeling horrible for how I'd left things with you, trying to figure out what I should do. I'd just started my summer job and the hours were long and grueling." My gaze cuts to him. "These aren't excuses. At the time, I wasn't focused on my body and when I actually stopped, I realized… I took a test."

My hand is now splayed on my middle. Nine months of both joy and strain.

"That's when I first tried to find you. I had to tell you. I didn't know what I would do—"

"Did you… did you have an abortion?" Voice rough and gravelly, it carries more than his words.

"No." My response comes out as a harsh bark. "An abortion never entered my mind. Even though a baby threw a wrench into my life plan, I wanted the child. And you had a right to know. To decide what part, if any, you wanted in raising the child…"

Nausea swims all around me, its thickness filling my throat, and breathing is near impossible.

I reach to open the window and then pause, looking to him for unspoken permission. He nods and I push the frame up to let the cold, fresh air rush over me.

"I couldn't find you… and I still had to tell my parents. My father is a devout Christian. Sex before marriage is unthinkable. A sin. Let alone pregnancy. I knew all this before I even said a word and yet I was still stunned when he kicked me out."

"What?"

I glance in his direction and he's moving closer. His questions and irritation and his yet-to-be pain are all there in his troubled expression.

I'm doing this to him, and with every word, icy fingers of sorrow claw their way around my throat.

"Yes. He disowned me and no amount of explaining changed things. My mother didn't have a say no matter what her viewpoint was, she never did. And my sister, she was a couple years younger than me. She couldn't do anything.

"I was out on my own. I couldn't find you and I had barely any money. I needed the summer job, but how was I going to finish law school?"

All the anxiety and fear I felt back then thunders over me like a stampede of wild horses, and feeling unsteady, I grab onto the back of the chair.

"I stayed with a friend that summer, kept working and put my law degree on hold. My mother and sister scrounged up some money for me. It wasn't a lot but enough to go somewhere else. I went to California. I worked a lot during my pregnancy, saving every penny I could. I was going to do this. Be a mother and a lawyer..."

"And the baby?"

"She was born in February."

"She? What's her name? Tell me about her. Where is she?" His hands are balled at his sides, thumbs clenched inside his fists.

"Lucy Patricia St. John." A smile blooms on my face at the thought of her.

"Lucy?" A sheen of unshed tears coats his eyes.

"Yes. Your mother's name. I remember how you'd spoken of your mom... you'd loved her so much."

All he does is nod and my heart lurches for what I must be doing to him.

"Lucy was perfect. Everything I never knew I wanted. Holding her in my arms, I fell in love with her instantly. Adored everything about her."

He stares straight ahead, eerily calm, not saying a word.

"I'd spend hours marvelling at her tiny little fingers and tiny little toes. Just smelling her magical baby scent—it should seriously be bottled. From the moment I laid eyes on her little angel face, she became my world."

A tear spills from the corner of an eye and I wipe at it, blinking back the others. "I swear to God I wanted to share her with you. I saved up and when I had enough money, I got a private investigator. I tried to find you several times after that but..."

I lift my arms up in the air and drop them back into my lap at the futility of it all. "You know what happened."

His forehead puckers and he cocks his head to the side. "Mia, you keep saying *was*. Where is Lucy now?"

I'm on the verge of tears; my hands are shaking. "She died when she was six years old."

"What?" He collapses in a chair, eyes glittering with confusion. "Hang on. You were pregnant with my child, a daughter, but she's dead?"

"Yes. I tried to find you, Patrick, I swear to God." My voice chokes on the words. "And I wanted to tell you sooner but—"

"How did she die? When? Tell me."

"It was this time of year, December third."

His eyes widen and he straightens his spine. "Griffin's birthday?"

"I know. When I saw his plaque at the cemetery, I couldn't believe it. Six years ago... that's why I was in Montauk. I needed to be alone." I start to pace, needing to move.

"Emily, my sister, had moved out to LA several years before and we were close. She made it possible for me to get my law degree. Well, and the loans helped too. Lucy adored her. Once I passed the bar, I applied for a job in a law firm in Portland. Being in LA, entertainment law seemed like the smartest move, but lawyers like me were a dime a dozen. My sister was taking care of her for one night and I flew up there for an interview. It was the first time I'd ever left her overnight."

I stop moving, now back in the middle of the room, the fire burning bright behind me. He's on the couch, his frame hunched over, defeated.

My fingers itch and my heart aches to go to him, comfort him. If I do, I'll shatter, unable to finish this, and he needs to hear it all.

"Emily had picked her up from school. It was a freak accident on the freeway. A tractor trailer. The truck blew a tire, and it flew at the car my sister was driving. She was killed on impact and Lucy died on the way to the hospital."

Bowing my head, I cover my face with my hands, feeling as if a wall of vines and thorns are growing around my skin. Pricking and suffocating me.

"Fuck," he growls, dropping his head to his chest. My hands fall and his dangle loosely between his parted knees.

"Patrick." His name on my lips is heavy with regret and so many more emotions I can't name.

"Why didn't you find me? Tell me sooner? I could have..."

"I tried... and then when I'd lost her and Em... I was a mess for a long time. I didn't think about finding you then. I just couldn't... I got the job in Oregon, but I didn't take it. As much as I wanted to run away, I wasn't functioning."

I walk toward him, wanting to comfort him, but he flinches at my outstretched hand and presses back into the couch in a defensive move, fully in survival mode.

His rejection hurts but I get it. I rush over to my purse and pull out a picture of Lucy from my wallet.

"Here." I hand him the photograph. "This was taken about a month before the accident."

He cradles the image as if it may break, as if a baby in the palm of his hand. Fragile. One finger reverently glides over her silhouette.

Her wavy strawberry blonde hair and big blue eyes so like his, like my sister's, and the smattering of freckles across the bridge of her nose.

A primal roar of anguish rips from his throat and he drops the picture on the cushion beside him. His fists pound into his thighs and he clamps his lips tight, strangling his pain.

"I'm so sorry." I drop to my knees beside him, wanting to touch him but afraid to do so.

"Are you?" The harshness of his words cuts deep. "Why didn't you find me? Give me a chance to know her?"

TRIPP

She stills, curling her hands so tightly against her chest that her knuckles pale. "I am sorry. While I can no longer fully recall the smell of her, the sound of her voice or the feel of her smooth skin and soft curls, I miss her every day. And I wouldn't wish that loss and pain on anyone, but I wish you could have had the chance to know her."

"Lucy Patricia." Her name is sweet on my lips.

"Yes. I wanted her to have a part of you, even if she never got the chance to meet you."

"What did you tell her about me? How did you explain why her father wasn't around?"

Anger fills my chest just thinking about my daughter never knowing her father. How was my absence explained to her? Did she think I abandoned her? That I didn't want her?

"I told her the truth. She knew everything. Your name, how we met. I told her you were a wonderful man and that you weren't around because you didn't know about her. She knew I'd tried to find you. I told her if you knew she existed, you would want to be her father. You would want to be in her life."

"Did you believe that?" I have a tough time reconciling all she's saying with the reality—I wasn't there. I never had the chance.

"Yes. It wasn't hard to tell her I knew you'd love her. A lot. And want to be her dad. That's one of the many reasons I tried so many times to find you. Even if we had no future, I knew you'd be an exceptional father. She wanted to find you just as much as I did."

This knowledge should help but it doesn't. I'm empty. Again, she reaches for me and again, I instinctually back away, hands up and now on my feet.

I couldn't bear her touch right now. I'm afraid it might break me. And these emotions churning inside me. I'm not sure what to feel.

I thrust my fingers through my hair. "You lied to me."

"What?" Her brows pinch.

"You say you tried to find me and sure, I get it when money was tight. But what about when you became a lawyer? What about all these years you've been in California—a successful lawyer to movie stars?"

"I stopped looking after she died. I was numb. Devastated. And what good would it have done to find you then?"

"I had a right to know. And what about when we reconnected a couple of weeks ago? Why did you wait to say something?"

"Yes, you had a right. But what did you want me to do, Patrick?" Her cry catches in her throat and it's another punch to my chest. "The second I saw you in the coffee shop, what was I supposed to do? Say 'Hey, Patrick. Great to see you. Guess what? After our one-night stand—'"

I charge toward her, fury searing my blood. My hands grip her arms, holding her steady, close to me. "We were not a one-night stand."

It pisses me off she can even think about us like that. Especially now, knowing we made a child. Fuck.

"Fine. I was supposed to tell you I'd had a baby. Your baby. A girl." She swallows several times in rapid succession, her voice smaller, weaker. "But she died when she was six in a car accident. Is that what I should have said?"

I want to destroy something. To burn the world down, and my home suddenly feels like a coffin, small and tight. Constricting.

"I can't…" I grab the picture from the couch, bounding toward the staircase. "I can't stay here. Let yourself out."

She rushes after me. "No, let me go. This is your home."

I back up from the top step, making room for her, and she moves past me to the stairs. She pauses, hand on the railing to stare at me.

"Please call me. If… if you don't want to see me… I understand. But know that I'm here." Her gentle touch on my arm makes me feel more alone than ever before. And as if sensing my unease, she removes her hand. "I'm… I'm sorry."

Her flaming red hair is all I see, bouncing with each step she takes away from me. I don't hear the door click or close and I don't care if she's still here, I just can't be here. I can't be still.

The taillights of the cab Mia got turn off the street, now out of sight. I jump on my bike and speed away, wishing I could escape the past. Behind me is nothing but pain and loss.

I ride aimlessly, the streets slick from the snow earlier in the day, and I welcome the roar of white noise, drowning out my thoughts. I find myself on the doorstep of my best friends' house in the middle of the night.

Van opens the front door with Carys just behind him, peering around his large frame. They are half asleep.

"What's wrong?" Grabbing my leather-clad arm, she yanks me inside, locking out the cold.

I shudder, my chilled bones against the heat of the house. I'm freezing on the inside and wanting to crawl out of my skin.

Fuck, I had a daughter. She's dead.

Van leads the way, wordlessly. Towing me behind her, Carys deposits me into a seat at the kitchen table and helps me out of my leather jacket like I'm a kid. I don't fight her. I don't have the energy to.

Van yawns, perching his back against the counter, staring at me. "You okay?"

"I will be." It doesn't feel that way right now but I will be.

I always come out the other side, even when it feels like I'm drowning in quicksand. Right now, I'm stuck, fighting not to get sucked under, and wondering if maybe I should surrender and die.

No. Screw that. Despite the shitty hand life seems to keep dealing me, I have things to live for. People who care about me. My family. I just got Griffin back even if he wants nothing to do with me.

He's alive.

And there's Mia.

Fuck, Mia. She's finally back in my life... and then, this.

Anger surges up my throat, dragging my bleeding heart with it. I can't even think of what I'd say to her the next time I see her. *If* I see her again. It feels like she failed me.

Did she really try to find me? I'll never know. I'd like to believe she did. But it doesn't fucking help.

It doesn't ease this gut-wrenching pain ripping through me. It doesn't erase feeling cheated from the chance to meet my daughter, to get to know her.

I can't say I wouldn't want to know she existed. I can't say I'd be okay with Mia never telling me, because that, too, isn't acceptable. Nothing about this is.

Carys places a shot glass filled with an amber-colored liquid—my guess is scotch or bourbon—in front of me. And next to that, she sets down a steaming mug of tea.

"I didn't know what you'd want."

"Thanks." I finish the shot.

The uncomfortable burn sears its way down my throat and it's a welcome reprieve from the feral anguish I'm drowning in.

"What's wrong?" Carys asks. "Is it Griffin?"

"No." I huff dryly. "I have a daughter. Shit. No, I *had* a daughter."

"What?" Van pushes from the counter, striding to the table.

"Yeah, with Mia. Her name's Lucy, and she would have been twelve. Thirteen this February."

"Where is she? What happened?" Her voice is wobbly and mirrors my insides. Unstable and panic-stricken.

"It was an accident," I say, and she grabs my wrist.

The one with Mia's leather bracelet. I stare down at the band, unable to imagine what Mia went through by herself. To lose her daughter.

I tell them all I know, and I'm not sure if I make any sense. I'm confused, turned around and sick to my stomach at what's been stolen from me. My daughter.

With my last words, I fumble with my jacket, shoving my hand in the pocket and producing the picture of my little girl. She's beautiful. A mixture of Mia and me. I see us both in her bright shining face.

I so fucking wish I knew her. The photograph lies on the table and Van is the first to grab it.

"Fuck, Tripp." Guilt clouds his tightening features and he mutters under his breath before handing the image to his wife.

Turning his back to us, he marches to the edge of the room, running a hand through his hair before resting his head against the wall.

Their children sleep soundly upstairs, and I don't want them to feel anything but happiness for what they have. Their family.

"Don't ever feel shitty for your family. Don't." My voice is gruff and unforgiving. "I'm going to leave. I shouldn't have come here in the middle of the night."

"No, you're staying," Carys says, and Van strides back to my side.

"You're welcome here anytime, brother." His hand rests on my shoulder, fingers curling around the bone.

His hold is fierce, and it's what I need; his strong touch grounds me, settles the roiling in my gut. Both of them remind me of what I have.

"I don't know what to do. Where to go. First Griffin. He wants nothing to do with me. And now this… I thought Mia…"

"C'mon, let's get you to bed. You're exhausted and I'm not letting you get back on your bike like this. You need sleep." Carys pushes away from the table, taking my jacket.

I stand, shaking my head as if not wanting to intrude—it's too late for that.

"Don't fight her." His gaze narrows, daring me to challenge them.

My shoulders sag, giving into the bone-weariness of the night. I'm here, and while I've already pulled them out of bed, I'm not going to make this more difficult. I do need to just lie down.

She leads me through the house and quietly upstairs into the guest room.

"I'm sorry about the mess." She doesn't like to use this room for guests because it's filled with boxes and a mish-mash of other things. But there is a bed.

Typically, if I crash here, I sleep across the hall with Noel, their son. His room has two twin beds, but she's wise not to put me with him. I'm pretty sure I wouldn't be able to keep my shit together if I saw their beautiful boy sleeping.

"Don't care," I mumble, dropping onto the bed and she turns out the light before she leaves.

The ceiling shimmers with fluorescent stars and I remember Kiera, their daughter, had put them up about a year ago. She loves astronomy and anything to do with space. She wants to be an astronaut.

An unexpected smile creeps around my face, and I wonder what Lucy wanted to be. Was she too young to have even dreamed about a future profession?

What was she like? I want to know her favorite color, favorite food, what she liked to do. I want to know everything. What did she and her mom do together?

Mia.

I always come back to Mia.

My heart aches thinking about her. I'm barely dealing right now with the news that my daughter died, and I didn't even know her. I can't imagine what she went through. What she's still going through.

She had to escape for a few days. I only wish I could have been there for her.

My life is filled with too many regrets. It started with my mother's death. I was helpless to save her from cancer. And instead of being there, I lashed out. Mad at the world. My last words to my mother were angry ones.

When my father turned to the bottle after losing my mother, I did nothing to stop him. I blamed him for all that was wrong in the world.

Fortunately, I got my act together and stepped up for Griffin, was there for him. Until I wasn't.

Where was I when he needed me? I was too busy living my life. Undercover and running away from what I didn't have.

Mia. Lucy.

I didn't have them and I wasn't there for them either.

MIA

"Hey, you're back." Eli squeezes my shoulder from behind, pulling a mug from the cupboard just above my head. "I thought I heard you get in. It was late."

I twist to face him, a cup of coffee in my hand. "Yeah."

"You okay?"

The mug hovers over my mouth, covering my trembling lips, and I swallow past the lump forming in my throat.

"I've been better. I told Patrick about Lucy last night."

"Oh." He drops the spoon and turns to face me. "How'd that go?"

Eli knows all about Patrick, college, my pregnancy and Lucy. We became friends after I lost her and he didn't know me while I was going through any of it, so in some ways, it made it easier to talk to him.

After a great day with Crystal that dredged up a lot of feelings about my own daughter, I broke down and told him everything. We commiserated over our losses. He shared the struggles of being a single dad in a rock band after Crystal's mother died from an overdose.

Never in my life had I felt so unprofessional. Not only was he my client, and I'd already crossed a line by befriending his daughter, but here I was, spilling my guts about the darkest moments of my life.

And even still, it was liberating.

"It was difficult. He didn't see it coming. I mean, who would? And he's still processing." I sit at the kitchen table, still sick when I think about how we left things and desperately wanting to talk to Patrick. "He kept asking me if I'd really tried to find him. I swear to God, I tried."

"You did." His hand rests on top of mine. "Don't beat yourself up. We've been over this before. You did everything you could. He was with the FBI at the time and it explains why you couldn't find him. Don't go back there."

"Yes. I just feel like maybe I didn't try hard enough?"

"Mia, you did everything you could."

"There were years when I was so focused on raising my daughter and establishing my career, trying to build a life for us, that I'll admit he slipped to the back of my mind. But he was never far."

Eyes closed, I think back to all the years as a single parent. There wasn't a week, sometimes a day, that didn't go by without thinking about him, about me wondering where he was.

"I'd wished countless times that I could reach out to him and tell him. Even if he had a wife and a family of his own, he deserved to know. And I wanted to give him the chance to know Lucy. I wanted him in her life."

"He'll understand that. Just give him time. This is a lot to take in."

We both stop talking when Crystal enters the room, smiling when she sees me.

"Mia." She throws her arms around my neck and I bury my face in her silky hair.

"Hey, baby doll. I missed you."

"Are you okay?" Her small hands cup my cheeks, and I nod, blinking away the tears on the brink of falling.

Crystal knows about Lucy, and while death is a part of life, I try not to burden her with the grief and sorrow.

"I'm great now that you're here."

"Good. Can we have pancakes?" She beams at me and then her father.

"Absolutely." I push from my chair. "You grab the eggs." I point to Eli. "And can you get the griddle?" I motion to Crystal and she's already headed to the cupboard.

Breakfast is messy and fun. Our bellies are full and I'm smiling at the end of it all. Crystal always makes things more bearable, helping me see the simple but good things in life, even with the conversation with Patrick still on my mind.

We clean up and Crystal goes to make her bed and get dressed.

"I have to go." My foot shuts the dishwasher, anxious to get back to some kind of routine. I need off this emotional rollercoaster and something to focus on. "I've got work for days waiting for me."

"Remember, our flight leaves tonight. If you want, we can stay longer."

"No, I've loved having you here but you've got a ton of things to do back home before the big move. And Christmas is coming. I'll be fine."

"What are you going to do?" He glances into the other room, checking we're still alone.

"I don't know." My heart is raw from all we left unsaid. "I don't know where things are with Patrick. He'll have questions and I want to be here to answer them."

"Yeah." He shoves his hands in his pockets, rocking back on his heels. "Have you made any headway on whether to stay here or move to Nashville?"

I wipe the counter. "No. I've got Murray looking for places and taking me on virtual tours… I'm still undecided."

My voice peters out, confused about what to do. I could flee. I'd be moving, another chance to fill my nights and days with ramping up my firm and settling down. From a business perspective, my career would prosper as most, if not all, of my clients would stick with me.

But it's thriving here. All moving does is keep me busy, filling my life with distractions. I'd be running away, avoiding my grief. The constant state of upheaval, constantly moving like a treadmill without an off switch. No time to sit with my thoughts.

And then there's Patrick. I don't want to leave him. I don't want to run from him.

"Look." Eli cuts through my deep thoughts.

He takes the cloth from my hand, forcing me to look at him. "You may think this is a tough question, but what it all comes down to is—what do you want?"

"It's both simple and complicated. Everything aside. Tennessee, New York, Lucy. I want Patrick." My voice cracks and I inhale a slow and steady breath.

Deep down, I've known this for a while but with thoughts of leaving and challenging myself to ask why, this is the first time I'm admitting I want Patrick, out loud.

"I've always cared about him, and I want a chance to get to know him better. To see where things might lead."

"Then why don't you do that?"

"Not that easy. It's really up to him. I've given him this horrible news, and while I want to help him pick up the pieces, he might not want me in his life. I have to respect whatever he wants."

"He needs time. He'll come around. He won't push you away." The confidence in his tone gives me hope laced with a healthy dose of reservation.

"You're not exactly objective, now, are you?"

"Maybe not, but I stand by what I said. He'd be a fool to walk away from you."

"Well, thanks for the support. I mean it. Thank you for everything. I'm going to miss you."

"Hey, I'm coming back after the holidays." He cracks a smile. "For good. And for whatever it's worth, I don't want you going to Nashville. There's nothing there for you. And don't even think about going to LA, Hinton's a dick."

I purse my lips, the thought never crossing my mind. "I'm not going back there. Fraser *is* a dick. Fortunately, Patrick's firm dropped the case and told him to back off. It seems to have worked. I haven't heard from him since then."

"Good riddance. I want you here when we come back to live."

"Yes, stay in New York." Crystal bounces into the room and I wrap my arms around her, laughing.

"I love you. I'll see you later."

Before I burst into tears, I hug her once more and then leave to get ready for work.

My day is filled with conference calls, meetings and tons of paperwork. Before I know it, my phone alarm goes off at seven in the evening, a reminder to get home in time to say goodbye to Eli and Crystal.

I want to take them to the airport but Eli wouldn't hear of it, and truth be told, it's probably better this way. I'm liable to break down and cry in the middle of LaGuardia, and my concern isn't for making a fool of myself but more for Crystal seeing me like that.

When I get home, there's just enough time to cuddle with Crystal and change into more comfortable clothes before the airport limo arrives.

"Text me when you get in." I hand Eli his backpack.

"I will."

"And make sure to tell me what Crystal wants for Christmas," I whisper even though she's well out of earshot, wheeling her suitcase toward the elevator.

"C'mon, Daddy, let's go."

"Coming, sweetheart." He smiles at her and turns back to me. "You be good too and call me anytime if you need anything."

"Of course. And same goes for you." I hug him once more, pushing onto my toes to bring him closer. "Safe flight."

"Bye." He dashes down the corridor to his daughter, already inside the elevator, holding the door open.

I wave, tears blurring my vision as she blows kisses and Eli waves. I don't move until they are out of sight, the metal doors closing, and I return to my apartment. Alone.

Several steps inside and I drop to a crouch, pressing my forehead into the palm of my hands. Patrick has been on my mind all day.

I want to call him and make sure he's okay but I can't. He needs the time to digest the news. I have to wait and hope he comes to me.

Work screams for my attention and while I made a good dent in the pile today, I should do some more. I sit on the sofa and perch my laptop on my knees, opening the draft addendum.

I'm barely through the first paragraph when there's a knock at the door. Patrick comes to mind and hope sparks within my chest but quickly fizzles. It's likely too soon and I'm not expecting anyone.

Through the peephole, I see what I most hope for and maybe even dread, a bit. My hands shake and stomach flips at the vision of who stands on the other side of my front door.

Patrick.

A lifeless expression plasters his face as he stares at the door, unblinking. He's a little ragged around the edges. His hair is more mussed than usual and he's sporting easily a day's growth of stubble. Ocean blue eyes are shadowed by dark circles.

He looks almost lonely and worn-down, fatigued, but no less beautiful. I want him as much, if not more than the first day I saw him, fell for him.

The anticipation of seeing him in the flesh weighs heavy on my chest, painfully crushing my frantic, pounding heart.

TRIPP

"Hi. Come in." Her eyes glisten with unshed tears and she offers me a weak smile, stepping back to make room for me to enter.

I swallow thickly, casting my gaze down the hall before facing her anguish, so much like mine, I would think.

My lungs fill once more on a deep, broken inhale and a low growl rumbles through my chest. Why does my chest feel like it's going to crack wide open?

"Hi. I should have called…" I make my way to the living room and she follows.

"No, that's okay."

"I saw you come home earlier but waited for Eli and Crystal to leave." I've been outside for well over two hours.

"Oh." Breath sticks in her throat on a startled gasp.

"Yeah. I remembered you mentioned their flight left tonight."

"You could have come up earlier." Her tone is soft and eager, and maybe even a little nervous. "You're always welcome."

"I have questions." My gaze travels the room, pausing on the painting hanging on the wall. "Did Lucy paint that?"

Since learning about my daughter, the painting kept coming back to me, appearing in a different light.

"Yes. She'd made it the day I left for the interview." The watery smile doesn't stay on her lips and doesn't come near to her eyes.

She perches on the edge of a chair, moving a laptop beside her so I can sit. "You said you had questions. What do you want to know?"

"All of it. I want to know my daughter." My voice breaks but I don't waver from holding her gaze.

"Okay. Hang on a sec." She stands, a little jittery, and heads for the bedrooms.

She returns a few minutes later, the waiting interminable, with what looks to be an old cardboard moving box. Her fingers tremble as she sets it down and her body shivers, gaze flitting from me to the box.

"This is Lucy's." Bending, she drops to her knees, pulling back the flaps. "Most of her things are in here."

I force myself to breathe, such a simple, instinctual function that now feels monumental. My legs weaken and insides quake. This is more than just some cardboard box. Mia removes a photo album sitting on top and looks up at me.

Grief is a conniving, heartless bastard, sitting on my chest, showing up and unable to be shaken. Anger, fear, shock and sadness are on endless supply. The debilitating loss makes it hard to think straight, to move.

"It isn't possible to put my baby in a box… she's everywhere." She sobs, clamping her mouth shut and breathing deeply through her nose. She's trying to keep it together for me.

I slide across the sofa to peer over her shoulder at the open album. So many pictures of Lucy.

"These were taken when she was only days old."

Bright pink complexion, tufts of wispy red hair and big round blue eyes stare up at me. God, she's fucking beautiful. So like her mother, and I think, or maybe I hope, I see some of me.

"Tell me about her." Tears prick at my eyes.

"She was wonderful. A bright light. So funny and smart. Even on days when I was stressed, she could make me laugh."

Mia flips through the pages, fingers trembling, pausing when my hand drops to an image of Lucy and a rabbit.

"She loved bunnies and would bug me almost daily for one," she says.

"Did you get her one?"

Glancing up at me, she blinks and tears flood down her cheeks. She parts her lips, trying to say something, maybe to stop sobbing. It takes her a few beats to find the words and in that time, my heart claws its way up my throat.

"No. I worked long hours. The thought of a pet just seemed like too much on my already-filled plate. But I wish I had." Regret rings true in her tone.

I place my hand on her shoulder and squeeze, wanting to comfort her as much as myself. She thumbs the edge of the page, turning to pictures of a birthday party.

"Who is that?" I point at a woman holding Lucy as a toddler, maybe two or three, I'm not sure, in her lap, covered in icing. The woman has a massacred cupcake in her hand.

"That's Em, my sister." She half sniffles, half chuckles. "It's the funniest thing. For her first two birthdays, Lucy turned her nose up at cake. She wouldn't touch it. I didn't give her sweets—well except for fruits—and so she didn't have a taste for sugar."

"What changed? It looks like she's enjoying that cupcake." A small smile crests my lips.

"Yes. Daycare. Once Em got a full-time job, I had to put Lucy in daycare, and they had birthday parties for the kids. So she got an introduction to sugar."

My smile widens and falls all in the same breath. I want to fully enjoy these stories but I'm warring with myself. On the one hand, I'm a greedy beast, devouring every piece of Lucy Mia has to give. Wanting, no *needing*, to know my daughter.

And on the other hand, my soul slowly doubles over into a ball. Unable to bear the loss of Lucy.

Time passes, all too quickly and all too slow, as Mia takes me through several books of pictures and the other things in the box. Lucy's favorite storybooks, her first tooth, a curl from her first haircut and so much more.

Mingling with my grief is gratitude, indebted to hear memories of my little girl. A chance to see and touch her things.

"What's this?" I pick up a small leather braid entwined with strands of white and purple.

"That was Lucy's bracelet. They had to cut it off her at the hospital."

Mia's fingers run along the fine ridges of the braid, sometimes grazing my flesh, and our gazes lock.

Her raw, unfathomable sorrow meshes with mine and the electric current between us is still there, strong and alive.

Mia clears her throat, blinking and shaking a few drying teardrops from her lashes.

"She, uh… Em always wore one and for a while, I still wore my bracelet. She wanted one too, so I made it for her."

"What are these?" My finger lands on the colored twine.

"This is for the three of us—Em, Lucy and me. Em's bracelet had white and mine had purple. She wanted a bit of each of us in hers."

She swallows more tears, watching my thumb glide over the smooth leather. My baby girl wore this very thing.

"Why don't you keep the bracelet. She'd want you to have it."

I whip my gaze to her, pulse now pounding in my ears. I want it, didn't know it until she uttered the words. My chest swells with the compassion rolling off Mia, all for me.

"I'd like that. Thank you."

Mia wraps a hand around my waist, crushing her fingers into my flesh. "No thanks needed. I'm happy to know it's going to you."

She stands, stretching, almost as if to release or get rid of something. Does sorrow weigh her down, too? Suffocating and torturing.

"I've got more of her things around and in with my things." Her head and hands move around the room. "Like that painting."

She stops moving, pointing to the wall where the picture hangs. I squeeze my eyes shut, pinching the bridge of my nose, slowly shaking my head. Sorrow drags on my heart and lungs. And as difficult as it is, I don't want to let it go. The pain is proof I had a daughter, that she existed. That I created a life.

"I'd give up just about anything for a chance to go back in time. For the chance to find you and have Lucy meet her father before it was too late." Yes, she feels it too. Grief grips her voice.

The fissure in my heart widens and I lift my head to meet her gaze; she is closer now, within arm's reach. Tears pool in my eyes, and I grab at her waist, pulling her to me, and still seated, I burrow my face into her stomach.

She sucks in a jagged breath, giving herself to me. Her body is almost limp, willing, and her fingers thread my hair, holding me to her. I shake uncontrollably, sobbing, no longer able to keep it all in.

Dropping to her knees, she wraps her arms tightly around me as if knowing I need to be held together. As if knowing I fear I might fall to pieces or crawl out of my skin with the searing pain.

My face buries into her neck, my breath hot and ragged against her sweet, inviting skin. I shudder from head to toe, and her body echoes the vibration.

"I'm so sorry. You aren't alone," she whispers softly.

I pull back, eyes boring into her. Raw, broken and untethered.

Her lashes are damp, the tips pointed like spikes, eyes red and cheeks blotchy from crying. This is my Mia and the thought causes me to quiver.

The backs of her fingers brush softly along my jaw, snagging on my scruff, and something snaps inside me. My anguish shifts. Less suffering and more primal, sexual even.

I lose all control.

My arm snakes around her waist, crushing her against me. Her eyes widen and I can't get my hands on her fast enough. The anger, the bitterness, the betrayal rushing through me blends with my lust, my empathy, my love. All of it for Mia.

Mouth on her, I sink my teeth into her lower lip, needing to bring both pleasure and pain. She gasps in shock and quickly follows with a whimper of pleasure; both slide down my throat.

My fingers fist into her hair, holding her in place and kissing, stroking as if fighting for my life. There's nothing soft or sweet about me as I battle my emotions.

I want to punish her, pleasure her, and the turmoil is constant. Every purposeful, aggressive move is countered with a sane voice in my head, reminding me this is Mia.

Yes, she had six years with our child, six years I never had, but she also suffered. Mia also lost. We both mourn the death of Lucy.

My heart beats so hard that it's all I hear, like the drumbeat of my hostility. Powerless to change a damn thing, all I can do is indulge and try to keep my punishing desires in check.

Fingers dig into her ass and my tongue dives into her mouth. Kisses voracious, unrelenting. And Mia doesn't back down or cower from my dominance. Instead, her body bows to me, incredible noises spring from the back of her throat, and I nearly weep.

She's giving, no matter how demanding I am, and she fills my need. Even in my anguish, she's loving and kind. Fuck, I almost break in two.

I need her. Still want her. Always.

She betrayed me.

Can I forgive her?

Still lip-locked, I shift and hoist her onto the coffee table, knocking everything onto the floor. I want inside of her. All of her.

On my knees, I wedge my body between her legs, ripping at her top, urgent to get her naked. With her shirt off, bra shoved below her tits, I cup one, bringing her dusty pink nipple to my hot mouth. I suck so hard, seeking something only she can give.

Fucking sweet and everything I need. Mia bucks and moans, head falling backward, and clenches her thighs. She could easily break me if she hasn't already.

Mouth still on her breast, I get off both her panties and leggings in one fell swoop. She fumbles with the button and zipper of my pants, eventually sliding her hand into my briefs.

Her fingers wrap around my steel-hard shaft. *Sweet Mother Mary.* I hiss, pulling my lips from her swollen nipple.

"Fuck, Mia." My lips blaze a path over her heated chest, unable to stop from taking and tasting from her. "I don't have a condom."

"I'm on the pill," she's quick to say, stroking me, owning every part of me, body, heart and soul.

Another woman, another time, another place and I might have walked away. But this is Mia. There isn't a choice. I'm not going anywhere.

"I'm clean," I croak, hooking my arm under her knee and pulling my pants down further, taking my briefs with them.

"I trust you."

Three fucking words and tears prick at the back of my eyes. I grit my teeth and internally scream at grief to fuck off. Go back into the dark, dank depths of hell. Not now.

My mouth crushes hers, and I squeeze my eyes shut, shutting out everything but pleasure. But Mia.

We kiss and kiss and the tip of my crown glides through her folds. She moans, her legs trembling, and she looks down at where my hard cock pushes inside of her.

I suck in a sharp breath, and she widens her legs and curls a hand into the hair at the back of my neck.

Her gaze holds me hostage as I plunge inside of her, buried to the hilt. I've never felt like this. This is more than sex, more than physical. Our connection exists on a plane all its own. I thrust in and out of her, mercilessly.

Chasing a demon I can't name. Seeking solace I may never find. And wanting this woman more than my next breath.

"Patrick..." The table shakes and her fingers dig into my skin.

My forehead rests on her before kissing a path along her jaw and the back of her ear. "You're perfect."

She arches her back and a tear slips from the corner of her eye on a long shuddering moan. I kiss at the wetness, tasting her regret in the salt of her tears.

"Fuck, Mia." I grab her leg by the back of her knee, bringing it in to rest on my chest, the angle sharper as I drive into her, deepening our connection.

Faster, harder, every inch of me plastered to every inch of her. Somewhere close by there's a crash but I don't stop. Don't care.

I feel her everywhere. Her body shudders and clenches around me and a surge of not only euphoria but something deeper, more profound, stretches through my body. My balls tighten, muscles tense and I yell her name, climaxing.

Sorrow vanishes; only love and bliss wash over me, followed by a welcomed stillness. A solitude I haven't felt in a long time. Well before learning of Lucy.

She kisses my jaw, lips gliding down to the crook of my neck. I hold her close to me, wanting to stay joined like this forever. Still throbbing and hard, inside her, once isn't enough. I want to take her again. Fuck her senseless until there's no more pain.

Blinking back the ruthless vision of fucking her into oblivion, I sink my teeth into my bottom lip. I was rough, at times angry. This is Mia.

If my mind wasn't reeling and insides all turned around, I'd be a goner. I'm with the woman I've always wanted.

She rubs my back and murmurs soft things into my ear, and I can't take this. I have to move. That was both phenomenal and a mistake.

Lifting my head, her creamy bare skin gives me another reason to pause. I'm fucked and can't use Mia like this. Is that what I'm doing? Using her?

I pull out on a shaky breath, getting to my feet and turning away to fasten my pants.

"Hey, you okay?" The concern in her voice sears my chest.

"Yeah."

"Do you want something to drink? I'm getting some water." Her fingers trail across my back before she saunters into the kitchen.

"Nah." I turn to see her fixing her shirt and brushing back her hair.

She returns to lean against the doorway, her cheeks rosy and eyes sparkling. "Can you stay the night?"

No is on the tip of my tongue. It's the smart thing to say. My thoughts jumble and emotions fray. I still don't know what I think or feel about losing Lucy. In one breath I both discovered and lost a daughter.

Yet this is Mia.

I've wanted this. Her. For as long as I can remember. How can I walk away from this? From her?

Not trusting my voice, I nod and a lopsided grin steals her pink lips. "Good."

She takes my hand and leads me to her bedroom. The room doesn't feel like her at all. It's small and white. No color. The walls are bare.

A few boxes line one corner and the only personal touch is a photo of Lucy and her, resting on the bedside table. They're at the beach and both are sun-kissed, smiling in their bathing suits.

Mia catches my gaze. "She loved the beach. She'd make sandcastles, swim and surf."

I raise a brow, impressed, and the ache widens in my chest. Looking away, I drop my pants to the floor, adding my shirt to the pile, and slide under the covers, ready for sleep.

Ready to shut everything out and hopefully get a reprieve from the agonizing grief. How is it possible to hurt so much for losing someone I never even met?

If she notices my sadness, she doesn't let on and follows my lead. Slipping out of her pants, she walks to a wooden chair in the corner where she picks up the quilt draped over the back.

"When this was first made, it smelled like her and I'd sleep with it. Holding it to my chest like my baby girl." She gets in beside me, fanning the quilt over us. "Each patch is a piece of her clothing."

The rows of squares in varying fabrics and patterns are all brilliant colors and filled with hope. It breaks my heart. My head twists to the side, away from her.

"I'm sorry. If this is too much, I can put it away. I'll stop." She gathers the blanket and I grip her hand.

"No, I don't want you to stop. I wish we could rewind but don't stop. I want you to show and tell me everything."

She snuggles into my side, resting her head on my shoulder like she has every right to be there. As if we are meant for each other. And I don't know if that's true anymore. Shit, I'm messed up.

Fingers tracing a yellow square of material, she tells me a story about our daughter and then another and another. Every tale is different but the same.

Behind every shape or animal or object, there's a priceless memory. Both beautifully simple and terribly sad because we both know Lucy is gone.

Yeah, we all die. From our first breath, we're dying. But Lucy was only fucking six. And she was mine. And I never even got to say hello.

TRIPP

We fall asleep with the blanket over us and I cling to her even though I shouldn't. It isn't fair. I'm filled with anger and darkness, threatening to spill all over her, spoil her, and she's been through enough already.

When I wake, in the early hours of morning, Mia's still in my arms. My legs tangle with hers, her hair curtains her face and her sweet scent soothes me. But it's all too much. My emotions, the turmoil, are back, gaining speed in full force.

Yesterday I barely slept, and even in the few hours I did get, I would awaken, consumed with rage and bitterness at how fucking unfair life is. Listen to me, I sound like a stupid child.

I'm too wound up, ready to snap, and shouldn't be here.

Not wanting to wake her, I carefully remove her limbs from mine and roll from the bed. I'm not even at the door when she groans and I still. Shit, did I wake her?

"Is it morning?" She's squinting, one eye open.

"Yup. I was going to get coffee."

Fucking liar. I was making a quiet exit.

"Wait, let me go with you." She gets out of bed, throws on last night's clothes and stuffs her hair under an LA Dodgers ball cap.

I wrinkle my nose at her cap, her choice of teams, trying to shake off this cloud, at least until I can get out of here. She laughs, more comfortable.

Maybe it's because we had sex; to most women, that signals a shift in the dynamic with the other person. Or maybe it's because she finally told me about Lucy.

What the hell am I doing?

Once outside, she entwines her fingers in mine, curling into me to keep warm against the snowy December morning. My arms wrap around her slender frame and fortunately, we don't have far to go.

The coffee shop is just across the street and we're back in her place with pastries and coffee in no time. Rubbing her hands together, she keeps her coat on while going about setting the table.

"What are you up to today?" Her fiery hair spills from the ball cap and she runs her hand through her mane.

Fuck me. Despite my conflict and these disturbed feelings toward her—I. Still. Want. Her.

"Work," I grit out through my tense jaw. "And you?" I hesitate to sit, standing at the edge of the table with coffee in hand.

"Me too. I've got a bunch of meetings and I'm still catching up from the few days away. Do you want to do dinner?" She tears a flaky golden piece off a croissant and pops it into her mouth.

I'm mute.

I can no longer stand being here.

Everywhere I look, especially at Mia, all I see is what I missed out on. All I lost without ever having it.

"I have to go." I'm gruff and my movements abrupt.

"What, now? Okay." She pushes to standing, expression tightening. "Is everything okay?"

"No. Last night…" I hang my head briefly, blowing out a harsh breath. "I don't know what I want."

I can't get into this, explain this to her without sounding like I'm casting blame. Fuck, I don't think that's it… I can hardly make sense of this.

She crumples, falling into the chair, and her expression does the same. Her eyes dim and a frown crawls along her mouth.

"If you need more time, I understand."

"That's just it. I don't know what I need. You said you tried to find me—"

"I did." Her eyes find mine, and I feel her remorse like a physical pain, the jagged slice of a knife tearing me in two.

"I know, but…" I can't breathe with this crushing weight on my chest. "I can't get past it. I've got to go."

She nods, tears spilling from her turbulent brown eyes. "Okay. I get it."

"Do you? I fucking don't get it." My fingers curl around my hair and nails dig into my scalp. "I don't want to blame you."

"But you do."

A painful tension in my throat makes it hard to speak. "Dammit."

Cupping her cheeks, I bring her forehead to mine and she shakes with silent tears. My lips hover a few inches above hers, still drawn to her—craving and needing her—even when I'm rejecting her version of things. Even when I'm looking for someone to blame, to punish, and she's here.

Her eyes flutter closed, tears still breaking through her lashes.

I feel so damn much for this woman. Not all of it is good or right, and it should be. She deserves better than my doubts, pain and anger. She deserves more than I have to give.

"Mia." My lips lightly brush her wet, salty ones.

Releasing her, I leave, faltering when she says my name, drawing more mixed feelings from me, but there's no looking back.

Desperate for a distraction, anything to banish Mia from my mind and numb the incessant ache in my chest, I head toward HC. In the car, on the way, Tommie calls.

I hit the talk button on the car console. "Yeah."

"Guess who's doing work for Taya?" She skips any pleasantries, just how I like it.

"Griffin." My jaw clenches and hands tighten on the steering wheel.

"Riff." She refuses to call him anything else until we have proof. "He's been hanging with Taya's thugs for the better part of the night. I tried calling you, but it kept going to voicemail. Where were you?"

"I had to take care of something." I tense slightly but keep my cool. "So where is he now?"

"He's headed to HC with Van."

"What?" I pull into my parking spot and hit the brakes hard, jerking forward, the seat belt digging into my gut as it spasms.

"Yup. When we couldn't find you, Van went over there and picked him up. We want to know what he's up to. He says he wants out of that life but if that's so, and if he wants to stay out of jail, he needs to stay clear of Taya and her business."

"How pissed is he?"

"Let's just say he isn't too happy. They're about five minutes away. You coming in?"

"Already here. See you in a few." I end the call and get into an elevator.

Van arrives with my brother soon after, a hand wrapped around the younger man's arm. Tommie and I watch them enter the conference room and Griffin tears from Van's hold, snarling.

"Take your hands off me." He steps back sharply, hair flopping into his face.

He halts when he notices they aren't alone. His gaze is fixed on me. "Tripp. Tommie."

I nod and so does Tommie, offering a smile.

"What is this? Another interrogation? Where's Mia?" His tone is snarky, though it softens at her name like maybe her presence wouldn't be a bad thing.

"Mia isn't here and she isn't coming."

"How is she?" He's still tense, shoulders wide and stiff, but he seems genuinely interested.

"She's good, thanks for asking." A hard stone, a lie filled with regret and confusion, lodges in my throat. I don't know how she's doing but she's never far from my mind.

Not wanting to talk about Mia, I refocus on why he was brought in. "My question for you is, why are you working for Taya?"

His gaze darkens, brows knitted and lips a thin line. "I had no choice."

"You always have a choice." Van takes a seat at the end of the table, folding his fingers together and resting them on his stomach. "Told you it wasn't smart if you want out. Cops are crawling all over her business and people."

Griff folds his arms, walking to the furthest corner of the room. "Tiny and Franz have been hounding me to work. I told them I wanted out, they said I have to talk to the boss."

"Look, Taya is hard to shake. She's also bothering me and demanding we talk."

Van goes rigid, eyes narrowing in my direction, and Tommie's perfectly arched brows quirk. This is the first they're hearing about this.

"I never bothered to say anything because I'm not going to see her. We know what she wants—to play games. She thinks she's in a strong position—she's not—and she wants to make a deal or figure out what we know."

We've been here before with the woman and I have no intention of talking to her. "That's why you can't go to her either. She's going to try and manipulate the situation. You were her ace in the hole and now that she's behind bars, hopefully for good, she can only control you if you let her."

I lessen my intense glare, sensing his hackles are rising. "Listen, now is your chance to tell them you're out."

It is easier said than done, especially when we're talking about the mob, but it's the best move right now.

"Now is the best time. And like your—" Van stops, shifting in his chair and pressing his lips together for a beat. "Like Tripp, don't go to her. If they continue to harass you, call us. We'll take care of it."

"I don't need your help." He marches to the door, yanking it open and nearly crashing into Tate.

She jumps back on a gasp. The guitar in her hand smacks against the wall with a thud and he stills, glancing down at the instrument.

"Sorry, I didn't know you were there," he grumbles without any real sincerity.

"It's okay. How are you?"

He steps back into the room and she follows, looking warily at each of us seated around the table.

"Fine." Griffin backs up into the wall, acting every bit like a caged animal.

Sensing his unease, Van says hi to Tate and leaves; Tommie goes with him.

"What do you have there?" I dip my chin at the acoustic guitar, already knowing and not so sure it's a good idea.

"Ah, this is yours." She looks to my brother and his brows hike to his hairline.

"No, it isn't. I don't play." His apprehension suggests she's handing him a bomb and he needs an escape.

For a beat, she's discouraged by his rebuff, quickly recovering and holding it out to him. "Well, you may not remember but Griffin was a musician. His band signed a record deal. You guys were great."

Turning up his nose, he scowls. "I'm not Griffin."

A DNA test would fix that. None of us have broached the topic with him. I'm waiting for the right time, when he might be more willing, but so far there's no ray of hope.

"Maybe, and maybe you are. Look, I know we don't know each other, and you might never want to get to know me but…" She glances at me.

I'm not sure why. Does she want me to leave? Help her?

I'm just as much at a loss as she is. I couldn't keep my mouth shut when he talked with Mia at dinner and that didn't go so well.

"I'd like to get to know you. And if you'll allow it, I'd like the chance to explain what Griffin meant to me."

This is hard for her, difficult for all of us, and he isn't receptive to any of it.

"There's no need to explain something that never happened to me.

And I know exactly who you are. We've been over this." His expression is menacing.

"But there's more… there *was* more to us… I mean to Griffin. I was in love with him and I thought we would spend our lives together." She takes a seat, bringing the guitar to rest on top of the table. "My parents, and a man who would become my husband, Bobby Thornton, kidnapped us."

"Sounds tragic but not my concern." He's flippant and I want to knock some sense into him.

"Let her speak." I glare and he matches mine.

"Please just hear me out," Tate says softly. "I thought Bobby had beaten you to—"

"I'm not Griffin." His rejection is even more pronounced.

"Sorry. I thought yo—Griffin was dead. I was there. The beating and the injuries… it's hard to believe anyone could have survived that."

She's trying to explain, calmly, hoping he'll entertain the possibility.

"That only proves I'm not him. He's likely dead." He's resigned.

Shaking her head, Tate brushes back her hair and looks up at him. "I'm not looking for friendship, or to make you do something you don't want to do. I don't know… this made sense in my head. I came here because Ry said you were here, and he gets it."

"Gets what?" He cocks his head to one side, his expression softening.

"I feel responsible for what happened to Griffin. I just feel the need…"

"To clear your conscience. And you think I'll give that to you?" He pushes from the wall, stopping only a foot or two in front of her.

I stand, alert, unsure if he's opening up or ready to strike.

"I loved him and always will. Even if you aren't him, I just want to say that I'm sorry. I'm so sorry for everything."

My muscles tense, throat tightening at all the things she's saying, all the things I wish I could say, everything I wish he'd be willing to hear.

"Why are you treating me like I'm him when I've told you I'm not? What do you want from me?"

"We could put an end to this." I step from the table. "Take a DNA test and we'll know once and for all if you're Griffin."

He stalls, then scoffs. "Like I'd trust you."

"What do you mean?" Tate's troubled gaze flits from him to me and back again.

"You all want me to be him. What's to stop you from doctoring the results?"

"We wouldn't. You pick the doctor or facility. It's all in your hands." I shrug, hoping my casual attitude makes him more inclined to do it."

He shoves his balled fist into the front pocket of his pants, glaring. It's almost as if he doesn't have an objection so he's not saying anything at all.

"We just want you to be happy. To know where you came from." Tate breaks the silence, on a mission to clear her conscience. "I found happiness with Ry and our kids. We're a family. And as twisted and ironic as this is, I owe it all to you."

"Fuck." His voice booms in frustration.

"I think you are Griffin." She's bold, moving to touch his hand, curling her fingers around his. "I can see that you don't recognize me. Any of us, and I'm not expecting you to, contrary to how this may seem. Have the test..."

I wish she'd back off now. She means well but he isn't reacting well; he's even more tense than before and I'm hyperaware.

"I see Griffin in your eyes, your mouth. Your features may have changed but you're still him."

He jerks away from her grasp as if burned. His dark, feral gaze darts around the room until it lands on the guitar. His anguish and anger are clear.

In one swift move, he grabs the neck of the instrument, turning on his heel toward the door. Does he remember the band? Playing? Maybe she did get through to him?

My chest swells with hope, relaxing my shoulders despite his aggressive strides away. In the next breath, his arm holding the guitar smashes it against the wall.

I lunge for Tate, pulling her behind me as she screams. The wood cracks, strings pop and he tosses it to the ground.

"I'm not that guy," he says with such force, spit flies from his mouth. "You look at me like you think you know me. You. Don't."

"Easy." My voice is slow, cautious, as are my steps toward him, hands up in a non-threatening way.

He stills, fingers midway through his hair. "I don't know anything about Griffin. Stop bringing me his things." He points to the broken guitar on the floor. "Showing me pictures and telling stories. And as for a DNA test, fuck you both."

His rage is a punch to my gut. We're doing more damage than good by trying to reach him. He could walk out that door and disappear. *Fuck, I can't have that.*

"Okay." Tate's eyes glisten and she steps in beside me. "Sorry."

On shaky legs, she gives him a wide berth heading out the door. I want to yell at him, to go after her. None of this is easy and no matter what we try, we're pushing him further away. So much so he won't even consider being Griffin or taking the DNA test.

I can sympathize with Tate. He was her first love and she thought he died because of her. Now, she sees this strong, healthy man in front of her. Merging those two realities messes with your head.

And the man in front of me, he's also broken in so many ways. I can't imagine what it would be like not to know who you are or where you came from. To have all these strangers look at you as if they know you. It's fucked up.

MIA

"Let it go." I clench my teeth and curl my fingers around the edge of the open cardboard box. "The deal with Curtain Call has nothing to with my non-compete, Fraser. And you know this."

"That's bullsh—" His voice is a snarl and I can almost see his red round face in my mind's eye.

"No. The fact that they want to wind down business with you has nothing to do with me. I did not lure them away from you. And they've told you as much. Contrary to your warped way of thinking, my life doesn't revolve around you. And not everything is about you."

"Like I'm going to believe you."

"We're done. Don't call again. Lose this number." I hit end, frustrated.

Anger and disappointment courses through my body, prickling and bruising. Why did I pick up the phone? When I saw that it was Fraser calling, I foolishly thought he wanted to patch things up.

Apologize.

Stupid.

Not a chance. Instead he was calling to falsely accuse me of stealing another client. I heave the cardboard box off my desk, dropping it to the floor, without a care if I break something.

Fraser had dropped his suit. Patrick spoke to him and got him to back off like he said he would. But it looks like Fraser still wants to harass me. I'm blocking his number.

I don't need this on top of everything else. I haven't seen or talked to Patrick in nearly a week. We now share the love and loss of Lucy. Telling him had been hard but needed. A weight lifted, despite the pain it caused him. But I wanted to help him.

I thought he felt the same way. We slept together and that gave me hope we'd work through things together. But he's also dealing with Griffin. Maybe all of it is too much?

I'm unclear where we stand. I've called him once and left a message letting him know I'm here for him.

It hurt when he left but I understood. With my body, he'd been wild and unrestrained. Days after sleeping with him, my contented body still ached in every muscle. I'd loved every minute of being with him and could sense his internal struggle while we'd had sex.

I would help him work out his pain and sorrow in any way. Being with him was more than I'd ever imagined and had been made more meaningful by his knowledge and interest in Lucy. We talked for hours. Everything was out in the open.

And now I felt like I was in the dark. I wasn't so sure of anything. Slumping into my chair, I hang my head in my hands and close my eyes.

The phone rings. Shit. This better not be Fraser. I forget it's in the box and it rings a few times before I finally have it in my hand. It's an unknown number.

"Mia St. John," I say.

"Hey, Mia. It's Riff."

I sit up straighter, surprised by the call. There's silence on the line. "Riff? Hi. How are you?"

"I don't really know why I'm calling…"

"Hey, that's why I gave you my number. Do you want to talk?"

"Yeah… can we talk in person?"

"Sure. I'm at my office."

"It's Saturday."

"Yes, well, I don't have much of a social life. I was going through some boxes trying to figure out what I'm doing, whether I'm staying or going." Why am I still even questioning this?

"Going? You're leaving?" He sounds concerned.

"No. Yes. Maybe. It's a long story... I'll explain when you get here."

"Okay." His tone seems lighter, as if maybe my flakiness has made him smile. "It's nearly dinner, I was going to pick us up something to eat. What do you feel like?"

"Oh." I check my phone; it's almost seven. "Um, whatever's easy. Is there something close to where you are now?"

"I'm actually not too far from your office."

I pause, at first wondering how he knows where my office is. Did Patrick put him up to this and if so why? Then remember my business card has the office address.

"Do you know that salad place with the roast chicken?" he asks.

"Oh, yes. I like their Cobb salad, please."

"Sounds good. Anything to drink?"

"Water."

"Okay, see you shortly."

"Bye." I drop the phone on the desk, staring at the wall, wondering why Riff thought to reach out and call me. Should I call Patrick and let him know? Or will it look like a lame excuse to talk to him?

I'm not even sure where things are with Riff and Patrick. Does he know if he's Griffin or not? Patrick and I haven't talked about him. There hasn't been time.

Time.

Now that my January first deadline—should I stay or should I go?—is only weeks away, I feel like time is moving faster than ever. I'm running out of time.

It isn't even ten days to Christmas and I haven't made up my mind. Truth be told, I haven't really thought about it and maybe that's my answer right there.

Eli and Crystal will be here soon. My practice is thriving. In fact, the next week is filled with social engagements from clients—Broadway shows and holiday parties. There's plenty of reasons for me to stay.

And Patrick is here.

Will he call me soon? I hope, at the very least, we talk around the holidays. If not, I will call him. And how he reacts may be all the answer I need.

If I go to Nashville, my days and nights would be filled. No time to sleep, let alone think. But is that what I want?

I keep spinning in this cycle and don't seem any closer to standing still. Lucy died six years ago and just when I think I've processed that loss, that I'm in a better place, something happens.

Dammit. It could be the anniversary of her death, or her birthday, or the holidays and sometimes it doesn't even matter. It's just a day.

On any day, I could be knocked off my feet as if I've just lost her. Maybe it's too much to put on any one person but Patrick could help with that. We could help each other.

The phone rings. Again. Without looking, I answer, "Mia St. John."

"Listen, Mia." It's Fraser. "If you cut me in on the Curtain Call deal—"

"No. Goodbye." I grip the phone in my hand as if wanting to crush it. "Grrr."

"Hey," a deep male voice says, and sheer joy sprints up my spine.

As if my thoughts conjured him, Patrick stands at the door to my office.

"Hi." Hands flat on the desk, I push to stand, both anxious and thrilled to see him. This has to bode well for us.

I walk toward him, only stopping when it occurs to me that his body language is closed. Arms rigid, folded over his chest, his frame stiff, and expression neutral.

"Everything okay?" His tone gives nothing away.

"What?" I back up until I'm leaning against my desk.

"Whoever you were talking to pissed you off or something."

"Oh. Fraser." My look, in the direction of the phone, is fleeting. "He won't go away and is still accusing me of stealing deals and clients. I'm going to block his number."

"He's pressuring you and expecting you to fold."

"Yes."

"He's trying to force you into doing whatever he wants because of his threat of litigation. You know, pack up your things, move back to LA and partner up with him again."

"Did he say that?" I'm more annoyed than surprised.

"Not in so many words."

"What else did he say?"

"Nothing more than I already told you." He's talking about our brief conversation when HC closed the assignment. "He agreed to drop the lawsuit. But it was more what he didn't say. He was angry and not surprised that his claims were unfounded."

"What a piece of work. I can't even… and to think I was in business with him for five years."

"Often it takes time for someone to reveal who they are." His blank gaze shifts to a box on the floor next to my desk, trailing to the others scattered about the room.

"I suppose. I just feel like I was blind to—"

"I came to apologize for the other night," he interrupts, stepping further into the room.

Maybe there is hope. This is what I had hoped for. He opens his mouth as if ready to say more but closes it just as fast, hesitating. I've never seen him like this before. So indecisive, so tied up in knots.

"Apologize?"

Is he sorry for sleeping with me? My stomach churns and my chest aches. "You regret it."

He rubs roughly at the back of his neck and then just as quickly, he's on me. In front of me and cupping my face in his warm hands.

"I care about you and I'm glad you told me." His eyes are a wild blue, electric and tempestuous. "Shit, glad isn't the word but…"

He leans in until our foreheads touch; we're so close, I could kiss him. His lips are a breath away. I want to kiss him.

"I understand." My fingers wrap around his wrists, holding him to me as my insides melt. So glad he's here and we're finally talking.

"But I can't do this..." His forehead breaks from mine and he tries to move back. I don't want to let him go.

"Mia." His plea compels my hands to let go of him, falling to my sides.

He retreats, clearing his throat and looking away for a beat. "I thought I could, and I thought with time... but there's also Griffin."

Every word is a painful slice to my heart.

I'm fixed in my position against the desk, needing the support, transfixed. Nodding like a bobblehead, I'm unable to find the right words. Afraid to move or speak. If I open my mouth, I may burst into tears.

"The other night... you telling me about my daughter. I fucking resented you."

"Resented me?" Something cold and vise-like chokes my throat.

"Yeah, and it's screwed up. I shouldn't." He is now practically out the door. "You had something I never will, and I feel like I missed out."

"I'm sor—"

"It isn't your fault. I know that logically. I believe you looked for me."

"But you can't get past it." Icy claws of panic sink into my heart. Is this it? We're over?

"I don't know." His head dips and he shoves his hands into his pockets. "But it isn't fair for me to be around you. To take it out on you." His mouth twists. "I don't want to do that to you."

"And you think you will?"

"Maybe. I'm on edge and when I think—"

"When you think about Lucy... I was lucky enough to raise her, to know her, love her in the flesh... it hurts. It's too much." The force of my tears sweeps through me like a tornado.

He nods, eyes downcast, and his pain is a living and breathing thing. Ravenous and needy. His suffering spreading, infecting and suffocating me.

"O-o-kay. I understand." I press my lips together to stifle any sobs.

"This is goodbye."

My heart cracks and it takes everything in me to maintain his stare. Well, I have my answer.

He's dealing with a lot and I'm just too much.

He may have found his believed-to-be-dead brother, or not. That is a lot.

Losing our daughter. It's a lot.

And me. He looks at me unlike before. Almost guarded. Assessing my moves, weighing my words as if looking for a motive or hidden truth.

"Anyway, it looks like you're moving." He motions to the boxes.

I have decided nothing, but what's the point in setting him straight? Maybe that's what he needs to believe. This time he's the one leaving, moving on, and maybe he needs to see that I am too.

As much as it hurts, I can't fault him, and I'll do whatever it takes to make this easier on him.

I can't change the past. I did my best and if he can't live with that, I have to understand. Maybe these brief encounters we seem to have, meaningful but not lasting, are all we'll ever be.

MIA

"Hey." Riff stands at the entrance to my office, hands full with our food, and stops, eyes on Patrick. "You didn't tell me he'd be here."

Patrick turns his body in a way that affords him a view of both of us. Riff doesn't hide his scornful gaze.

Quick to defuse the mounting tension, I say, "He just dropped by."

"I'm leaving." Patrick narrows his eyes at me, and I feel guilty of a crime I didn't commit.

Am I not supposed to talk to Riff? Wasn't that why he introduced us in the first place? Or maybe I can do no right. Again, he needs someone to blame, and that seems to be me. So be it.

"You two have been hanging out?" He motions between us.

"Riff just called me today." I hate how I feel the need to justify our actions.

"Look. Mia, I'll just leave this." Riff holds up the bags. "And we can talk later."

"No. I'm leaving." Patrick stalks to the door and his maybe-brother steps to the side, out of his way.

Patrick's goodbye rings in my ears and I want to scream, run after him, but I don't.

My heart splits in two. I ache at the loss and what he must see as my betrayal. Or maybe failure is a better word.

My failure to find him. After Lucy's death, I did wonder if only I'd kept looking instead of letting the search for him lapse, maybe things would have been different. It's all pointless and painful. I tried my best and yet, guilt still eats at me.

"Hey, you okay?" Riff inches nearer, bending his head to make eye contact.

I blink back the burning in the corner of my eyes. "I will be. It's good to see you. I didn't know Patrick was going to drop by."

And now I feel like a shit for explaining myself to Riff. Shaking my head, I squeeze his arm and get to my feet, needing to move.

"It's cool and you don't have to explain to me why your boyfriend was here."

"He isn't my boyfriend." The reality is a sledgehammer to my already aching heart.

"Fine." His tone is disbelieving, and I avert my gaze, clearing some space on the desk, motioning for him to put down the food.

"I think that was the end of us. Goodbye." Breathing is hard and he stills, eyeing me with worry. "I'm not so sure we're anything to each other."

I don't add the one thing that we will always be to each other, no matter what—Lucy's parents.

"Well, not that it's any of my business but I see the way he looks at you." He hands me a bottle of water and removes cartons from the paper bag.

Settling into a chair, he opens his container. "I don't know him but it's plain to see he's crazy about you. And when he was talking about you the other day—"

"He was talking about me?"

"Yeah," he says through a mouthful of pasta. "I asked about you and there's a reverence in the way he says your name. How he talks about you."

I sit beside him and open the plastic salad bowl. "When was this?"

I shouldn't be paying him any mind. Yet here I am trying to figure out if this was before or after we slept together.

"The other day. They hauled me into their office with another attempt to make me believe I'm Griffin."

Well, that answers one question. They still don't know if they are brothers.

"What do you mean?"

"That guy, Van, grabbed me when I was leaving one of Taya's warehouses."

"You're still working for her?" I frown.

"I didn't want to, but her men are on me. She wants to see me. Her lawyer calls all the time and leaves messages."

"You aren't going to see her, are you?" All too well, I can relate to having someone on you like a monkey on your back. All I need to think about is Fraser.

"No. So long as they don't make me. She's doing the same to Tripp, from what I gathered."

"Wait, you said a lot there that I'm just hearing for the first time. What do you mean by her making you?"

"Mia, these people are dangerous. Taya Conrad is used to getting her way." He puts down his fork and faces me. "I've never disobeyed her before. Her men could force me to see her like they forced me to work this last job."

"Oh my God, Riff, what are you going to do?" Like a horse breaking from a barn, my heart gallops with the danger both Riff and Patrick could be in.

"Just keep doing what I'm doing. I want out and so I'm going to ignore them."

"And what about Taya wanting to talk to Patrick?" Nerves like a razor's edge cut into my stomach.

"He's doing the same as me. Tiny has been acting on her behalf."

I wrinkle my nose and cock my head to one side. "Tiny?"

"One of Taya's top guys. He says she even wants to see her daughter and son."

He finishes the last few bites of his meal and I close my container, too sick with worry and dread to eat. "What do you think she wants with Patrick?"

"I'm not sure. He thinks she wants to make a deal. Get the Feds to back off." He shrugs, getting up to discard the empty food carton. "I don't know."

"If she knows you're Griffin, what if she's planning on threatening him or bargaining with…" I trail off not wanting to finish the thought.

He could be in serious danger. This woman sounds lethal. Look what she did to Griffin and whoever was buried in that grave. There's nothing stopping her from more than threatening Patrick or Griffin, or any of them at HC.

His expression darkens and his lips tighten. "What? Bargaining with my life?"

He strides to the window and perches on the ledge, looking out onto the now-dark street.

"Maybe. She's desperate and maybe she thinks you're her get-out-of-jail card." I really try to lighten the threat but hear the trepidation in my voice. "It sounds like she's coming at it from all angles. With you, Patrick, Tate and Max."

"Yeah." He looks back at me. "Hey, I'm sorry for coming over like this. I've got a lot on my mind and talking to you helps."

"Don't be sorry." I'm happy for the distraction. "I'm glad you feel comfortable enough to reach out. Listen, I think breaking free of Taya is a really good thing, even if there are risks. Just be careful… have you and Patrick made any progress?"

"No." Bitterness blankets his features. "More of the same. He wants me to be Griffin and I…"

"Hey, I think it's more than that. He wants to get to know you and he wants…" My gaze drops to my lap, second-guessing my next words.

"What?"

"He wants for you to want to get to know him. Is that so bad?"

"No. But I'm not Griffin. And besides, I'm not staying."

"You sound like me." My laugh is hollow, and I scan my office, taking in the boxes that have become a permanent fixture.

"What do you mean?" He follows my line of sight.

"I've been in New York for almost a year now. Two weeks will be a year and I might move to Nashville." I have no conviction in the possibility. More and more, this isn't what I want, even with how things are with Patrick.

"Really? Why?" He wrinkles his brow.

"I don't know. Because it's a great city for my profession..." I wander the room, fingers trailing over the leaves of a plant, the ledge of a shelf.

I stop and turn to face him. He's still at the window, now fully focused on me. "Where would you go if you left New York?"

"Don't know. Maybe LA." He gives me a wry smile. "Or just set out and see where I end up."

"That could be exciting... or lonely."

"Tell me what's going on with Patrick."

I sigh, sitting and crossing my legs. "I don't know where to begin. It's a long story."

"Start at the beginning. I've got time." His smile is warm.

Pausing, I wonder if Patrick would be okay with me talking to Riff like this. If this man is his brother, maybe Riff's hostility or unwillingness to consider he might be Griffin could thaw once I tell him about Lucy?

But we don't know much about this man. What if he isn't Griffin? What if he's a con artist or worse, working for Taya?

I hate thinking this way, not fully trusting him when we get along, but I don't know. Instead of baring my soul, I give him the bare minimum, starting with how I met Patrick.

"You guys have known each other since college?" he asks, interrupting.

"Yes." I skip everything with Lucy and jump to bumping into each other at the coffee shop.

I avoid Fraser's claim, not wanting to give Riff another reason to not like Patrick. He was doing his job, and what Fraser did would have happened whether he chose to hire HC or another firm. I choose to think fate brought us back together.

My insides are a mess. If fate brought us together because we are destined to be together, then why is one of us always running from the other?

"He's got a lot going on right now and so he isn't sure he wants anything with me." I shrug, feeling bad for withholding the full story and downplaying how heartbroken I am.

"That's bullshit."

While I appreciate his support, I also get the sense Riff takes any opportunity to be angry with Patrick.

"Maybe."

"I just don't get it."

"Get what?"

The office has gotten darker and the only light is from the silvery moon rays filtering in through the window.

"Why is he walking away? Like I said, that guy likes you a lot. Cares for you."

Leaning forward, I flick on the desk lamp and a warm amber glow surrounds us. "Can we talk about something else?"

He interlaces his fingers behind his head, still studying me. "Shit, here I am, dumping my crap on you, and you're dealing with his crap. I should go."

"No, no. I'm glad you're here." I miss having people to talk to outside of work, and I want a connection to him for Patrick's sake.

"Truth be told, I'm glad I'm not alone after being dumped." My attempt at a smile is a big fail. "Maybe the best thing to do is just leave. Go to another city, get out of his life."

"Come on. You don't have to move to avoid him. This city is big enough that you never have to run into each other."

I nod, even if it hurts how easily we could co-exist in the same city without any interaction with each other. Sounds horrible.

"But I don't think that's good for anyone. He needs you." Riff's tone is candid, as is his gaze.

"Listen to you now." I need to lighten the mood before I start to cry, hoping what he says is true. "For someone who wanted nothing to do with him… suddenly, you're concerned for him and all up in my business."

He laughs. "Excellent point. I just think he's being an idiot and he'll come around."

"Maybe. Maybe not." I play with a loose thread on my sweater sleeve. "Do you want to hear something pathetic?" My voice is near inaudible, afraid to say it out loud.

Despite any reservations about Riff—not knowing if he's fully trustworthy—he is easy to talk to.

He leans forward. "What?"

"When I saw him earlier tonight… I thought or more like hoped he was here to invite me to Christmas."

I look up at him now, my vision watery from my stubborn tears. He isn't looking at me and that's what gives it away.

"He asked you to join them for Christmas, didn't he?"

Riff nods, still unable to look at me. "Yeah, he texted to ask earlier today. I'm surprised he didn't demand it." He snorts but there's something to his tone, as if maybe he's contemplating it.

An envious pang slides cold and uncomfortable through me. I have no right to be jealous or upset. Riff could be his brother, of course he would invite him.

"That's nice. You should go."

"Nope, I'm not going." He shakes his head resolutely. "Especially now that I know you won't be there. You're the only person who doesn't look at me like you want something from me."

"Riff—" I don't want to be the reason he misses out on Christmas, and start to say as much when he cuts me off.

"I'll make you a deal." He stands, walking around to where I am. "If he invites you, I'll go; and if not, let's spend the holiday together."

I'm at a loss for words, selfishly wanting company but also not wanting to get between Patrick and him.

"I don't care for the day, but something tells me you do and you'll be alone. We can't have that."

I'm still undecided about leaving New York City, although deep down, I have moved nothing along if I were to move to Nashville.

If I'm being honest with myself, I'm still holding out for Patrick.

TRIPP

Mia's leaving New York.

I can't believe she's leaving. Every time I stop to think about it, I want to break something. I want to stop her, but I don't.

Instead, I take an out-of-town assignment that will keep me occupied and away from her over the holidays. Griffin refused to join us for Christmas and while I love my friends, I'm in no mood for company.

All of them expect me to make Riff see reason. He refuses to take a DNA test; I've asked again via text and he's ignored me.

He's stubborn, likely because I suggested it. Tommie hinted we could get his DNA through our own means and while tempting, I can't do that. I'm busting my ass to earn his trust. If I go behind his back, my brother might as well be dead.

Text is the only way we've communicated in the last little while and he wants me to back off. Give him time. Fair enough, but I don't have to like it. And now, still processing the news of Lucy and that Mia is leaving—even if I did walk out on her—it's getting to be too much.

The assignment is in Miami and while I welcome the sunshine and change of scenery, the job is too easy. It isn't enough to get my mind off Mia or Griffin.

As if that isn't enough torture, Taya's lawyer keeps calling, wanting to arrange a meeting. She's insistent and doing the same with Tate and Max.

My guess is she wants to negotiate a deal—a reduced sentence or no jail—with Griffin as her bargaining chip. We've worked with the Feds and NYPD in the past and she might be banking on our ability to sway them if we feel we have a proverbial gun to our heads.

She likely has her own DNA results and can prove if Riff and Griffin are one and the same, or disprove it, depending on her angle. We don't need her for that. All we need is time and I'm confident Riff will do the test. Besides, we'd never trust anything she provided. Even still, Tate and I have agreed to meet her.

We want to hear her proposition. We have no intention of granting it, but we're curious. And on the off chance she has something of value, then we'll know about it.

I'm not proud to admit this but I've got someone watching Mia just until I get back. I want to know if she leaves the city while I'm gone. Why I'm torturing myself, I don't know.

And this is how I find out she spent Christmas with my brother. The news bothers me. Riff ignored all my invitations, and despite unresolved feelings, I still want to be with Mia.

I get back to New York City on New Year's Eve and as soon as I turn on my phone, there's a text from Tate, letting me know she's waiting outside. We're seeing Taya today. With no checked luggage, I'm outside getting into the idling SUV in no time flat.

"Hey." I drop my bag at my feet and her driver takes off.

"Hi, how was your flight?" Tate asks.

"Good. You ready?" I'm more than ready, wanting to put this woman in her place, once and for all.

"As I'll ever be." She glances out the window at the stormy winter sky.

"Ry's good with this?"

I hate asking as if she needs her husband's permission to see her psycho mother, but Tate does her own thing. I wouldn't be surprised if my best friend has no clue what his wife is doing, and I won't be put in the middle.

"Yes. He agreed, knowing you're with me. Otherwise, he'd be here."

Satisfied, I focus on our upcoming encounter with the ice queen. This is my chance to tell her like it is. Her years of pain and havoc are over.

We park and it takes some time to get through the security check and then more waiting in the visitor's room, arranged by her lawyer. Finally, two guards enter the room with Taya.

She's shackled and the guards secure her wrists to a metal bar in the center of the table, and her legs are then chained together around the ankles. She's aged in the mere weeks behind bars. An evil smile grabs at her bony features the second she lays eyes on us.

I stare back boldly, not giving an inch. She doesn't have the upper hand. Not this time.

"The time has finally come." She's always so dramatic and cryptic.

"No games." I pull out a chair across from her and Tate takes the one next to me.

"Games?" She arches a blonde brow, twisting her colorless lips. "I'm in no position to play games. It's more like you two are up to games. I wondered how long it would take you to come see me. You're in the position of power."

Oh, so this is how she'll play it. The victim?

"Tell us about Griffin." Tate interlaces her fingers as if in prayer.

"Griffin? Whatever do you mean? He's dead."

"Tell us." My tone is chilling.

"Tell you what?" She's coy.

"Mother, why did you do it?" Tate's jaw is tight, her teeth clenched.

"Why? Isn't that what we always want to know? Why someone does what they do? Why something went down the way it did? But do you really think you're going to get an answer that will satisfy you?"

"Stop these games or we walk out right now." Tate's threatening tone finally breaks through her mother's icy exterior.

She flinches before lifting her chin and sniffing like she's offended. "You were uncontrollable. Taking off for Chicago like you did. I was going to haul you back to the city, but your father thought we should indulge your impetuous behavior. Let you get it out of your system."

Taya sneers at her daughter with contempt before bringing her gaze to me. "If only you'd have outgrown him. Outgrown your rebellious streak. Then it could have gone down so much easier, and Griffin… he'd still be alive."

A growl rumbles from the back of my throat and my fingers ball into fists under the table. It's taking everything in me to keep my distance, keep my hands to myself.

"If only you'd have answered our calls when we reached out. You forced us to take matters into our own hands... to do what had to be done."

"I didn't force you into kidnapping us. Beating Griffin to near death." Tate's posture is stiff and tightly wound, as if she too is battling to hold herself back. "Why did you make me think you'd killed him?"

"Because I could." She slips for a second. "Or maybe you're delusional. Is Mark Stevens Griffin or not? Maybe this has been my plan all along. Make you think he's Griffin. I take it you still don't know for sure."

Now she's fishing, although something tells me she knows we haven't got definitive proof. No DNA test.

"He is Griffin," Tate is the first to say. "What else did you do to him?"

"You and I are so much alike," her mother says, and Tate recoils. "Griffin was the only way to control you."

She lifts her pointer finger, aiming it at me, even if she isn't able to raise her hand more than an inch from the table.

"He was right under your nose."

No surprise at her pleasure in hiding him in plain sight.

"Let's make a deal. I'll release him, leave him alone in exchange for my freedom. You can work a deal for me with the prosecution. I might even offer up another tidbit or two to make them happy." Taya now straightens, her posture almost regal.

I open my mouth, ready to tell her where to go, when she rushes on, her voice cold and controlled.

"Maybe he is Griffin and that may be enough for you, but he'll never be free. Not unless I make it so. This." Her finger once more waves around the grim room and she lowers her voice to a whisper. "Being in here won't stop my reign. My power. I don't have to be outside these walls to call the shots. He is proof of my victory."

Tate makes a furtive glance my way and I keep my eyes on the delusional woman across the table.

"You can't win when all I ever wanted was for Griffin to be alive." Tate's bluffing because we want him to be free even if he has nothing to do with any of us.

Living a life under her mother's control is no life at all.

"But he doesn't know who you are." Her statement falls short of its mark, the blade not even breaking the skin.

"That doesn't matter. He's alive. And we have him back. You don't wield any power over him." I lean toward her, elbows now on the table.

"He's done with you and if you so much as think about him, then all of this—" I wave my hands around the room "—will look like paradise compared to the dark hole we will dump you in. You'll have no contact. You may have power but you won't be able to get word to anyone."

There's a brief flicker of fear in her chilly stare but she quickly schools her features. Stoic and unmoving.

"Let's go." I hold out my hand and Tate slips hers in mine, and we turn toward the door.

"Patrick," Taya says. "Don't underestimate me."

I peer over my shoulder, eyes narrowed, and don't even acknowledge her threat. "Don't ever say my name."

Mia flashes in my mind; she's one of the very few who ever call me by my full name.

“He’ll never remember you.” Her smile is triumphant, and it’s pathetic to see this woman gloat as if she is in any position of power.

I should leave well enough alone but she won’t have the last word.

“And that isn’t the point, but as usual, you missed it. This isn’t about us.” Tate and I stand side by side facing the witch. “The point is, he’s alive.”

MIA

"I can't imagine what you're going through." I place a beer in front of Riff and sit across from him at my kitchen table. "What it feels like to not remember your past."

We have been spending a lot of time together, and underneath his indifferent exterior, there is a sweet man. I only wish he'd share this side of himself with Patrick.

"Yeah, when I dwell on it, it frustrates the shit out of me. And Patrick doesn't help."

As planned, Christmas came and went, and we had the holiday dinner at my place. While grateful for the company, I still missed Patrick like crazy, and still cried for Lucy, although the sorrow wasn't as sharp or as overwhelming.

The mention of Patrick causes my heart to beat a little faster. "Have you seen him? Talked to him?"

"Nah. He still texts, at least once a day. But I don't think he's in the city. I think he's out of town for work."

"Oh." Is this why he hasn't reached out? I don't know why I'm holding out for this when I'll most probably have to make the first move. I will if I have to.

"Did he tell you where he was going?"

"No. Carys and Tate also bother me." He grumbles, bringing the beer to his mouth. "They told me he wasn't here for Christmas, but they didn't say where. It was for work."

It's New Year's Eve and once again, we're two lonely souls helping each other through another holiday.

"Hey, I'm sure it's difficult to feel that kind of pressure but they mean well. They care about you."

"No." He slams the now empty beer can onto the table, crushing it with his fist. "They care about Griffin. I'm not him."

Much like Patrick, Riff is broken. If they are brothers, they share a similar past. They lost both their parents as teenagers and then Griffin's supposed death... none of that is easy to get past. And even if you can't remember it, it must leave a mark, alter your life in some way.

"Are you okay?"

"Fuck, I would be if they would leave me alone." He frowns, looking down at the table.

"You get why they can't leave you alone, right?"

"Yeah."

"Do you want a relationship with any of them?"

"Isn't that the magic question?" Now he holds my gaze and I swear there's a flicker of hope or something similar.

"I take it you haven't figured that out yet?"

"No. It would be so easy to just fucking leave this place. These people have so many expectations of me. Of a guy I don't even know, but they all look at me like I should. The fucking pressure is unbearable."

I nod, understanding the pressure but knowing there's more. He still clings to the story Taya Conrad told him. Fear holds him back.

"You're lost." I rest my hand on his arm where the bracelet I made him for Christmas wraps his wrist. "You must feel as if you don't know yourself."

He pulls his arm from my grip and stands, walking away from the table. "Mia, I don't want to do this again. If you're planning on spending the night talking about those people and what they want from me, I'm just going to leave."

"Okay." I try to shake off his rebuff. "One more question and then we move on. I promise."

His gaze narrows but he doesn't protest. Throwing caution to the wind, I stand and edge over to him. "What would you say to a DNA test?"

"Did he put you up to this?" His eyes darken and his mouth twists into a sneer.

"No. I haven't spoken to him since that night in my office. You know that." I take one more step toward him as if trying to calm a feral animal. "He's never asked me to do anything other than talk to you."

"Then why do you want me to take the test?"

"It would put an end to their pressure and answer some questions. We'd know for sure if you're Griffin. And if you are, you can decide one way or the other if you want a relationship with Patrick."

"What if I am Griffin and want nothing to do with him or his friends?" His voice is low and raspy, as if it hurts him to ask out loud.

I step back, not expecting his question. "Then that's your choice too. But this way, you've given them the answers they are desperately seeking, and you can move on."

"Fuck, what difference does it make? They will never leave me alone if I'm him." He shakes his head, running a shaky hand through his hair.

And there it is. The root of all of this.

"What is it you fear the most? That you are Griffin Townsend? Or not?"

I'm willing to bet this is the first time in his relatively brief life—he only has a decade of memories—that someone, a group of people, have cared about him.

Well, other than that wretched woman, Taya Conrad. And even at that, her kind of caring must equal manipulation. Until now, no one and nothing has required him to do any real introspection.

"Shit, you're good." He tilts his head to the side, a small smile dancing on his lips. "You ever thought about being a therapist?"

"No. Not for me."

"You'd be good at it, because that's the thing I don't know. I'm not sure what I want, and I suppose if I get the test then my choice is taken away from me."

"Yes and no. You can make your choice with all the facts. The decision is still yours."

The same is true for me. Patrick might want me out of his life, and while it still hurts, I'll respect his wishes, but not without trying to change his mind.

I'm giving him space. For now. Moving to Nashville would be easy —running away is far easier than facing what's in front of you—but New York is where I want to be.

Patrick is here.

Patrick is my home.

We may not be together right now, but once he's had time to grieve and process, I'll seek him out. When that will be? … Now that's *my* magic question.

"Fine. I'll do it." His tone is accepting. "But you have to be there."

"Of course." I smile, happy that he's finally agreed. "So how do we do this?"

"I don't know. I thought you knew."

"I suppose I could call one of my clients. Her father is a bigwig hospital administrator, they might be able to point us in the right direction." I search for my phone.

"Yeah, we could, or…" He has a deep in thought look to his expression before blinking, looking at me. "I think I know someone who could help us."

"Who?"

"Max Conrad."

"Max? Tate's twin." I think back to Thanksgiving when I met Max for the first time. "He's heavily entrenched with Patrick and the others. Are you sure?"

I'm not connecting the dots or feel like I'm missing something. How does Riff know Max?

"He's a doctor. He'd have to keep his mouth shut. Doctor-patient confidentiality, right?" There's a light to his face that I've never seen before, almost like he might be excited or maybe relieved to finally be getting some answers.

"That's true, but why Max? We could get a doctor that doesn't know anyone that knew Griffin."

"Yeah, but I don't like doctors." He scratches at the back of his neck, giving me a sheepish look. "At least I know Max, even if he's dating Tommie and friends with Tripp and all of them."

"How do you know him?"

"He used to work for Taya. We weren't friends or anything…" He trails off and he doesn't have to say any more.

There likely is a strange or inexplicable connection that Riff feels toward Max. During Thanksgiving at Carys's, while giving me more details on his friends, Patrick had mentioned to me, in vague terms, that Max had been forced to work for his mother.

I shiver just thinking about the lengths that woman will go to to control things, or more specifically, people.

"Okay, you have his number?"

"Yeah." Riff nods, taking his phone out.

While he calls Max, I want to call Patrick to tell him about the DNA test. I won't call him, I won't break Riff's trust, but I believe Riff is Patrick's brother. Or I should say, I believe and trust in Patrick. He believes it and so do I. And I want them to have a relationship, or at the very least, get the answers they both need. I can help with that.

And maybe by helping them, this may help Patrick get past his resentment toward me. And maybe there isn't a way for Patrick and me to come back from the loss of a child. I may not have fully wrapped my head around that possible outcome; I can't, just yet. But hopefully, he'll see that I only want to help him and love him.

* * *

I TEAR off the packaging tape from the bottom of the last remaining box and crumple it into a ball, tossing it in the garbage. Then I break down the cardboard until it's flat, folding it over several times and securing it in a tidy flat square with a piece of string.

Resting the now-flattened box on the pile with all the others, I carry them to the door for recycling. I haven't told anyone that I've decided to stay in New York. I'd like to tell Patrick first.

There's a light rap on the door and Riff sticks his head in. "You ready?"

"Hi. Yes." I grab my coat and lock the office door.

We didn't make it till midnight last night and Riff ended up going home at eleven. Today, the first day of the new year, is the DNA test. Max readily agreed to do the test and reassured Riff that he was under oath and wouldn't tell anyone.

To make this easier, less clinical, Max offered to do the sample at Riff's place, but Riff suggested Max's uptown apartment.

"So, you sure you're okay with Tommie being there?" I ask as we step into the elevator.

Tommie and Max live together and Max couldn't guarantee that she wouldn't be there.

"Yeah, she's cool." He fidgets, playing with the collar of his jacket as if nervous.

"You okay? You sure you want to do this?"

"Yes. Seriously, I'm fine with Tommie. I just don't want to do it at a hospital."

"Okay. Do you mind me asking why?"

We saunter out of the building and onto the street where the Uber we ordered is waiting. We slide into the car and confirm the address before the driver merges into traffic.

"When I woke up, all those years ago, after the attack…" He clicks his seat belt into place. "I spent way too much time in hospitals. I had many painful surgeries over a couple years."

A muscle in his jaw ticks and he glances out the window, giving his back to me.

"Oh." I hadn't even realized that might be what he was most concerned with. "I had no idea."

"Yeah." He rubs his flattened palms along the tops of his thighs, lightening and then darkening the denim of his jeans. "I don't want to talk about it."

"Of course."

The drive uptown is quiet and for the most part quick. The car pulls up in front of the building and the doorman calls up to Max, notifying him of our arrival as he ushers us into the elevator.

"Let's do this." Riff steps into the elevator after me and there's a nervous energy in the air.

When we step out of the elevator, Max stands outside of his apartment, waiting for us. "Hey guys, happy New Year."

"Hi, same to you." I smile and Riff mumbles something beside me, his unease growing by the second.

"Hey, you nervous?" Max asks.

"Yeah, just want this over with." He shoves his hands into his pockets.

We enter their apartment and a German shepherd stands at attention. I falter, startled and unsure.

"Don't mind Gunnar, he won't bite." Max runs a hand through his pet's ruff before sauntering further into his place. "And Riff, just relax. This will be quick and painless."

"You promise?"

"Yep. Just have a seat and I'll get washed up." He motions to the kitchen table and then rolls up his sleeves at the sink.

"Hey, guys. Happy New Year." Tommie enters the room with the dog at her side. Her gaze lingers on Riff, assessing. "You sure you want to do this?"

"Yeah. Why? You think I shouldn't?" He's defensive and I inwardly cringe. Riff said he was cool with Tommie but now I'm not so sure.

"No, I think you should but you're not looking so good."

Max chuckles from the sink, now drying his hands and then donning a pair of nitrile gloves. "I think Riff is expecting a long thick needle, when all it is, is this."

He holds up a clear, thin package that looks like an extra big cotton swab on a long wooden stick.

"Okay, I'm going to walk Gunnar. I'll see you guys later." She leans in and kisses Max on the cheek.

"See you soon." He rips open the package. "Okay, Riff, this is a buccal swab and all I'm going to do is rub it along the inside of your cheek to collect some cells for testing. It's quick and painless. Open wide."

He does as he's told and Max inserts the cotton end of the stick. "This won't hurt. I'm just going to scrape along the lining of your mouth."

The test is over in seconds and we watch in silence while Max places the used stick into a clear plastic bag, seals and marks it.

"It'll take a few days. I'll call you as soon as I have the results."

"How are you going to know if you don't have Patrick's DNA? He doesn't know about this, right?" Riff is now on his feet.

"Relax. We have Patrick's from HC." Max removes his gloves. "Don't stress. Try to forget about it and I promise to call."

"And this is just between us, right, doc?" For some reason, Riff is still wary.

"Absolutely. Neither Tommie nor I will say a word."

"Okay, thanks, man."

They shake hands and Riff takes the lead toward the front door.

"Thanks, Max. We really appreciate this." I follow them.

"No problem."

We say our goodbyes and Riff orders an Uber on our way down, where we wait on the curb.

"I tell ya, this is one thing I miss about my old job." Riff stuff his hands in the pocket of his jacket.

"What's that?" I look up at him, squinting in the midday sun.

"Well, apart from a paycheck, I miss having my own wheels. But I suppose having a car at the ready whenever I wanted isn't worth the trouble of Taya and her men."

"Ah, no. Any luck on the job front?"

He has been looking and even gone on a few interviews. All of his identification says he's Mark Stevens and I wonder what that will mean if all of that has to be changed. I don't say anything. There's no point mentioning it until we know for sure.

"Nothing solid yet. I got a call back on that bartending job. They wanted me to work New Year's Eve."

"Why didn't you take it?" The car pulls up alongside us.

"I didn't really want to work in a bar." He opens the door, motioning for me to slide in first.

"Well, if you're interested, do you want to make a few bucks for a few hours of work?"

He gives me a sideway glance. "Sure. What do you need?"

"My friend Eli and his daughter arrive in a week, and I promised to get a few things set up for them. I need help to put up curtains and things like that."

"You didn't tell me it's manual labor." His tone is teasing.

"Of course not—if I did, you might not have agreed to help."

"Fine, I'll help but I won't take your money."

I purse my lips, not impressed with his refusal. "We'll see about that. I've got the stuff at my office."

* * *

Something is wrong. In the hallway, only a step from the office, I notice the door is open. Fear paints my insides and sweat breaks out along the back of my neck.

I grab at Riff's wrist, stopping him. "I locked the office door."

"Shit, stay here," he whispers, cautiously walking through the doorway into the small reception area of my office.

With my phone in hand, ready to dial the police, I follow. He's going to need help if someone is in here.

Heart charging, bucking against the walls of my chest, I creep behind him. Nothing looks out of place. Maybe whoever broke in has already left, finding nothing of interest in my office.

I don't have any money here and unless they are looking for

employment contracts, investments or other legal agreements, I can't think of anything worth breaking in for.

Two burly men, holding guns, come out of my office and for a split second time stops.

My blood turns to ice, freezing my organs and locking my joints, but not before a small sob slips from my mouth.

"Shit," Riff mutters, quickly glancing over his shoulder to see me.

Remorse for not following his command slithers, cold and dense, in my stomach and then I remember my phone.

"Tiny, what the hell are you doing here?" Riff steps in front of me and while he's protective, I don't feel safe.

"Drop the fucking phone," one of the men orders, his voice as hard as his glare.

They have guns and I do as I'm told. My phone clatters to the floor and they stalk toward us, guns now at their sides.

Both sets of eyes blacken as they size us up. We're in trouble. Before I can react, scream, run or do anything, one lunges for me. A large, strong hand tightly grips an arm.

I struggle to break free. "No. Help!"

With a hold on me, he yanks me toward him. My back is now to his chest and he sticks the gun into my stomach, just above my belly button. A clammy hand slaps down on my mouth, fingers digging into my jaw. Like a sprinkler springing to life, my eyes leak water, my nose tingling from the cutting sting of nails in my face.

"Shut up, bitch," a deep, menacing voice says into my ear. The muzzle of the gun presses further into my abdomen, reminding me to obey.

Air stalls in my lungs and against every impulse to fight, I stop, still tense but no more moving.

Only a foot in front of me, Riff's fist socks the other man's face and he staggers back a step or two. The impact of bones and flesh is a crushing violence. But it barely slows him down. The man reacts quickly, raising the gun and throwing a beefy arm around Riff. There's a scuffle, the two men chest to chest and jostling back and forth.

Something black falls from one of the men, sliding across the floor and sailing under the coffee table. I seem to be the only one who notices. Was it a gun? Did Riff have a gun?

My no is muffled because of the hand over my mouth and at the same time, a female voice from behind us, says, "Hello."

For a beat, I'm elated, at the possibility of someone walking in on us. Help is here. But all hope is quickly dashed when the man holding me turns us to face the voice. Tate, wide-eyed and startled, stands in the doorway to my office.

"Oh my God." She backs up, hand diving into her purse for what I'm guessing is her phone. Or maybe it's a gun?

Another guy, this time pure muscle, appears behind her. I never saw him in the hall. Where did he come from? He grabs Tate by the shoulder, spinning her like a doll and his arm bands around her. I feel the constriction in my own chest. I can't breathe.

"Fuck. You're all coming with us," says the guy Riff called Tiny. "As for you." He stares at Tate. "We can't leave you here."

"Do you know who that is?" Riff points at a pallid Tate. She looks like she may vomit or pass out.

"Yeah, so?" The guy gripping me steps forward, hand still over my mouth.

My jaw aches and I'm having a hard time breathing. My chest heaves, water dripping from my eyes.

"That's the boss's daughter. Is Taya behind this?" Riff glares at all the guys.

The guys look to Tiny as if he's in charge and he says, "What do you think?"

"Get your hand off her, she can't breathe," Riff snarls, pointing at me, then the beast suffocating me.

"You gonna be quiet?" The deep threatening voice sends shivers down my spine.

Nodding violently, my tears spill faster down my face and he removes his hand. I inhale a gulp of air. Riff waits until I look at him, satisfied I'm okay, or as okay as I'm going to be given our situation.

"Look, you think the boss wants her daughter mixed up in whatever this is? Or Mia? Leave them here and take me. Her beef is with me."

"Griffin," Tate says as if she's in a trance.

"Nah. She wants Red." He tugs me into his side, and I get a whiff of his stale onion breath.

Taya Conrad wants me? Why? She doesn't even know me.

The guy in the hallway turns and drags Tate with him. She doesn't fight, stumbling to keep up, all the while glancing over her shoulder at Riff.

"Yeah. And the boss is sick and tired of you ignoring her." Tiny yanks Riff forward.

"Fuck. Look. Take me."

"Red was our insurance policy against those assholes at Hart Corporation. Especially against that asshole, Tripp. Boss wants him on his knees. I think we're golden with both of you and now, Tate too." Tiny laughs, the last to step into the elevator, and the other two guys join in.

Tate is stoic, almost catatonic in contrast to my quiet cries. I'm getting more freaked out at how eerily silent she is, looking to Riff and his captor. Tiny has a hand wrapped around Riff's arm and the gun pokes into his side. Her troubled gaze is fixed on the gun.

Does she know what's in store for us?

"This is just like all those years ago," Tate mumbles more to herself but everyone stares at her. She's in another world and terror fills her eyes. "We've got to get out of here."

"We will." Riff's determined tone doesn't change her demeanor.

Afraid, but more so at the way Tate's acting, I have a horrible feeling we're not getting out of this alive. At the basement level, we're ushered through a corridor to the loading dock.

No one is around and there's not a sound. Not even the revving of car engines. I'd consider yelling for help but each of us has a gun at our backs. Tate's a zombie, Riff's angry and I'm terrified and confused.

At the back doors to the van, Riff's pushed in, smashing his shin on the bumper, and he curses. I'm next and I scurry on my hands and knees to get away from them. Before Tate can be tossed in, she bends over and throws up.

The large guy holding her leaps back from the splash. "Fucking bitch!"

He raises his hand with the gun, winding up to backhand her when I scream "No!" at the same time Riff's cutting tone stops him. "I wouldn't if I were you. The boss hears about it and you'll be dead."

Whether that's true or not, the threat works, and the guy drops his arm to his side, shaking his head in disgust.

"Help her." My demanding tone causes Tiny to echo my sentiment to the idiot closest to her.

He isn't gentle and doesn't bother to ask how she is, only pushing her in the back of the van. One guy climbs in after us, grabbing my arms and stretching them behind me and I whimper, fearing he'll rip them from their sockets.

"Easy," Riff grits out, but the guy ignores him, securing my wrists to a metal bar lining one side of the vehicle.

He moves on to Riff and then Tate before jumping out of the van and slamming the door, shutting us in.

It's dark back here. I can hear the gruff muffled voices of the two guys in front. There is a small rectangular cut-out up at shoulder height to the front seats. If the two in the front cab wanted, they could peer down on us.

The vehicle starts to move, and the drive isn't smooth. I'm jerked, shaken and wrenched from side to side, and with every little bump, my arms are tugged one way or the other. The plastic ties burn, slicing into my flesh and pulling at my bones. My wrists feel as if they might snap in two.

"Fuck, I'm sorry." Riff's regret-filled gaze lands on me and then Tate.

"This isn't your fault. It's mine." Tate wipes her chin on her shoulder.

Quiet, I try to stay upright as best as I can, holding back my tears, fighting down the fear-curdling nausea clawing its way up my throat.

I don't see how we'll get out of this. The only hope is if someone figures out we're missing.

It's New Year's Day, a lot of things are closed. The building was unusually quiet. Chances are slim that anyone saw or heard anything. Dammit.

And it isn't like Patrick will come looking for me, realize I'm missing. We aren't talking.

And Riff isn't exactly chummy with him either.

Our only hope is Tate. Ry will eventually realize she is missing. In the meantime, we have to stay alive.

TRIPP

January second and Mia is still in New York. This is good news. When I got back from Miami, while I was busy seeing Taya, I had Tommie check with Mia's landlords for both her apartment and office, the leases are still in effect.

Maybe she's changed her mind about living in the city or maybe not. Either way, I want her to stay. I spent New Year's Day holed up at my place, wallowing. Going over the past several weeks with Mia and Griffin, the news of Lucy and the years from college to now.

I'm not usually introspective or morose but it seemed appropriate with it being a new year and all. I was fucking miserable and Mia is the brightness in it all. Even with everything else with my brother and lost daughter.

"I need your help," I say to Carys over the phone, sitting in my car outside Mia's apartment.

"Sure." She sounds groggy and I cringe, realizing it's only eight in the morning. "What do you need?"

"Shit, I didn't realize the time. Were you working late at the bar?"

"No, it's fine. I have kids, they don't know what sleeping in is." She snorts and I laugh. "So what's up?"

"Promise me you will not get all weird and sappy."

"Now I really want to know what this is about." I can hear the smile in her voice.

"I fucked up with Mia and got all turned around with news of... Lucy." It hurts to say her name.

But the more I do, the easier it is to grab any bit of joy I can squeeze from everything Mia's shared, all her precious memories. Focusing on that, on my little girl, is better than dwelling on what I have lost.

"She'll understand." Her tone is softer, and no longer carries any of the humor it had moments ago.

"I hope so. I said goodbye, turned my back on us and the possibility of a future before we even began."

"Oh, Tripp." I can almost see the puppy dog eyes she would give me if she were here with me. "If you're asking if there's still a chance for you two, I say hell yes. Mia, of all people, can understand how you feel and that you'd need time."

"Look, what I want to know is..." I stare down at the leather bracelet around my wrist. "Is sorry enough?"

"Yes. Be honest with her. You were brave enough to do so when you first found out about Lucy even when it wasn't the easiest thing to do."

"Yeah." I huff, clenching my jaw. "I was so honest that I pushed her away. Idiot."

"Maybe... I've often said you aren't smart." She's teasing, trying to inject levity into the conversation, and I'm grateful to her. "But you also gave her a part of yourself that few see. You let her in even when you were struggling with the news of Griff. She'll see your actions—walking away for a while—and your apology in the same way."

"You seem sure. Why?"

I want to believe her. Believe that there is still hope for Mia and me.

"Because she loves you. And from the little I know of Mia, she'd do just about anything for someone she cares about. Just look at what she's doing for Griff."

I nod, forgetting she can't see me. "Yes. Okay, well, I better get this over with. Go spill my guts and hope I wasn't too much of a jerk for us to salvage our relationship."

She laughs. "You don't need it, but good luck."

"Thanks."

I shove my phone in my pocket before running a finger over the leather bracelet Mia made for me all those years ago. I never gave it any thought to why I never took it off, but now it's so obvious. I never wanted to say goodbye to her. Not back then, in college, and not now. Even with all that I've learned.

After she gave me Lucy's bracelet, I added it to the one Mia gave me, weaving my daughter's leather and twine into mine. It's a minor adjustment to the band, and it may not seem like much, but it made all the difference to me. I feel closer to Lucy, as if she's with me at all times.

A wave of sadness washes over me every time I think about Mia and Lucy. Together, without me for all those years.

But it isn't in an angry or cheated way, like I first felt. It's more sorrow for all of us. We were all cheated of being together and that isn't on Mia. No one is to blame.

Done wallowing and stalling my mea culpa, I get out of the car and march into Mia's building.

I knock several times on her front door, even calling through the wood to let her know it's me. She isn't home, but it's Saturday. There's only one other place she could be. Her office.

The tail I had on her was only during the time I was away on business. Despite walking away from her, I needed to know the second she left New York. Desperately holding my breath, and secretly wishing she wouldn't leave.

Now, as I head to her office in weekend traffic, I wish I had known where to find her from the outset of my decision to make things right. The longer it takes to see her, talk to her, the more my nerves wreak havoc on my internal organs.

I push through the stairwell door and Mia's office is in sight. The door is wide open and the hairs on the back of my neck rise, heart rate speeding up. This doesn't feel right.

Quickening my pace, I step into the office and stop when faced with a phone on the carpet. The reception area looks intact, nothing out of place from what I can tell. I pick up the phone, hitting the home button. It's Mia's phone.

Her home screen is a picture of Lucy, one of the many she shared with me. Her office looks much the same. But why would she leave the door open and phone on the floor?

Fuck. What happened?

I can't even call her. The first person to come to mind is Fraser Hinton. He's Mia's biggest threat, but he isn't violent. This kind of thing isn't his style.

It doesn't take me long to jump to Griffin. They've been spending a lot of time together. I don't think he'd hurt her but fuck, I can't say so for sure.

And if not him, his known associates and former employer… a disappearing act is their kind of thing. It's a hunch and a long shot, but it fits.

And there's the possibility she left, but that doesn't make sense. She wouldn't leave her phone here and her office unlocked. There's no one to call that may have seen Mia last… well, that's not true.

There's Griffin. I dial his number and as it rings in my ear, there's a ringing in the office. Bending, I move toward the noise and under a coffee table there's another phone. Griff's.

Shit.

Did something happen to both of them? Of course, with Griff, Taya is the first person to come to mind. But Mia isn't on Taya's radar. Despite warning Taya to back off, she may not have listened.

And she's desperate, facing many years in prison. At one time, Griffin might have been the answer to her freedom. Even now, if she were to kidnap him… fuck, that's likely what happened.

I need more information and hit the call button for Tommie. She answers on the third ring.

"Hey, Tripp. We have a situation. I was just going to call you."

"What happened?" I'm terse, wanting to get to my need first.

"Tate's missing." As if hit by a wrecking ball, my legs shake.

"Mia and Griffin might be missing too. Tell me about Tate."

"The boys were at Ma's yesterday and spent the night too." She's talking about Ry's mother. "Ma thought something was off when Tate didn't call to see how the boys were or to say goodnight, but she also thought Tate may have gone to bed early. Catching up on sleep. Ry had the Boland job."

Tension grows in the pit of my stomach. We all take turns over the holidays. HC never closes and this year Ry and I were up to work on any assignments that might have fallen during that time.

"Ry got home at a little before seven this morning and discovered Tate wasn't there. The bed wasn't slept in. He checked their security cams and she left the house yesterday afternoon and never returned. So far we don't have any leads." Tommie's grave tone matches how I feel. "Tell me what you have on Mia and Griff. This can't be a coincidence."

I walk around, examining every inch of the office, looking for anything I may have missed, any sign of what happened while I tell her what I found. "Can you tap into the building security?"

It might be our only lead. I stare up at the small black bubble on the ceiling, covering the surveillance camera outside her office door.

I've counted three on her floor alone and the elevator and lobby also have cameras. It's got to give us something.

"On it." Sounds of movement and her choppy breaths filter through the phone line. "Just give me a sec."

"Okay. In case there's nothing from the front, I also think there's an area for deliveries at the back or in the basement. There must be cameras there too. But start with her floor first."

"'Kay."

My gaze drops to the floor, hanging my head, frustrated with the time it feels like we're wasting.

"Fuck." I bend to pick up a shiny circular object, no bigger than a quarter, lying on the carpet in the hallway. "Shit, Tate was here too."

I'm wound tight and can't breathe, fearing I may explode.

"What?" Tommie asks.

"I just found something that I remember hangs off her key chain, or purse, or something." Images of one of Tate's little boys playing with this glittering ball flash in my mind.

Shit, if Taya is behind this and they grabbed Tate, they hit pay dirt. Nabbing her daughter would change things. Ry would fight to the bitter end, make any deal—even let Taya go free—to get his wife back.

Foolishly, it then dawns on me. Griffin holds a lot of sway with getting me to cooperate. Taya would be smart to bet on that.

I can't stop my brother if he wants to continue working for that woman. And I can't stop him if he walks away from me, so taking Griffin is one thing but not a sure thing.

Nabbing Mia... that's a different story. It ensures my cooperation to the bitter end. I'd make just about any deal or go to any lengths for the woman I love.

"Oh my..." Tommie says over the phone.

"What is it?"

"It's Taya's men... Tiny, Franz and another guy. They have Mia, Riff and Tate."

"Fuck." My fingers curl around the phone and I catch myself before I do any damage to the device.

"They got into a white cargo van. I need a few to see what direction they went... if I can find them."

Locking down any emotion, my voice comes out flat. "You will find them."

"Yeah. And I'll alert Ry and Van."

"Good." I race down the stairs and out the front doors.

A blast of frigid air hits me and it's the jolt I need to focus, determine our next move.

"Tommie, give me what you have. I'll start driving."

"Okay. I'm sending coordinates to your GPS—"

The beeping in my ear alerts me to an incoming call and I cut her off. "Ry's on the other line. I'll call you in a few. Keep sending me directions."

I hit the speaker and start the car. My voice is thick, drowning in fury, as I tell Ry, who Tommie must have texted while we were talking, the little that I know.

Not too long into our conversation, Tommie calls with more information. She's brought in the authorities—Feds and NYPD—and we've got the full extent of the law helping us find them. This isn't going to be easy. While the security footage gives us a head start, that's about it. We need more intel. It's like trying to find a specific granule of sand in the Sahara Desert.

The downside to working with law enforcement is now we have to do everything aboveboard. We don't call the shots.

We work well with the authorities; many of the HC crew started their careers as cops, Feds or in the military, and we know our place. But in situations like this, I want to use any means necessary.

Tommie confirms Taya is still in jail. She didn't escape—thank fuck—which had been a brief consideration. While there was slim to no chance of that happening, it was a possibility. She must be orchestrating this from inside.

I'm riled, ready to pay her a visit and wring her neck. What she hopes to gain isn't clear. Sure we have pull and connections with law enforcement but we have nothing to negotiate with them. There's absolutely no reason for them to reduce her sentence or even consider some kind of plea.

She hasn't offered anything, no details about her operations, nothing on another mafia boss or anything else to even start discussions. And while kidnapping them certainly gets our attention, it's pure evil with no endgame that I can see. Other than to wield her considerable power, even behind bars, and toy with us.

I'm scared shitless. Her men have Mia. Griffin. Tate…

Mia.

My family.

History can't repeat itself. This woman took my brother, beat him and let us think he was dead for a decade. I can't explain it, but now more than ever, there's no question Riff is my brother. Taya's actions prove it. She wouldn't have taken him otherwise. Same goes for kidnapping Mia and Tate. They are valuable, an easy way to get Ry and me to cooperate.

Mia… I don't even want to think about what might happen to her.

Shards of panic cut heavy and sharp into my chest. I can't have found them both only to lose them again.

MIA

One night. So far. Captive. Most of it spent bound and gagged in a warehouse overnight. I shiver and sniffle, freezing and achy. My lips are cracked and dry tears have streaked down my face, pulling tight at the flesh of my cheeks.

A golden ray of sun flickers through a sliver of glass, where some of the newspaper has peeled away to reveal it's a new day. The windows are covered in faded newsprint, blocking out the light or any sign as to where we are.

It's now morning, and the night was long, cold and uncomfortable. Riff sits on the cold, hard concrete, leaning against a wall at least thirty feet, if not more, from me.

His head is bent at an odd angle, chin to chest, sleeping, although it isn't a deep sleep. Every few minutes, he twitches and winces. And once or twice, his eyes flutter open for a moment before he groans and shuts them again.

Catatonic, Tate rests with her legs out in front of her at the far end of the room, eyes glazed, mascara marbling her smooth, pale skin. She doesn't blink or shift a muscle. If not for the up and down of her chest, air moving through her lungs, I'd think she isn't real. A mannequin.

She's been gagged the longest. Still is. Unlike me, where only my arms are bound, she has both her arms and legs tied up. I hope she's okay.

I worry about her the most. Funny, considering I'm in the same boat as she is and don't know what's going on. Yes, this is scary. I'm petrified of what's going to come next, but Tate was in a state of hysteria, and now seems almost comatose.

Yesterday, there was no way to tell how long the ride was from my office to the warehouse. It seemed short, definitely not hours, but it was long enough. Once parked, Tiny opened the back of the van and one of the other guys climbed in holding a small bundle of dark cloth.

A black swath of fabric is shoved over Riff's head. A mask. And the man is quick to do the same to Tate. That's when it happens. She loses it.

Screaming, her head swivels like she's in the Exorcist, piercing my eardrums with the high keening wail, more animal than human, and unlike anything I'd ever heard before.

Her sounds, that can only be described as some kind of plea or cry for help, still reverberate in my mind. The scariest feeling unfurls in my chest, finger-like tentacles grip my spine, and I've been unable to shake this bloodcurdling sensation ever since.

Legs like lead balls fired from a cannon, she knocks the guy back onto his ass while chanting Griffin over and over again. Her body moves are quick and jerky, as if convulsing. It takes two men to get a hold of her.

A familiar burn of fear spreads like a brush fire through me. Uncontrollable and fierce. Incinerating my insides while I sob, pleading with them to help her. I'm next. The mask is pulled over my face. Everything goes black.

I brace myself, afraid I'll react the same way she did, but I don't. It's terrifying to not be able to see but her freak-out was something else, maybe a fear of the dark? Or… I don't know. But whatever it was, it was chilling.

Tate's whimpering is all I hear; she must be muzzled, over and above everything else, as we are shuffled out of the van. Riff's close by, swearing and demanding they let us go. Both Tate and me, and he's nothing but protective. There's no doubt he's as much a victim as we are.

Once inside a large, empty room in what looks to be a warehouse, our masks are removed and we're placed in various spots, not at all close to each other. After Tate's outburst, Riff and I are also gagged. Satisfied we can't get away, the men step into a room off to one side and shut a door behind them.

For hours, I'm huddled in a corner, trembling. I share troubled looks with Riff; we have no other way of communicating and Tate's in no state to understand.

The waiting, not knowing what they'll do to us, is the worst. At some point, Riff is hauled away, taken into the room. Panic, like a tsunami, sweeps over me. I fear this is it and whatever they're going to do to us has begun.

Holding my breath, I hate to admit it, but I anticipate a gunshot. Shoulders tight, chest constricted, tears prick at the back of my eyes and I wait. And wait. Nothing happens.

I can't hear anything. Not even the slightest hint of Riff's voice, or any voice for that matter.

An hour, maybe more and he's brought back in, looking unharmed. The guy with him has a bottle of water in one hand.

Surprised it's even possible, paltry traces of saliva gather in the recesses of my arid mouth as Riff's the first to get a few sips. Then the man strides over to me.

The gag is ripped from my mouth and I stifle a painful cry, my lips dry and near bleeding. The plastic rim presses into my bottom lip, cutting, and cool liquid hits my scorched throat.

Heaven. And hell. It dampens and then burns my throat, all in the same swallow. Greedily, I try to wrap my lips around the opening of the bottle, to gulp a few more measly drops of the lifesaving water.

But the offering is over before it even begins. Barely three sips and he's gone. Precious drops trickle down my chin and onto my shirt as he marches over to Tate.

I weep, no tears coming, at the loss but also grateful he didn't resecure the gag. Sitting quietly, I rest my head against the wall as the warehouse is plunged into darkness.

A shaving of light glows from the base of the closed door and at times, dark shadows cut through the beam, showing movement from behind the barrier.

And now it's daylight and we haven't seen a single soul.

"You okay?" Riff's voice is a raspy croak.

His one eye is red-rimmed and puffy. Dried blood is caked on his forehead from the scuffle in the office when we were abducted.

"Yes." The single word is glass cutting up my throat and tongue. "What did you find out?" I try to move my stiff neck, dipping my chin toward the room where the men were last seen entering.

"Taya's behind this. She wants Tripp or Ry or anyone at HC to work their connections with the Feds or NYPD to give her a break—"

A sharp sound like furniture moving comes from the room and Riff stops talking. My muscles tense and I dare not look in the direction of the door.

When a few minutes pass without sound or movement, I whisper, "What do they want with us?"

"They're going to kill us." Tate's voice is a hushed whisper but flat. She isn't looking at either of us, just staring straight ahead. "This is just like when Griffin and I were kidnapped in Chicago."

I stiffen, heart leaping into my throat. From the very little that Patrick told me, Griffin was beaten within an inch of his life. Tate witnessed it and thought he had died.

That's why she's a mess.

It all fits and my heart breaks for her. I can't even imagine what she's going through. I'm a wreck, scared and panicked, and she's got to be a hundred times more so.

"Fuck." Tiny bursts from the room, eyes narrowed and lethal.

He's headed for Riff while the two other guys scurry after him, looking almost scared.

Boom. Crackle. An explosion rocks the foundation and walls.

I scream, shoulders folding into my body, protecting myself from whatever this is. As I turn my head to tuck it into the wall, away from the blast, I catch sight of Tiny stumbling, falling to his knees.

The two other guys are grabbed from behind and lifted clear off the ground. They shout and fight, but it's useless.

Large dark figures, covered in black gear from head to toe, invade the warehouse. Helmets, goggles and guns the size of my full-length arm. These creatures look like storm troopers and everything is happening so fast. Coming at me faster than the speed of light, it's hard to tell if they are here to help or harm.

TRIPP

Stay put my ass.

Ry and I rush into the warehouse where Mia, Griffin and Tate are being held. The SWAT team leader and the commander of this operation shouts into our earpieces.

"Get your fucking asses back here!"

I ignore the order, sliding in behind those lined against the wall. There is no chance in hell I'm sitting this out. My family is inside that building.

An explosion blasts open the large warehouse doors and the team charges into the building.

In those brief albeit agonizing minutes, I rush in behind them, scanning for danger, mainly concerned with finding Mia and Griffin. Alive.

Ry rushes to Tate and I'm briefly distracted, taking in his wife who is bound and sobbing, strange guttural cries muffled by the dirty rag in her mouth. Chilled to the bone, I stare, shocked and scared to even fucking even consider what happened to her.

Riff is being hauled to his feet and one of the SWAT team is removing his binds. My gaze collides with Mia's and a gleam of happiness—or maybe that's what I want to see—flickers to life in her troubled eyes.

She's in one piece; another team member is at her back, snipping a cable from around her wrists. My feet carry me to her, running or flying I don't know. I'm consumed with Mia. I need her in my arms.

Like magnets, our bodies attract, and she leaps at me. Our chests hit, her legs curl around my waist and my arms and hands grip, squeeze, crush her to me.

A rush of relief slams into my body. Air floods my lungs and lightens my brain. I can breathe again.

"Patrick." I feel her moan, my name on her lips, seeping into my neck and echoing through my chest. "I thought I'd never see you again."

I press my lips to the curve of her ear. Feel her, all of her, needing this to be real. She is safe. Mia is in my arms and all the pieces, once razor-sharp, strange and disparate, slide into place. All is right with the world. I only ever feel like this with her.

"Are you okay?" I pull back a few inches, gazing down at her.

My hand traces the sides of her face, searching for any sign of injury. She looks like she's been through a tornado. Mussed hair and face streaked with makeup are the telltale signs that she was crying. Is she hurt?

"I'm fine. They didn't hurt me. They tied us up." Tears spring to her eyes. "They had guns."

One of the SWAT team taps me on the shoulder, ushering us to leave the building. They need to clear the area and start gathering evidence and details of the abduction.

"You can put me down," Mia murmurs into the crook of my shoulder, voice shaky.

No fucking way.

"Not a chance. Even if you don't need it and feel good enough to walk, I need this." The gruff rumble of my voice reflects just how exposed and shaken I still am even with Mia in my hold.

My hands dig into her hips and the underside of her ass, needing her solid flesh and muscle to ground me. She presses her face into my neck, and I feel the hint of her smile against my skin, bringing one to my face.

Now in the midst of the organized chaos of NYPD, Mia wriggles in my grasp and her feet find purchase on the ground.

She searches, stopping once she sees Griffin being led to the ambulance.

"Is he hurt?" I ask, now focusing my concern to my brother.

"There was some fighting when they took us from the office and he has a cut on his face." She peers up at me. "Can we go check on him?"

I nod, swallowing my relief. We stay back and let the EMT do her job. Fatigue lines Griffin's face and his unreadable eyes watch us.

There is a slight cut above his left eye, which is cleaned and then the attendant places a steri-strip over the wound to hold the skin together. She gives him the all-clear and he hops from the back of the vehicle.

The tiny lines around his mouth are taut as he nears us, staring at me. We're both assessing. I want to tell him I'm glad he's fine but worry that may only tick him off. I've lost the ability to reach him.

But I am happy as fuck he's okay.

There was a time, before his supposed death, when he would listen to me. He respected and looked up to me. Those days are over, and I doubt we'll ever get back there.

"Are you okay?" Mia touches around the white strips on his forehead.

"Yeah. I'm fine. No stitches." He gives me a tight-lipped smile. "Tripp, I'm sorry. Had I known Mia would be in danger hanging out with me, I would have stayed clear."

A strange warming stirs at the base of my spine, surprised at the apology, giving me hope that maybe things aren't as estranged or lost as I thought.

"You were both in danger and I don't think any of us saw it coming. We missed it."

She wraps both arms around my waist and rests her forehead against my chest. "None of you are to blame."

Griff is the first to chuckle, shaking his head. "Yeah. You're right. You okay?" He squeezes her hand and she nods. "And Tate?"

I peer over to where she clings to Ry and his expression is grim. Mia sighs. "I think what happened tonight was hardest for her."

My blood turns to ice and I stiffen. "How so?"

"They left us alone in a room for most of the time. We were bound and had masks over our heads for some of it. Tate flipped."

Masks. Tied up. A warehouse. The similarities to her kidnapping in Chicago ten years ago are starkly apparent.

"Shit."

"She, ah, kept saying 'Griffin.'" He's uncomfortable, rubbing a hand at the back of his neck and avoiding eye contact. Does he remember his abduction with Tate? Or what?

My knees weaken, only now realizing the full magnitude of what that would have done to Tate, and hope that maybe my brother remembers.

"Do you remember?"

His sharp gaze is brief and at first, I fear he's going to yell that he isn't Griffin, but he doesn't. I'm surprised.

"No. But Tate… she was torn up. I can't imagine what she endured the first time and then…" Smashing his lips together, he stares at the couple, clinging to each other.

His features are tight and concerned, but there's no sign of recognition.

There will never be.

He will never remember his past, his life before the day they kidnapped him. And while I've accepted that logically, I realize on some level I've been holding out, hoping for him to prove the doctors and specialists wrong.

I've been expecting him to remember.

Ry looks over, motioning they are leaving, at the same time we're asked to come into the police station to give our statements. Tate isn't in any condition to do so now and will try tomorrow.

Mia and Griffin ride with me and many hours later we're finally given the all-clear to leave.

"I can give you a lift to your place," I say to my brother on the way out of the building.

"Sure, thanks."

I was lucky enough to sit in on Mia's statement and she mentioned he'd been taken into a room. While he's agreed to a debrief in the morning at HC, I want to know now.

"Hey, Mia mentioned you were with Taya's men for a while. What did they say or do?" I glance at him through the rear-view mirror.

"Basically, they wanted to make sure I understood I'd never be free of Taya. She was going to get out and hunt me down so if I thought I could run, I should think again." He's monotone and I wonder if he believes her threat or sees that she was trying to scare him.

"How was she going to be free?"

I don't understand her logic. The case against her is solid. A really good lawyer could shave some years off her sentence, but her chances of walking away free are non-existent.

"That's what this kidnapping was about. She wanted to force you or Ry to work your connections with the Feds or cops. She was looking for a moment of freedom. Sure, she'd love a pardon or reduced sentence, but she would have settled for bail."

I'm puzzled and spare another glance at him as I turn down his street. "All of this for bail?"

It didn't make sense when now they'd be adding kidnapping and a number of additional crimes to the charges against her.

"She was planning an escape. I told the police the pieces I picked up from Tiny while in that room. That guy doesn't know how to keep his mouth shut."

"She is something else," I mutter, shaking my head and stopping the car in front of his building. "You going to be okay?"

He opens the door, puts one foot on the street and glances back at me. "Yeah. Thanks. And Mia." He places a hand on her shoulder, expression solemn. "I'm sorry and so glad you and Tate are okay."

Mia grabs at his hand, patting it. "I'm glad we're all okay. We'll see you in the morning."

"Yeah. I'll call you."

He shuts the door and we sit in silence, watching him saunter up to the front of his building where he stops to pull out a cigarette. He waves at us to go and we drive away.

"Aren't you taking me home?" She peers out the window onto the street, nowhere near her place.

"I thought we'd go back to my place. If that's okay with you?" My heart lurches in anticipation. What if she wants me to take her home? Alone.

I'll respect her wishes, but she'll be in for a surprise because I won't be going anywhere. I'll camp outside her door. She may be safe but I can't or won't go far.

"Oh, sure." She gives me a sideways glance. "How did you know something was wrong? That they had taken us?"

"I went to talk to you. To apologize."

I park the car outside my house and turn to stare at her. She's bathed in moonlight and her gaze is uncertain.

"Mia, I'm sorry for leaving like I did. I should have asked for time and not said goodbye." Leaning over, I angle her jaw, leading her mouth to mine and lightly brush my lips against hers. "I could never say goodbye to you."

Her eyes flutter closed on a shuddering breath. "Really? I feel the same way. My biggest regret, even more than getting on that plane to Portland, is leaving you that morning back in college."

A watery smile floats across her face and I press my lips to hers once more. "You do know that even if you didn't go to Portland, things might still be the same?"

She nods, a tear dropping onto her cheek, and I wipe it away with my thumb. "I've played the *what if* game with myself, and what happened to Lucy might have… no, *would* have still happened had I been there. Em always picked her up, and that was her route home. My being in LA wouldn't change that. It wouldn't have prevented the accident that took their lives."

Something shifts inside me; the tight fist lodged in my chest starts to crumble, now comforted to hear she no longer carries that guilt.

"Don't you wonder why life can be so cruel?" My voice cracks and I pull back, part awkward and part irritated at myself.

"Sometimes. But there isn't anything we can do about it. All we can do is try to build a beautiful life. One where we can be happy and proud of what we've created."

Her hand rubs against the stubble on my jaw, her tender, innocent touch magnifying the truth of her words.

I lightly kiss the inside of her palm, the sweet taste of her warming my insides.

We hop out of the car and I take her hand in mine as we enter the house, heading to my room. I don't have any expectations. I only want her near me. We have a lot to talk about and I'm unsure if we should do it now or tomorrow. She's been through a lot.

Mia readies for bed, stepping from the bathroom in an old sweatshirt of mine. It's like a dress on her, hanging down to her knees.

The sight of her sweetheart face, rosy cheeks, button nose and lush mouth command my attention.

A magnet, modest and sultry at the same time, delicate curves and gentle lines, and I want nothing more than to have her in my arms.

She hesitates at the doorway. Almost as if uncertain if she will stay.

"What's wrong?" The urge to stride over to her is fierce but I linger at the side of the bed, not wanting to spook her.

"Nothing. It's hard to believe we're here, like this." She motions between us, together. "Just yesterday, I thought we were over and that I'd have to force you to see reason. To give us a chance."

"Force me?"

Her smile is so small I'd barely call it that. A disquiet unfurls in my belly and I will myself to stay positive, let her talk, and to not let the darkness take root. My stubborn heart loves her, always has, and can't bear to lose her.

And no matter what she has to say, I won't lose her. This is Mia. We belong together.

MIA

"I thought I'd lost you. For so long you were this dream, one that I'll admit I thought was so silly that I almost gave up on it. On you. And then when we found each other here, I didn't realize at the time, but more than telling you about Lucy, I was afraid to have my dream come true. It felt like I didn't deserve it."

"Oh, Mia, you deserve to have your dream come true." He takes a step, still several feet from me and then stops himself, releasing a low, frustrated sound from deep in his throat. "Come here. You're driving me crazy being all the way over there."

His need for me lightens the growing heaviness in my chest and I give him a lopsided grin. "Come and get me."

A grin stretches across his handsome face and he's on me before I can even take another breath. He sweeps me into his arms, depositing me onto the mattress, still in his embrace.

I laugh, throwing my head back onto the pillow as his lips roam the column of my neck. He lifts his head to stare down at me and his smile widens.

I barely remember a time when he smiled without restraint. It's a beautiful thing.

My fingers trace the upward curve of his warm lips. "I love your smile. You should do it more often."

"You make me smile." He kisses the pads of my fingers before playfully nipping at them. "Continue. Now that I have you here, I think I can handle whatever it is you have to say."

I study him, only now realizing he didn't know what to make of my words. They worried him.

"It isn't bad. You ended things and at first, I accepted it even though I hated it. But eventually, I realized I couldn't leave it like that."

I pause, unsure if I'll be able to explain myself when most of my actions until now have been about stalling my emotions, running from them.

"Riff and I had been spending a lot of time together and through our talks about what he was dealing with, I realized I'd been running from Lucy, or running from how to feel or deal with life after Lucy."

He pushes up onto his elbow, resting his head in his hand, still peering down at me. His ocean blue eyes are alert, memorizing every word, pause or breath I take.

"I didn't know how to do life after her, how to find and accept joy and love without her. I was stuck."

The heavy suffocation of grief and loss still lingers, pressing on my heart. And maybe it always will but I've got to learn a better way to deal with it.

"It felt wrong and the thought of staying put and making a life without her was unbearable. And that's why I didn't commit to staying here. And I could be wrong but I also think that's what you were doing."

I had years to come to this conclusion, and at times I was so blind, it's surprising I'm even here. I've got to remember this. Patrick and I are in different places in the life-long journey of loss.

"What?" His shoulders tense and features harden ever so slightly.

"After all the loss you've experienced—your mom's death, your dad and then Griffin—you shied away from any kind of joy, anything good, and I guess learning of Lucy only reinforced that.

"But life comes with loss. You can't have one without the other.

And you can't turn your back on all the good because you're afraid to hurt, to lose. You have too much to give and so much to gain."

I push up to plant a light kiss on the hardest, stiffest part of his jaw and then his chin before dropping back onto the bed.

"That's not who you are. That's not who I am. I was doing the same thing. When you came back into my life, leaving New York and losing Lucy were excuses I told myself as to why we couldn't pursue anything."

"I believe you were a gift from Lucy to me." I cup his jaw and kiss him. "We're a gift to each other from her. And I will not turn my back on that, on us."

His gaze softens, filling with tenderness. "Me neither."

His hand sinks into my hair at the back of my head and he slams his mouth on mine. We kiss greedily and he drives his tongue into my mouth, deepening our kiss, desperately seeking more of me as if trying to get closer, deeper, inside of me.

I open my body and heart to him, understanding the insatiable need to be one.

"Mia, I love you." His voice is a deep rumble. "No one has ever meant as much to me as you do. I was a fool to even think of saying goodbye. You're everything to me, Mia. Everything."

My world is turned upside down and righted all at once, sending me tumbling and falling with his admission. I never thought it possible to fall even more in love with this man.

From the moment we met, our connection had been substantial. Fierce. Inexplicable. And like now, always complete.

Patrick rolls us until I'm fully on my back and he hovers over me. A hand slides down my body, under his sweatshirt. Fingertips sweep across the skin above my panties, dipping below the waistband.

One touch and my head thrusts back onto the pillow. A hauntingly erotic moan fires from my lips and I spread my legs. My fingers weave into his soft hair and his mouth scorches a trail from my lips to my collarbone.

His rapidly hardening cock swells between my legs and with one hand, I pull at his boxer briefs and he helps to remove them. Lining up with my entrance, he runs his swollen crown through my slick folds from top to bottom and then plunges inside of me.

Moaning, he fills me. The power of him drums through me and I grab at his face, yanking him in for another blistering kiss. One hand clutches my throat, the other gripping the back of my head.

We're face to face and the way he looks at me, his expressive blue eyes bore into me, whispering secrets from his soul. I'm all he needs, and his abandon is my undoing.

"I love you." My lips move against his, breathing my love into his lungs.

"Fuck, Mia." His weight presses into me, grounding me and setting me on fire.

Butterflies beat in my belly; my thighs clench and my body shakes and shivers.

His love is a raw and frantic thing, like a wild animal imprisoned and wasting away with no food, water, or light. I feel it in the frenetic pace of his hips as they swivel and thrust into me.

With every stroke, he's desperate to bury himself deeper in me, fill me with all of him, take all from me. I'm drunk on him.

My body tenses, and every part of him is hard as steel. He roars, throwing his head back, and his name tumbles from my lips as he comes. I'm right behind him, core clenching, legs trembling as pleasure seizes and devastates me.

We lay silent and sated, tangled in the sheets until he moves to turn off the light on my side of the bed.

A crooked smile flirts with his lips and warmth surges through me at his happiness. At how happy he makes me.

"Mia, you're it for me." His lips ghost over my jaw past my lips, teasing me, and he pulls back.

"And you for me." I capture his lips.

The kiss is rough and sweet, so much like him. His exterior is rugged, demeanor rough-and-ready while on the inside, his heart is huge, protective, tender and loyal.

He flicks the light off on his side, and exhausted, I fall into a deep sleep, waking to Patrick staring down at me with the hint of a grin. He's fully dressed and looking like he's been up for a while.

"Morning." His voice is deep and gravelly.

"Morning. What time is it?"

"Ten. Time to get up. Van wants us at HC for noon."

"Okay. I need a shower."

"Everything is in the bathroom. Make yourself at home." He rolls off the bed, glancing over his shoulder at me.

"I need clothes." I peer down at my naked body and the thought of wearing yesterday's outfit, even with no other choice, isn't appealing.

"Already taken care of. I went by your place this morning."

I push up to sitting, bringing the sheet with me "You did? How did you get in?"

"Your keys." He points to them on the side table. "There's also breakfast and coffee downstairs. Come on down when you're ready."

He leans across the bed and steals a kiss before leaving. As I shower and dress, I dread reliving the whole kidnapping ordeal all over again.

Last night was wonderful and just what I needed. Not a distraction in that it was insignificant, but more something to blanket any nightmares and heal the scars from that horrible night in the warehouse.

Venturing into the kitchen, I find Patrick sitting at the breakfast bar, sipping coffee and doing something on his laptop.

I pick at my food and I'm restless and fidgety during the trip to HC. Not missing a thing, Patrick grabs my hand as we ride up in the elevator.

"We won't be long. We'll try to make this quick and painless. Your statement last night is what matters."

I nod, swallowing past my nerves and grateful for his presence and support. Riff shows up, and he's cooperative but quiet and uneasy like me. Tate isn't there but Ry is, and he shares details from her perspective.

Tate came by the office to talk about Patrick. From the little he had shared with her, she could tell things weren't going so well between us and she wanted to help.

I couldn't take on the guilt of her being there even if I wish she could have been spared the kidnapping. Ry was confident that the more time she had with her boys and his mother, she'd be okay.

The team then shifts their focus to Taya and how best to ensure she never does something like this again. They get an FBI agent and NYPD on speakerphone and I feel like I'm crawling out of my skin.

Patrick senses my growing agitation and without a word, we leave, going to his place where we are holed up for the next two days. Spending time with him is just what I need to move past the kidnapping. I have a ton of work and things to do to get ready for Eli's arrival, but for now, the world can wait.

We need this time alone to talk. He has more questions about Lucy and I'm happy to answer them all. He also shows me his new leather bracelet. It brings tears to my eyes.

"I don't know why I didn't think of this. It's perfect." My finger runs over the worn leather, now entwined with Lucy's thinner leather and twine.

"I feel like I have a part of her with me at all times." He clears his throat, pushing his lunch plate to the side, and looks down at his wrist. "If you're okay with it, I'd like to go with you to LA some time and see her grave. Do things she did."

"Ah, I scattered her ashes in the Pacific." Regret jerks at my heart for something else he missed out on. "I wanted to do the same with Emily, but my parents wanted her ashes. So I've got a stuffed dolphin and small turtle at home with some of their ashes. The Dolphin is Lucy and the turtle is Em. They are on my bed. I'm not sure why I didn't say something sooner, other than we've had a lot going on."

He nods, casting a glance to the side. "It's okay. I remember seeing them in your room. I'd still like to go sometime, and we could also go to Michigan, if you want. If there's some place to visit or be close to Emily."

"I'd like that."

"I was, ah, I was in LA when she must have been two. Undercover. I was on a case for almost a year with the FBI."

I drag in a ragged breath, not knowing if that news would have been better unknown. There were a few missed moments when maybe, if we'd done something differently, chosen a different path, maybe things would have brought us together sooner.

It's just plain torture contemplating those kinds of things and I shake my head, knocking the thoughts from my mind. They do neither of us any good.

"Sorry, I should learn to keep my mouth shut." He stands, taking both our plates.

"No, it's okay. We're here now, together."

He bends, lightly kissing the top of my head and then saunters toward the kitchen. My phone pings beside me. It's a text.

Riff: Max has the results. He wants me to drop by his office. Can you come with?

Me: Sure. How's thirty minutes or so?

Riff: Perf. Thanks.

I head toward the kitchen to let Patrick know I'll be going out when my phone pings again in my hand.

Riff: Don't tell Tripp.

Me: I won't lie to him but I won't break your confidence.

Riff: Cool.

When I enter the room, he's on the phone and it sounds like business. I finish cleaning up our lunch dishes and wait for him to end his call.

"That was Ry." He shoves his phone in the pocket of his jeans. "I have to go in for a bit."

"Okay. Looks like the world has come a-knocking." I step up to him and he grips me around the waist and bends his head closer to mine.

The force of his kiss sends me stumbling and I'm grateful for his firm hold. Our tongues war and I fist his shirt, uncertain if I want to pull him closer or push him away.

Maybe we could forget about Ry and Riff for just a little longer, forget about the world and its demands?

But common sense wins out when he breaks our kiss. "I'll be back in a few hours. I'll bring dinner."

"Okay." My hands clasp together behind his neck. "I'm going out with Riff for a bit."

At the mention of the man he thinks is his brother, he stiffens, and his lips press into a thin white line.

For the past few days, he hasn't asked about Riff or even ventured close to the topic. I imagine he's curious about the time I've spent with Riff. I would be if I were in his shoes, but it's as if the mention of his brother is a no-go zone.

Save for the debrief at HC, he hasn't even talked about Tate's traumatizing experience—her flashback of Griffin's beating—when Taya's men kidnapped us. I can't help but feel it's deliberate, his avoidance of all things related to his brother, and I'm not sure why.

Perhaps he's given up? No longer going to push the issue with Riff? I don't want to be the one to open that wound but like I told Riff, I won't lie to him. Not about my whereabouts.

"Everything okay?" he asks.

"Yes. It's fine."

With a peck on the lips, I grab my purse and jacket, hailing a cab to the hospital. Riff's waiting for me outside Max's office. He fit us in between appointments so the meeting is quick and to the point.

Before we leave, Max reminds us that this information is confidential and not even Tommie will know the results. This is Riff's news to do with as he pleases.

Outside the hospital, we stand shoulder to shoulder at the curb. There is so much I want to say or ask, but like Max said, this is about Riff. I'm keeping my mouth shut and waiting for his lead. He rubs at the back of his neck, glancing at me sideways.

"Fuck. Will you come with me to tell Tripp, Ry and Van?" He swallows hard, his eyes searching mine.

"Sure. When do you want to do it?"

"Now." He pulls out his phone. "I suppose I should make sure Carys and Tate are there too. They all deserve to know. I'll text Tripp and ask him to round up everyone."

"Are you okay?"

"Yeah. I don't know what I expected... nah, that isn't true." He pauses mid-text to look at me. "I'd hoped it would give me answers but all I have are more questions."

His attention is back on his phone, thumbs glide along the screen, and I nod, understanding the unearthing of more questions but not fully appreciating how he must feel.

"I hope this doesn't sound condescending."

"What?" He raises his head, brows knitted.

"I'm proud of you. This can't be easy and yet you're facing it head-on. You could have just as easily delayed or shied away from even talking to Patrick and the others."

He opens his mouth to speak, so I pause, and then he presses his lips together.

"You're being responsible. Even if you didn't ask to be in this situation, you're dealing with it amazingly well."

Now he barks out a harsh laugh and shakes his head. "I'm fucking bluffing. Good to know I'm doing a superb job."

I can relate and give him a small smile. "Whatever it is, I'm proud of you."

When we arrive at HC, everyone is there and all of them look equally anxious in their own way. Riff didn't share the reason for this gathering when he contacted Patrick.

"Hey, what's going on? Everything okay?" Van asks.

Riff nods, easing into a chair, and I edge closer to Patrick, resting my hand on his forearm. He's tense, arms crossed over his chest and gaze firm on Riff. He spares me a fleeting glance. His eyes are tender, happy to see me, and the corners of his mouth tip up.

"I had a DNA test done and the results are in." Riff's gaze lands on me and carries a glint of gratitude. "Actually, Mia was the one to suggest it, and I contacted Max to do the test. She's been a big help."

Patrick sucks air through his teeth, stiffening some more at my side. His eyes are fixed on Riff for a few beats before he tears his stare away, dipping down to look at me.

"Thank you," he murmurs, removing my hand from his body to drape his arm around me.

"What are the results?" Ry flexes his fingers on top of Tate's shoulders.

She's sitting and he stands protectively like a guard behind her. She tips her head back and they share a look.

Riff swallows hard. "I'm Griffin Townsend."

There's a collective release of their pent-up breath as if injecting life or change into the room. Carys is the first to move, bolting to him and stopping before it's too late, before she throws herself at him.

She reads him well. His posture is rigid, almost as if this news changes nothing. Does he still want nothing to do with them?

Her hands tremble and she raises them to cover her mouth. Silent tears slide down her cheeks. I think they are tears of joy. Her eyes shine and lips quiver upward into a watery smile.

"Griffin." She tries his name on for size, perhaps uttering it toward him, a living person, for the first time in years.

He shifts in the chair, keeping his nervous gaze on her and then thinks better of staying seated and he stands.

"I know I've been intolerable since you came… since meeting you. Even before knowing for sure if you were him, I reached out to you way too many times."

He scoffs, nodding in agreement, now leaning his butt against the table, and relaxing his stance somewhat.

"No excuses, my excitement and hope aside, you should have the time and room to figure this all out. I am sorry and I just wanted you to know that."

She shakes out her limbs, looking like a jittery toy before settling once more to stare up at him. "I'm happy about this news, as I'm sure you can see. But I am backing off, giving you space. I'm here to talk, if you have questions. Anything really. I'm here but I won't crowd you."

Her fingers interlace in front of her and she drops her eyes to the floor for a beat and in a blink, Van is at her side. His smile is slight, tight even, directed at Griffin as he wraps an arm around her.

"Me too. This is good news for us but we realize it may not be for you. We'll give you what you need."

He nods, clearing his throat. "Okay. Thanks."

"This might be out of line but I have to ask..." Carys trails off, looking back to Van and then Riff. "Can I hug you?"

Riff shuffles from one foot to the other, an awkward heaviness sliding over him. Then his eyes flick to me, as if searching for some support. A lifeline. And there's a strange pull in my stomach.

I can't possibly comprehend what he's feeling or experiencing yet I want to be there for him. Help him as best as I can.

"Hey, Carys." I stay at Patrick's side, in his arms, needing his support. "It might be best for everyone, if we..."

I hesitate. The hope in her open and gentle expression nearly undoes me. How can I shoot her down when she's hurting, missing her childhood friend and yet he's right in front of her?

"We should all take some time to sit with this," Patrick says, folding me tighter into his firm body.

Neither of us knows what Riff wants but can sense this, all of us here, might be too much. And I don't even know what this news means to him. We didn't talk on the way over.

He was deep in thought and I didn't want to push. Does knowing he's Griffin mean he'll stick around? Does he want a relationship with these people, or is he still going to leave the city?

Riff's uncertain gaze tracks the room, falling on each of us for a beat or two. All of them look on, eagerly staring at him, as if he's Santa Claus, and they're young children waiting for their turn. For him to make their wishes come true.

TRIPP

Griffin isn't angry nor is he pleased. It isn't clear if knowing who he is gives him a better sense of inner peace or if it only screws with him some more.

There's definitely an unease about him that hasn't disappeared. In fact, it's more front and center and it's understandable given the circumstance.

Carys nods and takes the cue to leave, giving me a hopeful grin on the way out. Van is right behind her. Ry and Tate have been silent, keeping their thoughts to themselves, yet they follow suit.

Then it's just the three of us. Mia breaks from my hold. "I'll leave you two alone to talk. See you back at your place?"

"Yeah." I tug her slender form against me, needing her breath, her scent. Needing her near me.

She glances up at me, pushing a stray strand of hair behind her ear. "You okay?"

We share a silent word and my lips brush against hers once before we break apart. She peers over her shoulder at Griffin. His expression is blank, and it isn't clear if this is part of a plan.

Did they talk about this on the way over? Giving us some time to talk? Or is she springing her exit on him right now?

"If you want to wait…" I trail off as she turns to look at me once more.

"No. Take your time." She pushes onto the tips of her toes and kisses the corner of my mouth.

Unable to resist, my tongue delves into her mouth, my lips capturing hers, and I take from her. I drink in her breath and inhale her subtle flowery fragrance.

My hand tightens on her waist and I shut my eyes, letting her breath fill me, give me her strength, calm and light.

Mia is what I need. Only Mia.

My brother being alive is a miracle and I couldn't be more ecstatic but I realize this may change nothing with this man. Brother. Family. These are words to him, maybe without meaning. Words he doesn't want to explore. Bonds he doesn't want to forge.

But Mia.

She's in my life again. The only person to center me, bring me peace and fill me with abiding love. And most of all, abolish any fear.

"I'm madly in love with you." My confession is a whisper for only her to hear but those words on my lips are freeing. Powerful.

She sinks further into me, saying back to me, "I've always loved you."

We break our embrace and her smile is bright and blinding, only for me. Then she turns, strolling over to Griffin and taking both his hands in hers.

She's the only one able to touch him freely. The only one he has accepted and let in. "Call me or text. Okay?"

"Yeah." His gaze dips to the floor and then back to her again. "And Mia, thanks for everything."

"Absolutely." With one last squeeze of his fingers, she walks out the door and we stare after her.

Silence consumes the air in the room, and I want to start the conversation. But I don't. I wait and fight to keep air pushing through my lungs. He cared enough to share the news with us, and I will respect that. This is his call. His news and his life.

Griffin is alive.

It's both surreal and expected. From that day on the streets with Tate, when we both saw him for the first time, something clicked inside of me.

Despite his vacant eyes, I could *see* my brother. Somewhere deep inside of him, almost forgotten. And I may never have my brother again—no, I will never have him as I knew him—but that isn't the point. It isn't what matters.

He is breathing. Alive. He will chart a path and be his own person, that's all I've ever wanted for him.

"I don't know what this means," he finally says, stalking past me to the window.

His back now to me, he stares out onto the city and I clear my throat, fighting to stay fixed to my spot.

"What do you mean?"

"I wasn't sure what I wanted the outcome to be." He turns, his back now on the glass. "Either way, I'm still fucking lost. I still don't *know* who I am."

He shoves his hands into his pockets and stares at me. Lost and vulnerable.

"Well, if it helps, I've already got what I wanted." I'm trying to lessen his burden. No expectations on him.

His brow knits and his gaze narrows, puzzled. "What does that mean?"

"We've had these expectations of you… I'm sure you felt it. And none of us meant any harm. I doubt we stopped to think how difficult it might have been for you. To have these strangers look at you with a hunger and need you couldn't possibly satisfy."

He pushes from the window, straightening and nodding. It's a subtle shift but his features and body open to me. More accepting of my words as he gifts me his undivided attention. Not a scowl or glare in sight.

"When I first realized you could be my brother, I'll admit… I wanted it all. I wanted every fucking bit of you back. Griffin, with the same look, the same childhood memories, the same friendship." I pause, swallowing past the grief-filled lump lodged in my throat.

"But it didn't take too long to realize he was no longer here. My Griffin. The guy I grew up with, helped raise... my best friend was dead."

Our matching eyes lock and we share a moment of understanding. It's brief and maybe I'm wishing it but I can't deny I feel the connection.

We share a loss.

His is for someone he'll never fully remember or know—a part of him lost forever—and mine is for someone I'll never see again.

"And then I only hoped to have Griffin alive. I wanted him healthy, breathing and strong. But alive was all I wanted. I wanted you to be him for that very reason. And I have what I want. There isn't anything else I will ask of you."

"Really?" His tone is disbelieving.

"Really." I rake a hand through my hair. "Sure, I'd like for us to get to know each other and maybe even have some kind of relationship. A friendship even, but I will not push. All of that is up to you."

He exhales a lengthy breath. "I have to admit. I kind of shut down when you and Tate told me about Griffin. I rejected it and wasn't willing to listen."

His expression is almost pleading, and I ask, "And now you are?"

"Yeah. I've got questions. A lot." He pushes off the glass, striding toward me and stopping short by a foot or two.

"Ask." My hands are open to my sides.

"Not right now. I've got to mull this over, but I will. We got off on the wrong foot and that's on me."

"Nah. I came in hot and heavy. I'm used to taking charge."

He chuckles and a wry grin creeps across his mouth. "No, really?"

His sarcasm pries a smile from me. "You don't need to be an ass about it."

"What can I say? I must take after you that way."

"Yeah." I'm bold and reach out to ruffle his hair. He lets me, stiffening a bit before relaxing.

"Listen, I can't promise anything. To any of you. But I want to know more about Griffin and this family."

"Cool." I attempt to come off calm while my hope explodes in my chest. This is all I've ever wanted—his willingness to want to know about Griff and have a relationship with me. "All of us will help. We want to, and I only ask that you go easy on them. Be up front with them. They'll understand that you're trying to navigate this, and we'll follow your lead."

"I can do that." He glances at the door and back to me. "I'm going to go now."

"Okay. Reach out when ready."

"'Kay."

On the drive home to Mia, my thoughts are focused on what comes next. It means more waiting, with Griffin in the driver's seat, and I'm fine with that.

But not with Mia. We've wasted too much time already and I don't want to wait a second longer.

I find her in the kitchen when I arrive. Something is cooking on the stove and she's sitting at the breakfast bar, sipping a glass of wine and reading what looks to be one of her long-ass contracts.

"Hello." I brush her hair to the side, kissing the sweet flesh of her nape.

"Hey." She shivers, dropping the papers and spinning to face me.

She widens her legs, inviting me to step in between her thighs, to get as close as possible. Her lips traverse the underside of my stubbled jaw and her warm tongue licks at what is likely salty skin.

"How'd it go?" Her fingers glide along my jawline and up, to trace my hairline.

"Good. He needs time and I'll wait."

"Okay. But how are you dealing with this? Your brother is alive."

I nod, a faint smile coating my lips. "That's all I ever wanted. If he doesn't want any more with me, I'll deal with it. I'll get by. Not you." I bury my face into her hair and my arms sweep around her back. "You, I want forever."

She laughs, tilting her head back and kissing the side of my face. "I like the sound of that."

"Thank you." Looking at her makes my heart ache, that's how

much I love her. "Thank you for being there for him and helping him decide to take the test. It ultimately helped all of us get the answers we needed."

I'm not so sure we'd have been able to get him to the same spot. We likely would have pushed him away with our desire for him to be our long-lost brother and friend.

"You don't need to thank me. I did it for him. I did it for you."

Mia St. John is a gift to me.

We may have taken a long and, at times, sad and lonely road to find our way to each other, but she's here now, in my arms, and while we have so much still to talk about and work on, there's no way I'm letting her go.

EPILOGUE

MIA

A year later

"Yeah, I'm taking excellent care of them." Patrick's deep throaty chuckle causes my eyes to flutter open. "You'd think you were her brother the way you're grilling me."

I must have dozed off. One hand still braces the tiny back of my baby, lying on my chest. His head is nestled under my chin and the sweet scent of him invades my senses.

A long pause follows the sound of Patrick's voice and footsteps near, climbing the stairs to where I am. Angling my neck from side to side, I stretch the muscles, working out any kinks from what was likely only ten winks, and yawn. Juggling motherhood and my practice keeps me in a constant state of tired.

"Yeah, you are like a brother to her," he says, closer still.

My little peanut stirs, fingers digging into the flesh of my collarbone and wiggling in my grasp. More laughter comes from the hallway, and then he stands in the doorway to the nursery, phone to his ear.

He's beaming from ear to ear, chuckling again and lowering his voice now that he sees our son is slumbering in my arms.

"Listen, I've got her here. I'll talk to you soon." He walks toward me. "Be careful, Griff."

He holds the phone to his chest with a crooked grin, happy to be speaking to his brother, and I can't help but give him one of my own.

"It's Griff. You up to talking?"

His hard-to-earn smiles are a gift from the universe but after these past months together, living with him and building a life, he now smiles easily, and all for me. More and more, and I can't help but feel lucky to have his smiles and his love.

"Yes. Can you take Cal?" I push to stand, and we trade.

Giving me the phone, he carefully lifts our son, Callum Townsend, named after his father and only a month old, from my chest into his arms.

The baby wriggles and moans and his father coos into his ear, bouncing him gently in the cradle of his arm.

I yawn once more, lightly pecking father and son on their respective cheeks. He pulls me close with his free arm, pressing a rough kiss to my temple.

"Hey, Griff, how are you?" I close the door to the nursery, hoping Patrick will get Callum to stay asleep, to nap longer than thirty minutes.

"Good. How's Mama Mia doing?" I can hear the smile in his voice.

"I'm great. Exhausted but not complaining." Entering our bedroom, I grab sweats and a hoodie, wanting a shower. "How are you? Where are you now?"

"Okay. Florida. Just got here."

"Nice. Planning a visit to New York soon?" My question is more a dream.

He came for the birth of our son, and while it was awesome to have him here, it was too short. He was here barely a week before he itched to be on the road again.

"Maybe in a few months. But no promises." As predicted, he doesn't mention Taya's trial.

He isn't looking forward to it, but he's testifying for the prosecution. He wants to, not only because of our kidnapping, but especially since learning more about Griffin's life and the impact of his supposed death from Tate and the others.

And there was also Mark Stevens. The DNA proved it was his body shipped back from Chicago and buried. We gave him a proper reburial before Griff left. Taya's manipulation and lies are hard to deny.

"I know, I know. But don't blame me for asking. As Callum gets older, we will want him to know his Uncle Griffin. We want you to be much more than just a name. You will have to seriously consider putting down roots."

I'm the only one who could get away with making that kind of request. To ask him to put down roots in New York, come back to the family.

"Yeah, and soon. I promise. I'm close."

"Close to what?" We've talked for many hours about his trip around North America.

He's looking for something and I can't say I don't get it. I do. But his journey is nothing like mine.

"To… feeling settled in who I am." He huffs and I can almost see his skeptical expression as if he isn't sure if he buys into this. "I guess."

"That's great. Take all the time you need. We're not pressuring you even if I'd love to have you here in Manhattan."

"I know. Mia, sorry but I gotta go. Love you and keep sending pics of my godson."

"I will. Love you, Griff."

"You too."

I end the call and peek my head back into the nursery on my way to the shower. Patrick's rocking with the baby in his arms, eyes closed. The frame on top of the dresser catches my eyes.

It's a picture of Lucy at Zuma Beach in a bright yellow bathing suit, strawberry blonde hair windblown, smiling with sprinkles of sand on one cheek. My smile is uncontrollable.

Cal will love his older sister and I like to think she's watching over us and already adores her baby brother. Lucy may not be with us physically, but I feel her in spirit every day and everywhere.

Closing the door, I head to the bathroom where I discard my clothes, turning on the shower, letting the water get hot. An easy warmth fills my chest at our conversation.

Shortly after the DNA test, Griffin spent some time getting to know his brother, Van, Carys, Ry and Tate.

He also got to meet Ma, Ry and Carys's mother and a second mother to Griffin and Patrick. They'd chosen not to say anything to her until there was no doubt he was Griffin. He even made friends with Tommie and Max, and along with me, we met Anna and Coop who returned from Italy.

Eli and Griff also bonded over music. While he hasn't played the guitar and says he won't, he talks to Eli often about the new music or bands he comes across on his travels.

But even with all this, he also kept a safe distance, making it clear he wasn't staying in New York City. He needed to find himself, and when he left, he still insisted on being called Riff.

It was only during his last visit for Cal's birth that he asked us to call him Griffin. Patrick was speechless and thrilled. They all were.

Patrick had meant what he said. He was content with having his younger brother alive. That was enough.

But Griffin wanting to be a part of his life. Griffin accepting his past even if he couldn't remember any of it... that was huge.

I stare at my naked image in the mirror, piling my hair on top of my head so it doesn't get wet, and smile. My tummy is still there. Not as big as I was at nine months, but a reminder of my baby boy and that he was inside me not too long ago.

This past year has been everything I'd hoped for. Shortly after the new year, I moved in with Patrick and right after that, I got pregnant.

Some worried I'd wanted marriage and then a family, and others, namely Eli and Tate, that being pregnant would be hard. I didn't care about the order of things. We have a healthy, happy son and are still to be married.

I don't need a document to tell me Patrick is mine and I am his. We'll be together forever.

As for the pregnancy and being a mother again—no, I never lost that honor. Even after Lucy's death, I will always be her mother. The pregnancy was amazing, terrifying, a tumultuous roller coaster of emotions.

And while Lucy was never far from my mind, and I cried for losing my little girl many times, I'd do it all over again.

* * *

TRIPP

Eight months later

THE WAY she looks should be illegal. She's divine. A knockout in the colorful sundress, falling to mid-thigh with barely-there straps resting on her sun-kissed shoulders. She's fucking edible.

My heart stops when her vibrant gaze pins me in place and everything and everyone else fades away. A hint of rose and vanilla wafts through the air, flooding me with a sense of home and peace.

Someone clears their throat behind me. "Ah, Mia, you look gorgeous." Carys steps up to my wife and hugs her.

"Thank you. It feels strange to be dressing up and going out." Mia fusses with her waves.

Carys's eyes widen, and she smacks me playfully on the chest. "Way to go, Tripp. Your wife needs a break more often."

She's making light of the situation, hoping to lessen Mia's anxiety. This is the first night we'll be out all evening, overnight, since Callum was born.

"Yeah." I huff, rubbing at my chest while walking to Mia's side.

"You're gorgeous. You ready?"

She nods, glancing to Carys and then Cal, resting on her hip. He's all gums and smiles, drool coating his chin. The poor guy's teething.

"Yes." Her voice is pensive, and her palm tenderly glides over one of his chubby legs.

I can sense her internal battle. She's trying to resist the compulsion to scoop him into her arms and never let go. She won't say it but she's tempted to call this date night, sleepover, off.

"Okay, let's go."

I'm ripping off the Band-Aid, for her sake as much as mine. We say our goodbyes, Mia more than once, and Carys reassures her they'll be fine. Van and their kids are downstairs in the game room and they're all staying the night.

Cal will have a blast with so many people fawning all over him. Especially the younger people, he loves watching older kids.

Mia wipes at the corner of her eye, biting her bottom lip as she slips into the car.

"You okay?" One foot rests inside the car and the other on the ground. "We can stay if this is too hard."

She shakes her head. "No, I want this. It'll be good for all of us. Let's go."

I get in and drive with one hand, the other clasping hers, hoping to convey it will be okay. Tonight is an enormous step. I get it and I don't.

She was away from Lucy when the worst thing that can happen to your child did. I can sympathize with her, but I don't really know how it feels, nor do I wish to ever.

This evening away was her idea. We had gotten married at the courthouse several months ago now. It had been quick and easy.

We then gathered at the Waters with our friends to celebrate while Ma watched our son, upstairs in her apartment over the bar. But we took him home with us.

Tonight we'll be in a hotel, just us. She's both excited and anxious. I'm nervous too, but mine is more because I've never done this before. I'm a dad now and the urge to love and protect my kid, at all costs, is fierce and constant.

We check into the hotel—our dinner reservations aren't for over an hour—and as we step into our room, I grip her upper arms, swinging her around to press her body up against the door.

Touching her, being this close to her, is electric. Tingles of pleasure shoot down my spine and I suck in a ragged breath. Nearly two years together and a lifetime to go, and nothing gets old with her.

Warm, plump lips latch onto mine and my insides coil with a burning need. My arms land on either side of her head, caging her in, and she deepens our kiss. Tongues tangle and her fingers curl around the fabric of my shirt, pulling my body closer. Our heat's combustible, our mutual want palpable.

"I missed this." Her hot, sweet breath skates over my mouth.

She's talking about the abandon with which we can give in to our desires. With a baby, there's been more planning and less spontaneity with sex, and this feels good.

"Me too."

Tension and anticipation saturate the slip of space between us as our breaths mingle. With each exhale, her lush breasts heave in and out against my chest.

"I want you, Patrick. Now."

"Want you too," I murmur against her lips, lifting her skirt, my fingers savoring the soft creamy flesh of her thighs.

I will always want her. This life.

Mia came into my life like a fiery starburst of light. Once I saw her, nothing and no one else mattered.

She's smart, funny, and compassionate. A remarkable mom, the mother of my two children. One in heaven and one on earth.

Mia St. John is a gentle, loving soul, and sometimes too practical in her approach. She grounds me, softens my gruff, sharp edges and has given me all I could ever dream.

THANK you for reading Broken Night! For an edgy, enemies to lovers romantic suspense, grab Prophet. Available at all major retailers and www.smwestauthor.com.

THANK you for reading and please leave a review on your favorite book site, including tell a friend. Reviews help readers find books!

. . .

For exclusive content, a free book and to find out when I have new releases, please sign up for my newsletter at www.smwestauthor.com.

OTHER BOOKS BY S.M. WEST

Scarred Hearts Series

All can be read as standalones

Prophet

Kit

Nomad

Griffin

Zero

New York Knights Series

Reckless Night

Fallen Night

Captive Night

Relentless Night

Broken Night

6ix Loves Series

All can be read as standalones

Trusting the Ex

Scoring the Player

Promising the Billionaire

Stealing the Billionaire

Falling for the Charmer

Winslow Grove Series

All can be read as standalones

Close to You

All of You

Here with You

Canyon Spring Series

A collaboration with Kimberly Quinn

The Cowboy Bargain

The Cowboy Hitch

Trojan Series

All can be read as standalones

Clutch

Reverb

Smash

Rush

Standalones

Made to Love

Resisting the Best Friend's Sister

ABOUT THE AUTHOR

USA TODAY bestselling and award winning author, S.M. West writes sexy, angsty stories about brave hearts and wild love, including, more times than not, heart-pumping twists and turns.

Apart from her infinite love of books, she's a self-professed wine, chocolate, and travel junkie. When not writing or hanging with her family, she's usually talking to her characters (in her head) or planning her next adventure.

www.smwestauthor.com

Pinnacle Book Achievement Award

Griffin - Best Thriller

Smash - Best Romance

Global eBook Awards

Griffin - Gold, Suspense

Scoring the Player - Silver, Romance

Global Book Award

Griffin - Silver, Romantic Suspense

Independent Press Award

Griffin - Distinguished Favorite, Audiobook, Fiction

Griffin - Distinguished Favorite, Romantic Suspense

NYC Big Book Award

Reverb - Distinguished Favorite, Romance

Finalist National Indie Excellence Awards

Griffin

For new releases, exclusive excerpts, giveaways and more, sign up for her newsletter.

www.ingramcontent.com/pod-product-compliance
Lightning Source LLC
LaVergne TN
LVHW091122080826
845145LV00008B/2011

* 9 7 8 1 9 8 9 8 8 1 0 5 7 *